Hidden Hills

By

Jannette Spann

Hidden Hills Copyright 2021 JANNETTE SPANN
Previously published in 2013 by Astraea Press
Cover Art by Brynna Curry
ISBN-13:978-1975685485
ISBN: 10:1975685482

Dedication

My husband, Mike, for his patience, Amanda Hosey, for my first deep critique, Tammy and Stacy for my story inspiration, Samantha and Morgan, the inspiration for my girls.

Chapter One

"Will there be anything else, sir?"

Jake was caught off guard—"wool-gathering", his mom would have called it—but he'd been unable to take his eyes off the cashier since entering her checkout line. The high cheekbones and clear green eyes with arched brows were the first things he'd noticed. Her pale, translucent skin appeared to be airbrushed by an artist with a delicate touch. When she turned to say something to the other cashier, he noticed her long slender neck and the mother-of-pearl clip holding back her smooth, auburn hair. His heart fluttered in response to her smile.

The register sprang open. "It's seven forty-nine, please."

Handing her a ten, he glanced at the name tag. Charlotte... pretty name for a pretty lady. How could he start a conversation with this flawless creature without a decent line? His flirting days ended with college, and here he was fifteen years later wondering what to do. There'd been a couple of short-lived relationships since Betty passed away, but those women had come on to him, not the other way around. When she closed the register, he noticed the gold band on her left hand—married.

"Here's your change, sir."

"Thank you." Jake nodded and slipped the money into his pocket, making his way to the automatic doors before he heard her call.

"Sir? You forgot your milk."

Her voice sounded impersonal, but the green eyes looking straight into his never wavered when he retraced his steps. She smiled again and his attraction for her escalated. "You must have a lot on your mind."

"Yeah, I guess I do," he replied, feeling awkward. The cashier slid him the bag containing the two jugs. It wouldn't do for her to know the real reason behind his walking out empty handed. She was off-limits.

A nervous energy seemed to surround her, like she couldn't wait to finish, probably eager to get home to her family. The magnetism faded before he put his groceries in the truck, but the memory of her eyes remained.

Driving with his windows down, he enjoyed the last dog days of summer. The train tracks on Dove Street held boxcars loaded with crushed coal. As a kid, he'd played along these same tracks, never realizing the danger. Now he sat listening to the bells ring, waiting for the train to pass and the crossing guards to lift to their standing position.

He'd spent most of his day on the phone, dealing with annoying customers' complaints and long-winded salesmen. The last thing he'd needed was a call from Jeremiah Hamner, the neighbor from two doors down, about a baseball busting his window out. It would be the fifth pane he'd installed this summer for the neighborhood because of his boys. With fall arriving and school already started, things should hopefully settle down. Easing across the tracks, he drove at a snail's pace the rest of the way home to give his boys time to get their story straight.

* * * *

Tiredness engulfed Charlotte on the trip home from picking up her girls at the sitter. Driving eighteen miles to Hillside everyday was bad enough, but the roundtrips had given her threadbare tires and the need for a quart of oil with every other fill-up. It was just a matter of time before the motor would need overhauling, providing the transmission didn't go first. Either way, it was money she didn't have.

"Mama." Becky's clear voice called from the back seat. "Julie Brown's having a skating party Saturday. Can I go? Huh, Mama, can I?"

"We'll see." Julie was Becky's best friend and Charlotte hated to tell her no, but she wasn't sure if they had rent money for a pair of skates.

"I want to go, too, Mama," Maggie said. "Can I? Huh? Please?"

"You're too little," replied the older girl. "I'm seven and you're only five. It's just for big kids."

Charlotte ignored the argument between the girls, focusing instead on whether there were enough leftovers in the refrigerator for supper. Thankfully, she didn't have picky eaters. Casserole surprise made mostly from leftovers tasted different each time she made it.

Easing off the gas pedal, she made the last turn before the road changed from pavement to loose gravel. Up ahead were the impressive iron gates of Hidden Hills, standing watch over the house as they'd done since shortly after the Civil War. There'd been a time when the gates welcomed her home, but not anymore. Without Mitch, they were a reminder of the loneliness awaiting her. It had started when he passed away, and it wasn't getting any easier.

Her closest neighbor lived two miles away as the crow flies—five if she traveled the road. Some days the isolation became unbearable. The winter months when darkness came early were the worst. She'd managed with Uncle Eli, the caretaker, living with them, but he'd moved in with his daughter because of poor health. Now every night was an ordeal.

Charlotte stomped the brake, her car skidding to a halt on the loose gravel. She remembered locking the gate before leaving for work—now it stood open. Her gaze darted back and forth along both sides of the drive. The thick undergrowth beneath the large oak trees made good hiding places for would-be attackers. Fear made her palms sweat, and she glanced over her shoulder to make sure the back doors were locked before driving on.

Mitch's parents hadn't set foot on the place in weeks, not since she'd removed the girls from their private school at Wills' Junction and enrolled them in Reader Elementary. They were the only ones with access to the key, and it wasn't like them to drop by unannounced.

The car gained speed after crossing the bridge, but her eyes continued darting back and forth, taking in the familiar scene of poison ivy and wild flowers lining the dirt road. Everything appeared the same. Her heart pounded in her chest when she rounded the last curve and glimpsed the silver convertible parked at the front door.

"Look, Mama. It's Grandfather."

Judge Tom McGregor, Mitch's dad, was hard to take any time. The dread she'd felt in recognizing the car multiplied. He was the last person she wanted to see.

Thinking back on her day, she tried to work herself in a better frame of mind before facing him. She recalled the man walking off without his milk and his expression when he'd come back, like he'd been embarrassed for being preoccupied. There'd been an instant connection the moment their eyes met. His were a dark, royal blue framed by thick, black lashes. Although she'd sensed him watching her while waiting to be checked out, he hadn't tried a come-on like some guys passing through her line. It was a relief, since a few seemed to think of her as fair game.

"It's about time you showed up." Judge McGregor's voice grated on her nerves. He rose from the porch swing, glaring down his nose at her jeans and tee-shirt. As usual, his appearance was impeccable—hair combed, shirt crisp, trousers creased—like he'd just dressed instead of having spent the day in court. "I have no idea why you waste the entire day getting home."

Charlotte's jaw clinched. "Afternoon to you too, Judge."

"We need to talk."

She locked the car before opening her front door. Becky and Maggie stopped long enough to speak to their grandfather, but when he showed no interest in spending time with them, they went inside to get started on homework. "It must be important to make you drive all the way out here."

"It is. You've got till the end of the month to come up with my thirty thousand. If you don't, I'm filing a claim against the estate."

"The estate?"

"You heard me. Charles should have left this house to Ellen. She's his daughter—his only child. It makes her the rightful heir, but the old cuss skipped her like she didn't even matter."

"Oh, she mattered, all right. It's you Grandpa kept it from."

"Well, I'll see about that. The skinflint's gone. He'll not dictate to this family from the grave—not anymore!"

"You know the terms of the will, or you should—you've tried hard enough to break it."

His chin shot up. "Next month, Charlotte. You owe the money, and I'll see to it you pay every dime!"

She held her tongue while Tom McGregor stomped off the porch. He stopped long enough to gaze up at the house before opening the door to the luxury car. "Next month, girl!"

* * * *

"It wasn't me!"

Jake had heard it before. As always, it was his middle son, Bruce, pleading his innocence. The boy should put it on a CD and save his breath.

"Mr. Hamner's window didn't break itself."

"But, Dad," replied the boy. "It wasn't my fault. The mower's got a bent blade."

"You're telling me the mower slung a baseball through his kitchen window?"

Bruce beamed. "Exactly."

"You're eight," Jake pointed out, giving the boy another chance to get his story straight. "You aren't supposed to use the mower until you're eleven."

"I didn't."

"So now it's Jeremy's fault? And remember he's bigger than you."

"Well..." The boy cut his eyes toward his older brother

and back again. "It wasn't me."

There'd been a steady stream of heated complaints over the summer from the neighbors: switched garbage cans, broken windows, and patches of dog poop on the neighborhood porches. The people of Robins Lane were fed up, with all fingers pointing toward his boys. He knew a short trip to the woodshed, like he'd gotten as a boy, would do wonders, but he'd promised Betty he'd spare the rod and spoil the child as much as possible.

"I want the truth about the window."

The older boy downed his juice. "What? Why you looking at me?"

"What happened to the lawnmower blade?"

Jeremy emptied the jug and left it on the counter by the sink, even though the garbage can was closer. "You said I could use the mower. Besides, Mrs. Wilson paid forty bucks for the job."

"The blade?"

"I hit a steel pipe somebody shoved into the ground next door. It didn't used to be there."

"It's a land marker. The surveyors left it, so spray it with red paint before you mow again," he said, trying to remember where the extra blades were hung. "Now, tell me about the window."

Jeremy shrugged. "It's the first I've heard about it."

That didn't surprise him at all. "You know the routine, four bucks on the table and go apologize."

Bruce groaned. "Aw, Dad. We didn't do nothin'."

The boys weren't guilty of all the problems of Robins Lane, but he was fed up with their nonsense. School starting should have helped, but it hadn't. "Mrs. Brown called again last night. There's graffiti on her garage door."

"It wasn't me!"

"I know."

"Her old garage has been peeling for years. She probably trashed it herself so you'd make us paint it."

"Now why would she do that?"

"Don't you get it, Dad?"

"Get what?"

"It's a conspiracy! She blames us—you pay for the paint, and we work for free. The same goes for those windows. They break them and blame us. We pay for 'em and you put in new ones."

"He's right, Dad." Jeremy slid his arm around Jake's shoulder. "These old folks are running a scam, and you're their victim. It's got to stop."

Bruce nodded in agreement. "I know it hurts to hear it, but we thought you should know."

There was a scam running, all right, but it wasn't the old folks. He was raising a couple of con men. Their thoughts meshed together to create ingenious plots, making it almost impossible to pick out the mastermind. As for the new scenario they'd just laid out, he would admit it was possible, just not probable. Elsa Brown was seldom seen outside of her home without a cane. It was hard to picture her spraying obscenities on anything. The boys did have a point though. It wasn't fair for them to have to work for free, if, and it was a big if, they happened to be innocent.

"It's worth ten bucks to each of you. Take the bucket of white paint from our shed and paint her entire garage. You should have enough, but if not, see if she has some."

"What about Andy?"

Jake sighed. "Give me a break, he's only three."

After putting his toddler down for a nap, he went outside to enjoy the clean, warm smell of late summer. This had been Betty's favorite time of the year; now it was the worst for him. She'd been gone three years, two months, and five days, but the ache in his heart felt as though it could have been yesterday. Sometimes all he had to do was close his eyes to smell her perfume. Shoving his hands through his thinning hair, he exhaled in an attempt to clear the cobwebs from his mind. There was work to be done. Lollygagging wouldn't fix anything, and it sure couldn't bring her back.

He was on his knees replacing the bent blade when he heard gravel crunch behind him. Since the older boys hadn't had enough time to paint the garage, he figured Andy had finished his nap. Busy with the job at hand, he didn't bother looking up until he saw tiny pink toenails poking out from a pair of white sandals. His eyes traveled upward over skinny legs and knobby knees to striped shorts with a matching fairy princess shirt. A little higher and he was nose to nose with freckles, green eyes, and red curls, glowing in the sun like new copper pennies. The girl was adorable. Her flawless skin reminded him of a pale peach.

"Whatcha' doing?"

"Working on my mower," he replied, breathing in the fresh scent of soap and cherry lollypop. Their foreheads were inches apart, and the child hadn't so much as blinked an eye.

"It tore up?"

"Uh-huh."

"Can you fix it?"

"Well," he said, blinking when her face began to blur. "I can if I'm not interrupted."

"I won't let nobody in'upt you."

"Okay," he said, trying not to grin. "That's real nice of

you, but don't you have some place you should be? I'll bet your mother's looking for you."

Copper curls swung in all directions. "Nope. Mama said I can look around."

Jake knew most of the kids in the area, but he'd never seen this one. "But did she say you could come over here?"

"She didn't say I couldn't."

Glancing over her head, he expected to see a frantic mother, but there was only the old hedge row. He studied the girl's demeanor. Cute kid. She didn't appear to be neglected, just momentarily unsupervised.

"Can I watch?" She shoved his wrenches from the work stool, and before he could disagree, her little bottom wiggled onto the greasy seat.

"I... suppose so. My name's Jake. What's yours?"

"Maggie."

"Nice to meet you, Maggie. Do you live around here?"

"Over there." She pointed to the house next door.

"That's the Parker house," Jake said, concerned she might have slipped away from her family. "It's been empty for a while. Want to try again?"

Maggie jumped off the stool, caught his face with her greasy hands and twisted his head around as far as it would go. "Over there. See?"

The row of overgrown hedges separating the yards blocked most of his view, but he could see enough to know someone was walking around in the adjoining property.

"Is your family buying the house?"

Her head bobbed. "Uh-huh."

He could see the white-haired realtor as her hands pointed to the features of the house. "Is your mom with Mrs. Wilson?"

"Uh-huh."

"Where's your dad?"

"In heaven. Mama said God needed a lawyer, so he took my daddy."

He was dumbfounded for a moment. Since when had heaven started having legal problems? "Has he been there long?"

"For ever and ever," she sighed. "I sure do miss my daddy. I wish God hadda took Grandfather instead. Mama wouldn't cry if he was gone."

Judging from her size, Jake figured Maggie to be maybe a year older than Andy. The right words were hard to come by in a situation like this. He wasn't usually soft-hearted but the girl's pain was similar to that of his boys. "Maybe God needed a special kind of lawyer."

The girl leaned closer, her warm breath tickling his ear. "Mama said it's 'cause Grandfather's going to hell! Where's hell, Mr. Jake?"

"Your mom said it?"

"Uh-huh." She nodded, her clear green eyes searching his, willing him to believe. "Mama told Grandfather to go there. I heard her."

His first instinct was to condemn the unknown mother. How could she say such a thing in front of the girl? But then her trusting face reminded him of things he'd said that his boys shouldn't have heard. At a loss for words, he used the same lame excuse he'd used with the boys countless times. "Maybe your mama was just mad."

Wiggling closer to his side, the girl pulled a wrench from under her leg. The greasy smear left on her shorts grew larger when she tried to wipe it away. "Mama cries when me and Becky are bad, so we're good, but sometimes Becky makes me mad, and then I'm not so good."

"You don't say?"

11

"Uh-huh. Do you think my daddy misses me even when I'm not so good sometimes?"

A lump the size of an ostrich egg made it hard to answer. He wanted to take her in his arms and hug the hurt away, but he knew it wasn't possible. Only God can mend a broken heart. "I'm sure your daddy misses you, no matter how bad you are sometimes."

Maggie's grin let him know he'd made a friend. The girl's inquisitive eyes watched while he reversed the socket wrench and braced his leg in an attempt to free a stuck bolt. He needed more leverage. "Hand me the board."

She handed him the wood and without warning, grabbed his hand. "You're dirty. Mama says I'm not to get dirty 'cause ladies don't get dirty like boys, and I'm a lady."

"Is that a fact?"

"Uh-huh. Do you like boys, Mr. Jake?" She didn't wait for an answer. "I like Cucumber, and he's a boy, but it don't count 'cause he's a cat, and anyway, he got lost, and now I don't got a cat. Uncle Mark says I can have another cat if Cucumber's squashed on the road with his guts smashed out, but Mama says ladies don't say 'guts', so I don't say 'guts', 'cause I'm a lady."

"You don't say?"

"Uh-huh." She scrambled on her knees for a closer look under the mower. "Not everybody's a lady 'cause they don't got red curls. Do you like red curls? Santa does, and I've got lots of them. Only Becky don't. I'm glad Santa likes red curls, since I got so many."

Jake burst out laughing at the pint-sized chatterbox. Before he realized what she was up to, her greasy hands pushed his lips away from his teeth. Gagging, he jerked his head out of her reach and grabbed his handkerchief. "What are you doing?"

12

"Do you got false teeth?" she asked, fascinated with his mouth. "Uncle Eli does. He don't eat corn on the cob, but I do. Sometimes Mama won't cook it 'cause she says I make a mess, and ladies don't suppose to make messes, and I'm a lady."

Jake spit again and again, trying to rid his mouth of the gritty motor oil. "I know, you told me."

"Oh yuck!" she cried. "You spit—that's not nice!"

"Neither is sticking your fingers in someone's mouth." He wiped his tongue. Quick as a wink, the girl plopped her bony rear-end onto his lap. Gone was the mowing deck. He was staring at Santa's beloved red curls.

"Why you stopping?"

"Because it's break time." He leaned back on his hands to keep her hair out of his mouth.

The sharp bones dug deeper into his legs when she twisted around. Her hand pushed his face sideways.

"Why's your face all dirty? Mama don't like dirty faces."

At the moment, Jake couldn't care less what her mama liked. He planted her feet `facing the hedge. "Go find your mama."

Maggie rotated on the spot, her hands firmly on her hips. "You not got no kids, Mr. Jake?"

"As a matter of fact," he replied, thinking this should get rid of her, "I've got three boys."

Her face scrunched up as if he'd suddenly grown two heads and a horn. "You not got no girls?"

"No, just boys."

"Poor Mr. Jake." Disappointment drooped her shoulders when she walked toward the hedge. Then, as if remembering her manners, she stopped and waved. "Nice to meet you, Mr. Jake."

He glimpsed her greasy rear end darting through the hedge.

The women came closer, and he listened to see if Maggie was with them. All he heard was Mrs. Wilson's soft voice, pointing out the property lines, but then—

"Maggie McGregor! Where have you been?"

He wondered if the kid's mother was as prissy as she sounded. What had Maggie said? "Ladies don't get dirty. Ladies don't make messes. Ladies don't say guts." His boys would eat her alive.

The closing of the car doors had Jake craning his neck for a glimpse of the woman, but the bushes were in the way. All he could see was the house, which had once been identical to his own. He listened to the car purr to life. Moments later, the sun disappeared behind the clouds, and they were gone along with the warmth of the afternoon.

The late August wind ruffled his hair as he continued to stare beyond the hedges. There were moments like this when his life seemed empty, like the old house. The peaceful afternoon began closing in, leaving him restless and out of sorts. As before, he took a couple of deep breaths, refusing to give in to the loneliness. He had his boys and it was enough. They were his sole reason for living.

Chapter Two

"Turn the racket off!" Jake thumped his thirteen-year-old on the head. "You going deaf?"

The music stopped.

"Man, Dad!" Jeremy flinched from the pain. "That hurt!"

"It was supposed to." His attention remained on the stove, not the boy, while giving the soup a final stir. "Somebody set the table. It's time to eat."

Pictures rattled in the hallway as the younger boys wrestled their way toward the kitchen. Bruce tossed Andy into the air, caught him by the seat of his pants, and swung him around in a circle.

"Airplane!" squealed the three-year-old just before his feet contacted with Jake's left kidney.

The racket was deafening, but he didn't mind. At least they weren't fighting, for a change. He could take anything but their constant bickering.

"What's for supper?" Bruce gagged after the first whiff. "Aw, Dad! Not soup again. It's all you ever cook."

"Soup's good for you."

"Not the way you cook it," he mumbled.

"I heard you."

Jeremy took the glasses and bowls from the cabinet, with Andy clinging to his back. "Did any of you see the pigeon checking out the dump next door?"

Jake shook his head in disapproval. "If you're asking if Mrs. Wilson showed the house to a client today, then yes I did."

Bruce rocked his chair on two legs before landing with a thump. "I pity the dope who buys the place."

"The Parkers' house isn't bad." He gave the boys time to settle into their chairs. "It just seems that way because they were old. How would you guys like it if someone your age moved in? You'd have friends to play with."

"Sure," Bruce said, sailing a spoon across the table at his brother. "There's nobody but old geezers around here."

Jeremy glowed. "How about some hot chicks?"

"Won't do you no good." Bruce ducked. The saltine cracker grazed his ear.

Jake's hand shot out, intercepting the airborne missile on its way to the floor. "We don't throw food."

The mischievous glance, passing between the older boys, made him uneasy. He'd gone through a string of housekeepers and sitters, hoping the right woman might have a calming influence, but none had lasted long enough to find out. They'd been on their own for the last three weeks and they'd survived.

"Mr. Parker was fun." Bruce rocked his chair back on two legs in an imitation of their former neighbor. "Remember the time his teeth fell in the toilet? It sucked 'em down so fast he couldn't get 'em out."

"And whose fault was it he dropped them in the first

16

place?" Jake said, wiping the smirks from their faces. "The next dentures I buy had better be for myself."

He filled the bowls and passed them around the table before sitting down. Andy frowned, shoving his away.

"Stinks!"

"No, it doesn't." He slid the bowl back to the pouting toddler. "Now eat your soup."

Andy stared at the bowl. His lips quivered and huge tears pooled in his blue eyes. "At least try it, son."

The dreaded spoon passed the pouting lips, and tomatoes spewed in all directions. The older boys shoved their chairs back, exaggerating the situation. Defeat was something Jake had faced several times over the past few years.

"All right, calm down," he said, taking charge again. "Wash your faces and get clean shirts. We'll go to the Pizza Plate."

He waited until the boys left the table before tasting his soup. "Soap!"

* * * *

The local hangout was usually packed, but he didn't have a choice if they were going to have a hot meal. Smelling the warm, garlic-filled air starved him, and after forty-five minutes of standing in line, his stomach introduced itself to his backbone. They were seated at their table, waiting for the pizza to arrive, when he noticed a little girl with red hair. He instantly thought of Maggie.

"Give it back!" Andy cried.

Bruce held the pizza-shaped placemat out of his brother's reach. "You're such a baby. I'm just looking at it."

"Am not! Daddy, make him give it back."

"Cry baby!"

"Daddy!"

"That's enough." Jake retrieved the paper from the older boy. He felt a slight tug on his sleeve and for the second time since lunch, found himself gazing into cool green eyes. "Hello, Maggie. What a nice surprise."

The girl's eyes traveled from one boy to the next, clearly unimpressed. "That your boys?"

He beamed with pride in spite of the way they'd just behaved. "This is Andy, Bruce, and Jeremy. Boys, say hello to Maggie."

Andy stared, Bruce nodded, and Jeremy winked, causing Maggie to blush until her face matched the red hair. To his surprise, the girl ducked her head and ran.

Bruce jabbed an elbow into his older brother's ribs. "Idiot. You embarrassed the poor kid!"

"All I did was wink," he said, craning his neck to see where she'd gone. "Can I help it if I'm hot?"

"Hot?" Bruce replied. "Geek's more like it."

"Moron."

Jake's sigh was one of despair. Puberty—the awkward age where testosterone runs rampant, and boys think with their bodies instead of their brains. With a five-year age difference between the three, the next fifteen years would pass before he could relax. A wiry grin twisted his lips. He sympathized with them.

"I don't think four-year-old girls count."

"You tell him, Dad," Bruce said. "She's no babe—just a baby. Jeremy can't get a real girl."

"I get plenty of girls, you snot-nosed jerk!"

"You take it back!" Bruce shoved Jeremy against the wall. The older boy came back with his fist aimed at the eight-year-old. Jake's hand shot out to intercept the lick.

Reaching across the table, he clamped his hands on the boys' shoulders to get their attention, then continued in a tone they knew all too well. "That's enough. Now finish your meal and get to the truck—pronto!"

"But, Dad…"

"What?"

"Our pizza's not here yet."

He rubbed his face, the five o'clock shadow reminding him of the time. "All right—we'll wait. But if either of you give me another ounce of trouble, you'll get a pound of cure you'll never forget. Are we straight?"

They eyed each other and slumped in the booth. "Yes, sir."

Jake found it hard to recall the peaceful calm he'd felt earlier. It got even worse when the afternoon crowd began to leave, and the room packed with loud, boisterous teens. The music and laughter echoed from the rafters, while the urge for his sweats and a recliner became too much to ignore. Had kids always been this bad?

His eyes scanned the crowd in search of Maggie's red hair before finding her at the other end of the large room near a plate glass window. An older girl with long brown ponytails sat across the table. The smeared window blurred the woman's reflection, but her backside was nice and trim. He liked the way the navy blouse narrowed at the waist, not to mention the sleek shoulder-length, classy auburn hair.

"Nice butt, huh, Dad?" Bruce mumbled around a mouthful of pizza.

"What?"

"Her butt. It's round like those girls in the magazine."

Jake choked on a breadstick. "What are you talking about?"

19

"Maggie's mom. She's stacked."

Jake hid behind a napkin to clear his throat. "Don't say that—someone might hear you."

His eight-year-old seemed confused. "I didn't mean it ugly. She has as many curves as the centerfold."

Jake's mind reeled. "Centerfold? What do you know about centerfolds?"

"Jeremy's mag—uh, I don't remember," he lied, amnesia coming from a swift kick to his shin.

"Jeremy?"

"I didn't waste money on it, Dad. Honest! It's worth every cent."

Jake shook his head. "What are you guys up to?"

They swallowed hard and shoved more pizza into their mouths. Forget the age difference, these two were shooting through puberty at the speed of light. Why had he taught them basic economics but failed miserably in the more important things? He realized his mistake of depending on others for their moral raising, but it was going to change.

"There's more to a woman than a pretty face and the way she's built."

The pizza was forgotten. "There is?"

Jake watched his boys, while loosening his already-unbuttoned collar. How had he gotten himself into this mess? He'd covered the basics with Jeremy when the boy had been ten or eleven, but from the look of things, something hadn't registered. There was only himself to blame. The women he'd dated since Betty's death had been someone to talk to and nothing more. He searched his mind, hoping the right words would fall from heaven. They didn't.

"Women are…"

"Hot!"

20

"No, I meant…"

"Dad, was Mom hot?"

Finally, something he could talk about. His boys only knew Betty as "Mom," and now they wanted to know her as a person. Their mischievous eyes glowed and it dawned on him, they were waiting for intimate details he had no intentions of spilling. Some things were too special to share with anyone, even his precocious sons.

"Your mom was the hottest woman I've ever known."

"Wow!"

He leaned his elbows on the table, basking in their attention. "What do you remember about your mother?"

Jeremy smiled. "She smelled good, like flowers, and she always laughed at my jokes."

"And she was soft," Bruce added. "She gave big hugs and lots of kisses."

Jake remembered Betty's last night on earth, when she'd had the boys in her bed. It was a good memory. "Your mom was that and so much more. She was the most caring person I've ever known and she loved you boys, all three of you."

"Was she stacked?"

"Yes, Bruce," he said, to satisfy his curiosity. "But it wasn't what made her a woman. Now finish your pizza so we can leave."

The rest of the meal passed without incident. When it came to eating pizza, his boys left only a handful of crust. He put his usual tip on the table and started for the door with Andy in his arms. Glancing back to make sure the other boys followed, he saw Bruce pick up the money.

"What are you doing, son?"

"Ah… you forgot this?"

"No I didn't," Jake replied. "The money's for the

waitress who took care of us. It's a tip."

"But she didn't do nothing."

"How many glasses of tea did you drink?"

"Four."

He took the money from the boy's hand and put it under an empty glass. "Our placemats were on a clean table. The waitress brought our pizzas and refilled our glasses several times, and now she'll come back and get the table ready for the next customer. I'd say she deserves the tip, wouldn't you?"

"Well," Bruce said, his thumbs hooked in his front pockets. "Since you put it that way, then I guess she does."

"I'm glad you agree." He placed his hand on the boy's shoulder, removing the temptation of taking the tip by walking him outside.

The crowded parking lot held mostly sports cars and four-wheel drives, the only exception being an old blue hatchback parked next to his truck. He suddenly felt as dated as the car.

"Did we get any mail today?" He unlocked the doors and waited for his boys to get in. "Maybe a brown envelope?"

Bruce jumped into the front seat, beating Jeremy by a good six seconds. "Not a thing."

"Except a letter from Principal Ruff," Jeremy added to get back at his brother.

"I'm gonna kill—"

"Hold it! Nobody's killing anyone," he said, defusing the fight before it got started. He rubbed the sharp pain forming in his temple, then adjusted Andy's seatbelt before latching his own. Just once, he'd like to start the school year without the principal in an uproar. It didn't take a genius to know which kid was in trouble. "You didn't hack into the school's computer system again, did you?"

Jeremy reached across the seat to shove his brother's head against the window. "Yeah, dimwit. Did you delete the test scores again?"

Bruce slapped back. "I told you it wasn't me!"

"Stop it!" Jake wasn't sure if sitters had been the right approach. What they'd needed was a referee.

"Why me, Dad?" he cried. "You always think it's me."

"No, I don't."

The boy's sullen expression was barely visible in the dim interior of the truck. "Andy and Jeremy are so-o-o precious. They never do nothing wrong. It's always me."

"Boo-hoo," chirped the backseat agitator. "Are you gonna cry me a river?"

He slowed for the caution light on Birch Street, the nerves in the back of his neck tightened from tension. His head pounded as war raged on between the boys. "That's enough, Jeremy."

"Andy's climbing out of his harness, Dad."

His teeth clenched. "You're bigger than he is, Jeremy, so put him back in!"

"Well, shucks—whatcha yelling at me for? I didn't do nothing wrong."

"I wasn't yelling," he replied, lowering his voice to a more moderate level. He'd give a lot for a nerve pill the size of a watermelon. Thank goodness it was almost bedtime. "You guys think you can tone it down a bit?"

"It's not always me," Bruce muttered.

"I know it's not, son."

"Jeremy called that woman," he said, the confession coming a month late.

"Well, you gave me the number," Jeremy reminded him, spreading the blame. "How was I to know it came from the wall in the john? You're not supposed to be at Al's Garage anyway."

Jake stood his ground, trying to avert another full-blown argument. "It's okay, guys, just water under the bridge."

Jeremy refused to let it die. "How was I supposed to know what she was?"

"You weren't." Jake remembered the voluptuous blond in red spandex at his front door. So much for his mother's idea of him hiring a cleaning woman. The boys had taken it upon themselves to find one.

Bruce's foot landed on the dash in an attempt to retie his sneaker in the dark. He gave up, shoving the strings inside the shoe. "Dad, why did the woman say you owed her money when she didn't do nothing? She didn't even wash dishes. Is that why you told her to leave, 'cause she wouldn't wash dishes?"

"No, you termite." The thirteen-year-old laughed. "It's 'cause she's a hooker!"

Jake glanced at his middle son, hoping the remark had flown over his head. Innocence was a wonderful thing, and he hated to see his kids lose it.

Robins Lane was quiet when he slowed to enter his drive, the only racket riding in the truck with him. Floating through his mind was the plan to let the boys unwind for a few minutes while he shredded Jeremy's girlie magazine, and then it was baths, bed, and peace at last.

He slid the key into the deadbolt and stepped aside while Jeremy and Andy shoved their way in. He'd yet to figure out why being first in the house was so important. Bruce hung back, deep in thought.

"Dad," the boy said, cocking his head to one side. "What's a hooker?"

He'd known it was coming. "Well, son," he replied, not wanting to say too much. "It's a bad woman who sells her body."

"Oh?"

"Yes, so just stay away from anyone like her."

Bruce frowned. "I thought they just hung-up coats."

"Who?"

"You know—hookers. Ain't it what they call the girls who hang up coats in fancy restaurants? Not here, but I watched them do it in an old movie. And hats, they hung up hats too."

Jake grinned. He'd been worried about confusing the boy. "Uh—yeah. That's what I meant."

* * * *

"This is getting old." Jake took a deep breath before starting up the flight of granite steps in front of the stately old building. It had taken some juggling, but he'd managed to shift things to make the three o'clock meeting.

He'd made more trips to the principal's office since his boys had started school than in all the years he'd gone there himself. Not only had the building remained the same, but so had the lady in charge, and he knew from experience she didn't like to be kept waiting. He glanced at his watch and opened the door—ten minutes early. That should make her happy.

Bruce sat alone in the outer office, his chin buried deep in his collar and a worried frown marring his lovable face. Jake eased down beside him, placing a reassuring hand on the boy's shoulder just as he'd done years ago, for the

25

kid's mom when she'd sat in this spot.

The bell rang, dismissing school for the day. Kids of all ages poured into the tiny room, shoving their way to the single phone on the desk. Jake felt he would drown in the noisy pint-sized whirl of humanity.

He caught a back-sided glimpse of a woman with long auburn hair leaving the room just as his name was called. She was tall, like the cashier at the grocery store, and she dodged backpacks with the grace of a dancer. It might have been her...but she was married so he had no business thinking about her. Maybe the woman from the Pizza Plate? After thinking about it a moment, he dismissed the idea. Those little girls weren't old enough to cause trouble.

"Mr. Weatherman," repeated the secretary. "Mrs. Ruff is waiting."

Jake held Bruce's shoulder as they worked their way through the throng of kids. He glanced down at his son when they reached the closed door. Something wasn't right. For a kid in trouble, Bruce was suddenly showing a remarkable lack of fear.

"You're late, Weatherman!"

"No way," he replied, face to face with the woman who'd terrified him as a kid. "I had trouble getting through the delinquent pen."

Referring to the outer office by its old name would have gotten a chuckle from most people, but not this woman. The situation called for charm and tact, but Jake was fresh out of both. He forced a smile.

"How's it going?"

"Could be worse," she said, tossing her glasses on the desk while getting right to the point. "Let's have a seat and hash out Bruce's latest problem."

The woman sounded tired, but so was he, and there

was a load of paperwork waiting in his truck to be dealt with tonight. "Bruce says he's been accused of hitting another student in the hall."

Instead of answering him, she pinned Bruce with a cold stare. "Is that what happened?"

"I was just getting a drink of water."

"But you admit you were in the hall," she continued.

"Like I just said, I was…"

"Did you hit Brandon Hunter in the eye?"

"Why would I hit him? He's bigger than me."

"He's got a point there," Jake commented for the record.

"True," she conceded, looking at Jake for the first time since the interrogation began. "But Brandon has a black eye, and he swears Bruce gave it to him."

Jake knew the Hunter kid. The only way Bruce could have reached his eye was if he'd stood in a chair. "Anyone else in the hall when the fight supposedly happened?"

"Only one girl, and she claims she didn't see anything."

"Maybe she was too far away." Jake said it as a reminder. The water fountain could be seen from anywhere in the hall. "If she didn't see anything, maybe it's because nothing happened."

The principal rocked back and forth slowly, fingertips pressed together so tight her hands were shaking. "I see your point."

It appeared as if thirty years of dealing with kids was taking its toll on her nervous system. He could have been more sympathetic to her case had he not been where his son was now.

Long lashes framed the blue eyes gazing up at him as if to say, "It's not always me," and he was inclined to agree with the boy. It boiled down to one kid's word against another, and he was beginning to wonder why he was here.

"Anything else?"

She scribbled a few words on a notepad before looking at Bruce again. "There was a frog in the salad bar at lunch on Friday. Would you know anything about it?"

"I don't eat salads."

She chucked her pen. "I didn't think so."

Jake rose from his chair. They'd wasted enough time. As far as he was concerned, the meeting was over. "Are there any other problems I should know about?"

"Not firsthand, but his teacher has sent a couple of notes home you've not responded to."

He nodded. They'd finally reached the heart of the matter. "Son, you want to tell me about those notes?"

Bruce squirmed. "Wasn't nothing important."

"I'll be the judge of that," he said, then turned to the principal. "I'd like to talk with his teacher if she's available."

"Ordinarily you would have to make an appointment," she said, clearly satisfied justice was finally being served on the boy. "But in your case, she's been waiting for you."

Jake's meeting with Bruce's teacher was more to the point. The boy had missed homework assignments, disrupted the class, and last but not least, had generally poked his nose where it didn't belong.

"Son, you're lucky you weren't expelled," he said, after they'd reached the truck.

"Aw, Dad—"

"Don't 'aw, Dad' me." He flipped the radio off as fast as Bruce had turned it on. "You're grounded."

"But—"

"And who was the girl in the hall?"

"Her name's Becky. She's just a little kid."

"What's her last name?"

Bruce shrugged. "I don't know. She just started this year."

"She pretty?"

"Aw, Dad. She's just a baby!"

"Babies don't go to school."

"You know what I mean. She's not big."

Jake let it slide. The boy was in enough trouble without looking for more.

Arriving home, the first thing he noticed was the open windows in the house next door and an old hatchback in the drive. The place had come alive.

"Look, Dad!" Bruce cried, coming out of his sulk and seatbelt at the same time. "The sign's gone!"

Jake glanced back, but his view was blocked. He thought of red curls as he pulled around to his back door.

"I guess Maggie was right about the house." He tried to imagine what life would be like raising girls instead of boys. Chances were he wouldn't have spent the last hour in the principal's office because of a black eye.

Bruce bounced around. "You mean the girl from Saturday night?"

The kid's excitement warmed his lonesome heart, and he felt a renewed pride in the boys. Okay, so maybe they were a handful—but he wouldn't have it any other way.

"She said it's her new home."

"Awesome!" Bruce hit the ground running and never looked back.

Jake wasn't as enthused, gathering his invoices. He glanced up and saw Maggie waving from an upstairs window with Andy and Jeremy making faces behind her back. Smiling at the threesome, he thought about introducing himself to the girl's mother, but the weight of the folder in his hand reminded him that he was wasting time. Returning the wave, he went inside alone to get started.

It had been one of those days when he wished he could punch a time clock instead of worrying about making payroll and competing with the larger stores. He liked staying behind the scenes leaving Sara, his mother-in-law, to deal with customer complaints. Unfortunately, she'd been on a four-day buying trip in Atlanta, so he'd had no choice but to smooth the ruffled feathers himself. High maintenance women were a pain in the neck.

He'd grown up on the farm in the shadow of his older brothers. Their parents believed if they wanted to be happy, they should each follow their own dreams. His included degrees in business management, marketing, and Betty Barlow—the girl next door.

It seemed he and his brothers spent much of their childhood rescuing her from angry cows, swollen creeks, and the occasional bully. When ninth grade rolled around, Betty, the tree climbing tomboy with a passion for trouble, warped into a fashion-conscious girly-girl. A year later she stole his heart and never gave it back.

The week after he'd left home for the university, she'd opened a little consignment shop in their hometown of Hillside, Alabama. By the time he'd finished college, Betty's Hole in the Wall had gone from consignment to first-quality women's wear.

Instead of moving to Birmingham or Atlanta like most of his friends, he'd come home to Hillside and married Betty. The next eleven years had been the happiest of his life, with his world revolving around Betty and his boys. Together they grew the business to include children's apparel and changed the name to Bett's, because she'd thought it sounded more sophisticated.

He'd thought seriously about selling out after Betty died, but it had been her dream, so he kept the store and poured himself into making it grow. Now they were in the process of opening a men's shop in the new Four Corners Mall near the Interstate. It had been a risky gamble with the slow economy, but it kept the lonely nights from driving him insane.

Chapter Three

Charlotte stretched her back, admiring the kitchen floor with the afternoon sun reflecting off the faded hexagonal print of the linoleum. The appliances, though yellowed with age, were as spotless as the white cabinets. Her aching body, along with the dirty mop bucket sitting by the door, provided a living testimony to the floor's cleanliness. She'd scrubbed on this room for most of the day and it showed. Pity was, no one except her girls would see it, and they were too young to care.

The back door opened, and a boy with dark hair crashed through on a collision course with the bucket. Charlotte screamed, but it was too late as the nasty water sloshed across the room, taking the kid with it.

"Whoa, cowboy." She caught his arm before his head smacked the floor and steadied him on his feet. He tried to wiggle out of her grasp, but she held tight. "Where I come from, we clean up our messes."

"I ain't cleaning that up!"

Charlotte gritted her teeth, fighting the urge to pop his smart mouth. She'd dealt with attitudes like his before with some of the foster kids she and Mitch had cared for. "Yes, you will."

"You're not my mama!"

"You got that right," she said, counting her blessings. Her fingers tightened on his shirt as he twisted his shoulders, trying to break free. "This is my house and you made the mess, so you're cleaning it up."

His jaw clenched as he eyed her with anger. "I said, I *ain't* cleaning it!"

"Oh, I think you will." She raised the stakes for the obnoxious brat. "Either you mop up the water, or you can't play with Becky and Maggie. Your brothers will be welcome, but you won't be allowed to come over."

After his shoes stopped sliding, he stared at the dingy water and then at her. She held the mop in her outstretched hand and waited as the indecision on his face gave way to her dogged determination.

"Now." She refused to take no for an answer. "Clean. It. Up."

"Aw, man," he groaned, the mop fitting his smaller hands.

The boy's expression was almost comical, as if his day had been as bad as hers.

"I suppose you're Bruce?"

"Unfortunately."

"Any more of you guys at home?"

Bruce frowned, more subdued than before. "Just Dad. I'll get him, but my hide will be hamburger."

"Because of this mess?" she asked. The boy leaned against the handle, his head tilted to the side while he eyed her up and down. There wasn't a doubt in her mind... he was sizing her up.

"Are you a hooker?"

Her breath caught. Had he been older, Charlotte would have popped his jaw without giving it a second thought, but according to his big brother, this kid was only eight.

"Bruce, do you know what a hooker is?"

"Dad says it's a bad woman."

She folded her arms across her chest and did some sizing up of her own. There was nothing slow about the blue-eyed, shaggy-haired, snaggle-toothed kid. He was as cute as a button and sharp as a tack. "And you think I'm bad because I'm making you clean up your mess?"

Bruce stood his ground, tossing the mop handle back and forth from one hand to the other. Then with long lashes blinking his innocence, he looked her in the eye. "You sure are pretty."

"Nice try, kid," she said. "Now finish your job."

Bruce sulked, but he didn't give her any lip, which was a good thing, considering how tired she was. With each stroke of the mop, his brain was probably plotting revenge, but she didn't care. His "trust me" expression had been too angelic to be real.

With the spill cleared and the mop in the bucket for the final time, Charlotte bragged on his work and sent him to play with the others. The house was quiet except for the children. Without realizing it, she found herself listening to their voices while she dusted the door facings.

"Man, she's tough like Mrs. Ruff, only pretty!

"Who?"

"Becky's mom," replied the eight-year-old. "Look at these hands. I got blisters!"

"So go home," said his older brother. "Nobody invited you anyway."

"Not until I see Becky. Where is she?"

"Upstairs, why?"

"I owe her one. She saved my butt today."

Charlotte wanted to hear more from the eight-year-old, but the voices faded when they climbed the stairs. It was getting late, and although she'd promised herself to finish the living room floor before calling it quits, a slight twinge in her lower back gave her second thoughts.

The aroma of freshly brewed coffee began to fill the air when terrified screams coming from overhead sent chills down her spine. She ran, taking the stairs two at a time on legs made of jelly.

"I'm telling Mama!"

"Shut up, Red!"

"You can't make me!"

"Oh, yeah. You just watch me!"

"Mama, Bruce did it!"

Five kids locked in mortal combat she could handle, but an eight-year-old struggling to hold onto a pair of ankles inside a wall opening the size of a small microwave brought terror to her heart, especially since she recognized the legs were Becky's. She'd thought the old laundry chute would save steps, not realizing it could be a death trap for a child.

Each step toward the chute came slowly, like she was trapped in a fog. Fear robbed the remaining air from her lungs. The boy's arms had to be throbbing when she reached around him and grabbed the squirming legs.

"I didn't mean it, honest!" he cried, blue eyes wide with fear.

"Becky!" Charlotte called. "Are you okay?"

"Mama!"

"Don't let go," she pleaded with the boy. Becky was fifty-six pounds of dead weight and Charlotte's wrists

35

burned, ready to snap. "Help me, Lord!"

"I'm pulling as hard as I can," Bruce cried. "Honest!"

It was no use. Becky was getting heavier by the second. Even together they weren't strong enough to lift her more than a few inches. "Where's your brother?"

"He's coming."

"Mama, get me out of here!" Becky's voice echoed in the ductwork.

"I will, honey," Charlotte promised, knowing it would take a miracle for her throbbing hands to hold on much longer. In answer to her prayer, she heard heavy footsteps bolting up the stairs. Expecting the older boy, she was relieved when a stranger put his arms around her from behind and clamped his large hands on Becky's legs.

* * * *

Reaching as far into the opening as his wide shoulders would allow, Jake was able to work his left hand down to the girl's waist and catch her leg above the knee with his right. On the count of three, he lifted while the woman pulled.

Something caught.

"Ooh! You're hurting me!"

"What's wrong, Becky?" Charlotte asked.

The girl screamed. "Mama, it's got my hair!"

Jake felt an involuntary tremor course through the woman's body. The situation was even worse than he'd thought. Becky had been upside down for several minutes and regardless of losing a few hairs, they had to get her out.

"Becky," he called, keeping his voice calm. "Can you move your arms?"

"I'm scared."

"Can you free your hair?"

"It's dark!"

"I know, sweetie." He heard the tears in her voice. "But you're a brave girl."

"No she's not," Maggie said, trying to see into the opening. "She's scared of the dark."

"Maggie, please!" scolded the frustrated mother. "Get out of the way and hush."

As the woman pressed into his side, the combination of honeysuckles and pine cleaner whiffed upwards, tickling his nose. It was then he noticed the color of her hair—auburn. He tried to ignore her, but even the job at hand couldn't stop the excitement of liquid fire shooting through his veins. Becky kicked, bringing him back to reality.

"Is your hair free?"

"Uh-huh," came the muffled reply.

Jake saw the white knuckles on the woman's clinched fingers. No doubt she was terrified, but he was glad she'd kept her cool. A hysterical female would have been worse than the kid stuck in the wall. He bent his knees for more leverage and buried his nose in her wild mop of a ponytail.

"Ready?"

She pulled while he lifted, and a moment later the screaming girl was out of the wall, staggering as the blood rushed from her head. The woman sank to her knees, wrapped the girl in a tight hug and showered her with kisses.

"Mama, you're hurting me!"

"Sorry." She kissed her again on both cheeks before releasing her.

He had been trying to catch a glimpse of this woman for days. Now that he'd finally caught up with her, he couldn't believe his luck. Even without makeup, there was a proud elegance in the way she held herself. Her green eyes and porcelain skin reminded him of Maggie, but the dark auburn hair was more like the older girl.

"Thank you sounds lame after all you've done." She stood, still breathless from the exertion. "How can I ever repay you?"

Several ways came to mind, but none involved having the kids around. While he'd been drooling over her, Jeremy and Bruce had been backing toward the bedroom door, making their escape. Before he could say anything, the woman was pointing an accusing finger at Bruce.

"Hold it, young man!" she said, the anger in her voice unmistakable.

"What's he done?" Jake dreaded the answer.

"Your son has been one disaster after another, since coming into this house!"

Bruce shoved his hands deep into his pockets and dropped his head.

"Let's try to be rational," Jake said, hoping to defuse the situation. The woman was furious. He knew his boys could be brats, but they were *his* responsibility. He didn't need a stranger telling him how to raise them.

"Rational? You want to talk rational? He tried to push Becky down a laundry chute, and I'm supposed to be rational?"

"Bruce?"

"I didn't push her, Dad, honest. Becky wanted to see the bottom, so I helped her."

"Helped her?" The woman's voice rose in anger. "I don't think so. There's no way Becky could have gotten so far into the wall without being pushed."

"I just said I helped her. Don't you listen?"

"Bruce!" Jake jumped in at the first sign of disrespect.

"But, Dad…"

"That's enough, son. Come here." He motioned for his boys to cross the room. It was time to put a lid on this hornet's nest. "Care to explain how this got started?"

Bruce squirmed, kicking the toe of his sneaker against the carpet. "Do we have to?"

"It's the ghost!" Maggie said, tugging on his arm. "He tried to get Becky, but you wouldn't let him!"

"It was just a joke, Dad." Jeremy spoke up in his brother's defense. "We didn't mean to hurt her, honest."

"We'll talk about it when we get home," Jake said, knowing the punishment had to be severe. "Becky could have been hurt or even killed. Do you realize that?"

"Sorry, Dad."

Jake rubbed the back of his neck where the muscles had tightened into iron bands. Up until now, their pranks had been aimed at grown-ups in the neighborhood, but things were getting out of hand. This was more than an ordinary prank.

"Sorry doesn't cut it this time. Girls aren't as tough as boys, and you'd better not do anything to hurt these two."

"Aw, Dad, you know we wouldn't hurt 'em on purpose."

He believed them, but the stunt had scared the daylights out of the girl's mother, and rightly so. What-ifs were running through his mind.

"We're sorry, ma'am," they said in unison. Jake knew they were trying to lessen the punishment by apologizing without being told. If they were to be neighbors, then he wanted to start on good terms.

She appeared to accept the regret in their apology. "I'm just tired and this… well, it aged me by ten years," she said, rubbing her forehead. The dark circles under her eyes affirmed it. "Sorry I blew up."

"You have a right to be upset. I promise it won't happen again. Isn't that right, boys?"

"Yes, sir."

"Wait a minute." She placed a hand on his arm. "Don't I know you?"

Jake nodded. Her knuckles weren't white anymore, but warm to the touch. The connection he felt was undeniable, much like when their eyes had met. "I'm the guy who forgot his milk the other day."

"I thought you were familiar," she said. "It's nice to meet you. I'm Charlotte McGregor, and these are my girls, Becky and Maggie."

"I'm Jake," he said, relieved she appeared to be cooling off.

She smiled again and this time, it was directed straight at him. "You never did say how I could repay you."

"That isn't necessary, but I believe my sons have worn out their welcome."

"It's over and done—" Her hesitation led him to believe she was more shaken than she let on. "Becky's fine. Aren't you, dear?"

"Yeah, it was fun! Can we do it again?"

"No!" her mother cried vehemently. "And don't any of you go near the door again."

Jake followed Charlotte to the kitchen where she filled mugs with steaming coffee. The liquid sloshed, but he pretended not to notice her hands shaking.

"I brought the extra cup from home in case a neighbor stopped by," she said, the empty pot resting in the sink. "But to tell you the truth, I was expecting a woman."

"Guess I'm the only welcome wagon you're likely to get today."

He relaxed on the floor of the empty room, his back against the cabinet and his long legs stretched in front of him. Taking his time, he studied Charlotte through the steam rising above the rim of his cup. From his vantage point, he could testify she had the longest, shapeliest legs he'd seen in ages. The messy hair and dark circles only added to her feminine appeal.

She took time to hug Andy and give him a cookie, before finding her own square of linoleum. He couldn't believe his usually shy toddler snuggled into her lap and laid his head against her chest. The boy scrunched his shoulders, giggling when she kissed his neck.

"I love hugging this guy. He's such a happy little fellow."

"Most of the time."

Her attention focused on him after the toddler lost interest and ran off to play. "I'm glad you're here. Becky's small for her age, but she was getting heavy. I should nail the door shut on the laundry chute."

"There's no need, I'll do it," he said, smiling when she tried to hide a yawn. It wouldn't take him but a minute to have it fixed. "Have you been cleaning all day?"

"Except for a little while this afternoon. I had to meet with Becky's principal."

Jake nodded. "So it was you."

"Beg your pardon?"

"At school today," he explained. "Unfortunately I was there for a meeting, too. I saw you leave Mrs. Ruff's office."

Charlotte frowned. "I'm sorry, but I don't recall seeing you."

"I was in the corner."

"Oh."

41

"But I knew it was you."

Her expression clearly said he wasn't making any sense. "I recognized you from Saturday night."

"Saturday night?"

"At the Pizza Plate."

Her face paled. "Are you the guy in the window… the one who kept staring at us?"

She was looking at him as if he was some kind of wacko nutcase. He held up his hands in surrender. "Wait a minute, you've got me mixed up with your other stalker. It's true I glanced your way, but only once. It doesn't mean I was staring. Maggie came over to my yard when you were inspecting the house. I recognized her red hair."

Charlotte's eyes locked with his for what seemed like an eternity. He'd never thought about how vulnerable a woman on her own with small children would feel.

She visibly relaxed, giving him what seemed to be the benefit of the doubt. "I'm sorry. My husband was a lawyer, and a lot of his cases involved children. I just panicked."

He felt like a heel. Here he'd been fantasizing about this woman since the first time he'd seen her face. Her voice wasn't impersonal, like it sounded at the grocery store, or prissy, like when she'd talked with the realtor. She seemed real, and he wanted to get to know her. "I'm the one who needs to apologize, and I should've introduced myself, but our food arrived, and well, you've met my boys. It would've meant starvation if I'd left the table then."

"Apology accepted. So you had to see Mrs. Ruff, too — wait a minute, that's where I've seen Bruce. He was in her office this afternoon, wasn't he?"

Jake frowned. "Do you think their rooms are on the same hall?"

"It's possible. And I could be wrong, but I think our

42

kids might be teaming up with each other."

His suspicion was tweaked. "What makes you think so?"

"Voices carry in empty houses, and I heard Bruce telling Jeremy something about Becky saving his skin."

"I knew it!" His anger simmered just below the surface. He'd been had by an eight-year-old.

"What's wrong?"

"The little rascal didn't give a straight answer all evening. He lied to me!"

"Well," she said. "If he lied, then so did Becky. But to be fair, Mrs. Ruff didn't call any names."

The girl wasn't his problem. "I'll have Bruce's hide for this!"

"Now wait — we aren't sure they lied. It could be something entirely different."

He emptied his cup and stood up, offering her a hand. "We'll see. Right now, I need to finish some paperwork I brought home, and the boys have homework."

"Thanks again," she said. "You were a Godsend."

"No problem."

* * * *

Arriving home to an empty house the following afternoon, Jake had a good idea of where his boys would be. They'd talked of nothing else since the night before. Charlotte's back door stood open so he knocked as he entered, carrying a basket loaded with fruit and nuts. "Welcome wagon."

"Thank you. We love fruit. As a matter of fact, I think the paint I used in here is apple green."

He glanced around, taking in the clean cabinets and

bright color on the wall. It was hard to believe how much the place had changed. "Nice."

"Looks different, doesn't it?"

"It sure does. Reminds me of the day we moved in next door. Elsie Parker invited us over for fresh apple pie."

"How long ago?"

"Right after Jeremy was…" Jake's reply became lost in the chaos going on upstairs. He was fast on his feet, but Charlotte beat him to the bathroom at the head of the stairs by a good five seconds. Following her in, he herded kids out of his way.

"It hurts, Mama!" Maggie screamed, tears streaming down her blotchy cheeks.

He crouched beside the girl, trying to calm her fears, but his stomach tied in a knot at the sight of her little arm trapped in the antique toilet. It was twisted at the elbow, the wrist and hand completely out of sight.

Her shrill voice pierced his ears, causing his eyes to cross momentarily, but he knew the ringing in his ears was nothing compared to what she was feeling. The screams corkscrewed in his head when he touched the arm just above the elbow.

Bruce leaned in for a closer look. "Hey, Maggie, can you feel any doo-doo in there?"

Jake jerked his head toward the door, a warning to the boy, but it was too late to stop Maggie's green eyes from filling with terror. "Mama!"

He wasn't sure if her arm was broken, but he was positive he'd gone deaf in his left ear. If his boys were responsible for this, they'd be grounded for life.

Charlotte distracted Maggie for a moment by drying her tears. "How did it happen, honey?"

"Su-Susie doll dropped her shoe." She sniffed. "An-

44

and I tried to get it."

"Had you flushed the toilet?"

Her lips quivered. "Uh-huh, and it got me-e-e."

Positioning his shoulder, he tried to work so the girl couldn't see what was going on while maneuvering her arm. "It's beginning to move. I just don't want to do any more harm."

"Mr. Jake," Maggie said, looking up at him with trusting, tear-filled eyes. "Do I still got a hand?"

"Sure you do, sweetie. You'll see it in just a minute."

Her green eyes sparkled. "Am I your sweetie?"

His heart melted. "You and Becky can both be my sweeties."

A mischievous grin replaced her tears. "Can Mama be your sweetie, too?"

Charlotte's face glowed. "Two sweeties are all he needs."

He couldn't help but grin. For years, his boys had occupied every inch of his heart, but now, in two short afternoons, Charlotte's girls had plowed their way in.

"Thank goodness!" He freed the arm at last and spread her small palm open in his. "I can see all five fingers."

Maggie's nose wrinkled in disgust. "It's nasty!"

"It'll wash off. Now wiggle your fingers."

Fresh tears shimmered. "They don't move no more."

Jake intercepted Charlotte's worried glance while waiting for Jeremy to return with a clean towel. She held Maggie's arm under the faucet in the sink to wash away the slime, then carefully placed the towel around it. He picked her up and carried her to the car. "I'll lock up. Do you want me to go with you to the emergency room?"

She slid into the driver's seat. "It isn't necessary. I'm

used to doing things by myself."

He and his boys stood on the steps watching while Charlotte and her girls backed out of the drive. She'd seemed a little put out, but he couldn't blame her. After a couple of long, hard days, not to mention the near misses with her girls, he figured she had a right to be a little flaky. Besides—she was absolutely gorgeous.

* * * *

Supper came from leftovers, but the kitchen was still a mess. He loaded the dishwasher, wiped the table, and tossed the dirty towels into the laundry hamper while the older boys finished their homework. The afternoon's distraction had been a welcome change from their usual routine. Instead of the toddler pestering his brothers, Jake found him at the living room window with his nose pressed against the glass. At first glance, Andy appeared to be watching the stray cat searching for mice under the hedges, but then he saw the tears on his cheeks.

"What's wrong, son?" Jake asked, crouching beside him.

"When Mama come home?"

He hugged him, breathing in the faint scent of pine and honeysuckles still lingering in his hair and clothes, a sure sign of Charlotte getting her hugs in. Andy didn't know what it was like to have a mother. The older boys had memories, but his baby had nothing.

"Mama's in heaven. She's not coming back."

Andy's head bobbed. "Uh-huh! Her bring Maggie back."

"No, she…" Jake stopped. It hadn't occurred to him that Andy was watching for Charlotte. "She's the girls' mama, but her name is Charlotte, and that's what we'll call her."

"Mama Char'it."

"No, just Charlotte."

Andy stomped his foot. "Mama Char'it!"

"She's not your mama, Andy," he said, losing his patience at the first sign of a temper tantrum. "Charlotte and the girls are our neighbors. They'll live in their house, and we'll still live in ours."

"I go see her?"

"If you're a good boy."

"I be good. I like Char'it."

"Yeah," Jake agreed, concerned his three-year-old might get too attached. "She's nice. I like her too."

Jeremy deserted his books. "You know what, Dad? It'll be cool having Charlotte next door. Did you know she works two jobs? And she says I can babysit sometimes and earn extra money… if it's okay with you and I keep my grades up."

"You hate babysitting."

"Yeah, but I like making money."

Something in the boy's babbling clicked—two jobs. Now why would a lawyer's widow need to work two jobs, especially with small children? There should have been a boatload of insurance. Of course, she could have blown the wad on—on what?

It was his job to know clothes, and while hers had been of good quality, they'd seen better days. He pictured the porcelain skin with the perfectly arched brows and clear green eyes, adorned by the longest lashes in town. Hers was a natural beauty, not the high maintenance type of woman he dealt with on a daily basis.

"What else did she say?"

Jeremy shrugged as if he'd already lost interest in the subject. "She likes chocolate."

"Most people do."

"Dad," Bruce said, not wanting to be left out. "Becky says they live in a big house, and they've got a swimming pool and a creek in the yard. Boy, if we lived there, I'd never want to move. We could swim and fish all the time."

A whiff of Andy's hair was another gentle reminder of Charlotte's closeness. She hadn't been the least bit forthcoming about herself. If Bruce was right and they lived in a ritzy neighborhood, then why would she want to move to Robins Lane? He'd bet money there was more going on than a change of scenery.

* * * *

The house came alive after school each day. Jeremy washed windows while the younger boys made peanut butter and jelly sandwiches for everyone. Other than their initial battles, Bruce remained a perfect gentleman, and even though she hadn't asked for help, she wasn't about to turn it down either. As for the girls, they'd managed to avoid any more accidents since she'd put the upstairs bathroom off limits and explained in no uncertain terms what would happen if anyone leaned out a window or slid down the banister.

The week flew by with her aching body crying "foul" along the way from the cleaning and packing. Now there was nothing left to do except let the movers in at the other house. She glanced around with pride at a job well done.

Taking the checkbook from her purse, she frowned at the balance. Everything would have to fit into a single load, since it's all she could afford.

Bruce sniffed the air. "You're right, Charlotte."

"About what?"

"This house. The old people smell is gone."

She put away her checkbook. "Then we're finished. Let's call it a night."

"Do we have to?"

"I'm afraid so. Tomorrow's the big day."

"But, Dad said to keep you here until he got home."

"Why would he want me to stay?"

The eight-year-old crossed his arms, heaving an exaggerated sigh of the put-upon. "I don't know, but we're in big sh… uh, trouble if you don't."

Charlotte frowned at the kid. "Oh, yeah? Well, you're in bigger trouble if you don't watch your mouth. Are you guys afraid to stay by yourselves?"

"Shucks no—I mean no, ma'am. We do it all the time."

She glanced at her watch when Jake came through the door with his feet dragging. He tossed his keys on the counter and picked up his youngest son.

"It's about time!" Bruce said, as if they'd been waiting for hours instead of minutes.

He shifted Andy on his hip. "Sorry I'm late. Can you wait a little longer? There's something in the truck."

What could he possibly have she might need, other than a million bucks? Since his house appeared to be an updated version of this one, she ruled it out.

It wasn't long before he and the oldest boy brought in a large, cardboard box and set it at the foot of the staircase. Standing up, Jake grabbed his back.

The younger kids gathered around for a closer look, but Bruce backed away, staring at his dad with eyes full of hurt. Was he jealous of the girls? It was understandable, if he feared losing more of his dad's time. From what she'd seen this past week, the poor kid had precious little to spare. Her heart went out to him as memories came to mind of Becky, fighting for Mitch's attention when the foster kids happened to be boys.

"Would someone tell me what's going on?"

"It's a gift," Jake replied. "Actually, it's a toilet."

Things costing so much usually had ulterior motives attached. She studied his dark blue eyes, but came up blank. "Well, it's a nice gift, but I'm afraid I can't accept it."

"Why not?"

"Because it's too expensive."

"Expensive?" Jake clutched his heart, staggering backward. "It's just a toilet, not a jet plane. Would it make you feel better if I said it was stolen?"

Charlotte shook her head at his ridiculous antics. Jake Weatherman could possibly be the best neighbor in the world, but it didn't change the fact he was a man. To her dismay, he ignored her protest.

Crossing his arms, he rocked back on his heels and grinned. "Girls, would you like a new commode?"

"Sure," Becky replied. "Mama likes flowers and candy."

His dimples sank deeper into the lean cheeks as he winked at the girls. "I'll have to remember that, won't I?"

"About the commode." She pointed to the large box in the hope of getting the subject away from her likes and dislikes. "As I was saying, I can't afford it now, but..."

"It's not costing you a cent." The interruption came before she could finish her excuse for not accepting the thing. "Remember, you're renting. I'm sending the bill to John Parker. He's known for years the commode needed replacing. Besides, this was a window display. I was able to get it at a discount."

She didn't know what to say. Why was it so hard to trust him? "You're sure it's not stolen?"

He burst out laughing. "I'm sure. Haven't you ever given something because it was needed? You've got to be the most skeptical woman I've ever met."

"Maybe so," she said, her past a constant reminder. "But I learned a long time ago not to expect something for nothing."

He shook his head. "Well, this is the exception to the rule. The only catch is you'll have to help me install it."

"I haven't said…"

"I'm not listening to your excuses," he said, interrupting again. "Maggie's running around with her arm in a sling because of the monstrosity upstairs. Now we're installing this commode before somebody else gets hurt."

He had a point, even if he did have an attitude to go with it. The grin had been replaced by the stubborn resolve a man gets when he knows he's right. Charlotte knew it was time to stop looking her gift horse in the mouth.

"Thank you."

He blinked. "What?"

"I said thank you."

"But . . ."

She walked away, returning shortly with an old shoebox. Most of Mitch's tools had disappeared shortly after his death, and she'd assumed his father had taken them, but without proof, it was wiser to say nothing and make do with the few she had left. "Here's my toolbox."

"Never mind," he said, after seeing her hammer and bent nails. "I've got my own tools."

"Then we only have one problem left. The kids ate peanut butter sandwiches after school, but it's almost suppertime. They're probably getting hungry."

The kids giggled when Jake scratched his head, making funny faces while pretending to study the situation. Fingers snapped over his head, indicating the light bulb clicking on, and he reached into his pocket, took out his cellphone and tossed it to Bruce. "You know the number. Order enough pizza for everyone."

The boy's eyes lit up. "We're going to the Pizza Plate?"

"Not tonight, son. We've got a commode to install."

Chapter Four

The shiny white commode fit the décor in the fifties-style bathroom with its claw tub and pedestal sink. Even the linoleum floor appeared in good shape, except for a slightly worn traffic area. Looking around, she made a mental note to pick up some lace curtains to cover the blinds on her next trip to the thrift store.

"Dad's back with the pizzas. Come on, slowpoke. Everybody's at our house."

"I'm coming," she said, using both hands to lift the heavy tool box. She knew from experience how picky Mitch had always been with his tools, so she'd made sure Jake's were all accounted for before closing the lid. It was the least she could do.

The cellphone rang, creating another distraction when she went through the kitchen. Thinking it was the kids, she sat the toolbox on the counter and fished the phone from her pocket. "Hello."

"Charlotte."

The distinctive voice of her father-in-law hit a raw nerve. Her eyes rolled. Had she checked the number, she would have ignored the call. Now it was talk to him or risk him showing up on her doorstep again. "How are you?"

"I believe I should be asking you that," he said, the cultured cadence grating on her nerves like chalk on a blackboard.

"Why?"

"I heard you're leaving Hidden Hills. Is it true?"

"It is," she replied, wondering how he'd found out since no one, other than Mrs. Wilson and the utility companies, knew she was moving. "I've rented a house in Hillside. It's close to the girls' school."

"That's no reason to move."

She bit her tongue to keep from telling him to mind his own business. "Look, Judge. My girls need other children to play with."

"Those girls are fine. You need to focus on your obligations to this family. If you can't afford your mortgage, just how do you plan on paying rent?"

"It's my problem, not yours," she said, ready to stand her ground. She'd thought long and hard before making her decisions, even though the money she'd save in gas would cover the rent. The last thing she needed was Mitch's arrogant, silver-haired father giving her orders.

"Don't even think about neglecting the mortgage." His demanding voice was accompanied by what sounded like a fist, pounding on a table. His angry tone had her imagining purple veins popping in his forehead and his blood pressure skyrocketing. "It comes first, and I'll not let you give the impression our family is in financial trouble. Everything you do reflects on me."

"I'm not neglecting anything."

"Well, I'd like to know what you call it!"

"Survival."

"Don't get sassy with me, girl!"

"Then don't preach to me! If you hadn't dangled the fake partnership in front of Mitch, I wouldn't be in this mess."

"The partnership was real, but he still had to earn it. Nothing is free in this world. It's a concept a little gold-digger like you wouldn't know anything about!"

"Earn it?" she said. "Mitch spent the better part of his life trying to earn your approval. It wasn't until he married me that he realized your approval wasn't worth having!"

"I'm going to ruin you," he said. "Do you hear me? When I get through with you, nobody will give you the time of day, much less any kind of a loan. You'll be lucky to buy a piece of gum!"

"You do it, old man. And I'll see what I can leak to the local papers."

"Now you listen to me, young lady," he said, biting the words out. "I'm running for state senate next year, and I'll not have the family name dragged through the mud. And another thing, don't even think about filing bankruptcy! Do you hear me? Don't even think about it!"

"You old goat! Why don't you leave me alone?"

Charlotte snapped the phone shut before he could start on her other debt, the one he'd claimed was due today. Mitch had told her the money was a gift, a part of his inheritance. She'd known it was a golden carrot dangling in front of his nose to get him to accept his legacy of Hidden Hills. Why had she given in? There would be no freedom from his family until she repaid every cent.

"You'll get no help from me!" Tom McGregor had stated emphatically when she'd asked for his help, shortly after Mitch's death. She'd needed legal advice, not his money. By turning her down, he'd blown his chance.

Whatever decisions she made concerning the estate had nothing to do with him.

With the economy in the pits, a lot of people had opted for bankruptcy instead of waiting for the foreclosure on their loans. But it was a choice she couldn't afford. Mitch occasionally worked at a reduced rate, if a client was desperate or broke, but the only lawyers she knew cost money. Maybe, as a last-ditch effort, it was something to consider. She wasn't trying to hurt Mitch's family, but the money from his life insurance was almost gone—and then what?

* * * *

Crumbs, along with dirty napkins and paper cups, littered Jake's kitchen table, the pizzas now a pleasant memory. Their kids lay spread-eagle in front of the television set, while he and Charlotte cleared the table.

"I'll bet you didn't think I could install a commode."

She stopped. "Tell you what, since you did such a nice job on our pot, I think I'll let you clean up this mess."

"You're all heart." Jake sat, rotating the empty glass in front of him. They'd made a good team, working side by side, to install the commode. She'd even agreed to pick up the tools while he went for pizzas. Now to sit and relax at the table with her seemed right. He hadn't been this comfortable with a woman in a long time.

The dishtowel landed next to him. "Make yourself useful."

He couldn't shake the feeling something had upset her while he'd been gone, but he wouldn't press. They'd just met, so her private life wasn't his business — yet. The questions would be answered in due time, but it didn't stop him from wondering. There had to be a way to get her to confide.

She stacked the empty boxes, stuffing them into the garbage can along with the napkins and cups. "Do you realize how much cheese our kids just ate? Three large pizzas seemed like a lot of food, but they had no problem wolfing it down."

Jake thumped his chest in hopes of relieving the heartburn brought on by too much pepperoni. "I know… I'm stuffed. Just look at them, sprawled on the floor without a care in the world."

"Peaceful."

His mind drifted back to the days when his family made a meal off one pizza. "I wonder what Betty would think of her boys now…"

"Was she your wife?"

It took a moment for him to realize she was talking to him. The green eyes gazing into his held a world of understanding, as if he'd found a kindred spirit.

Charlotte crossed to the sink where he'd made the coffee. She reached into the cabinet and removed two mugs. He wondered if being in his kitchen felt as right to her as it did to him.

"Jeremy said his mother died when Andy was born."

"The timing probably seemed that way to him." His somber tone had come from thinking about Betty. He seldom talked about her or how she'd died, but for some reason, it seemed okay to tell Charlotte. "It happened a week later. I was at work when she had an aneurysm. By the time the ambulance got her to the hospital, it was too late."

"You must've had your hands full." She poured coffee for each of them before sitting down. "Raising three boys, and Andy being a newborn, how did you do it?"

He watched her add cream to the cup, slowly stirring with a teaspoon before taking a sip of the strong brew. "I've had some help. The grannies deserve jewels in their crowns. Then the ladies from our church pitched in, and I can't remember how many housekeepers we've had."

"Well, somebody's done a good job," she said, looking up from her coffee. "We couldn't have managed this week without their help."

"My boys? It's an uphill battle to keep dirty socks in the hamper."

She nodded. "Well, all I've heard this week is yes ma'am and no ma'am."

He frowned, glancing from her to his boys and back again. "My boys?"

"I don't see any others."

He shook his head. "They're up to something."

"Talk about me being skeptical. At least I've got a reason."

"And I don't?"

"Not that I can see." She picked up the dishcloth he hadn't touched and leaned close, wiping crumbs into a pile.

Jake fought the urge to take her in his arms, taste her soft lips, and feel her silky hair slide through his fingers. Her pale skin was inches away, but he didn't dare; she was already skittish. If he worked too fast, she might think he was a scumbag and with good cause. She moved away, leaving the faintest hint of pine and honeysuckle in the air.

He thought about telling her some of the stunts the boys had pulled, but he knew she wouldn't believe him. One thing for sure, she wasn't the prissy pushover he'd first thought. Maybe being around her would be the steady influence his boys needed—a woman's soft touch when they needed it, but firm if they goofed up. Knowing she'd send them home in a heartbeat might make a difference.

"You're too quiet. What are you thinking?"

"If you're going to let me in on it."

"On what?"

"Your reason for being skeptical," he said, determined to learn something about her, even if it took some old-fashioned meddling. "You act like nobody's ever given you anything just for the joy of giving."

"It's been a while."

"How long?"

"Long enough," she said. "And if you're interested, Mitch and I weren't close to any of our neighbors."

"Why not?"

"Our house was rather isolated."

"Not like this place?"

Charlotte released a lengthy sigh. "Is something wrong with me?"

He took the opportunity to stare openly at the curves he'd been admiring all week. "Not from where I'm sitting."

"Not my body!" She threw the dishtowel in his face. "I'm talking about me. I've spent entire afternoons here this week, and you're the only neighbor I've seen."

Jake arched his brows and leaned his elbows on the freshly washed table. Had she blushed? This side of Charlotte was new to him, and he liked it. Underneath the cool, confident exterior, there just might be a lonely soul, looking for a friend.

He wasn't sure if he should burst her bubble or let her down gently. "Well, let's see. There's Mrs. Brown. Her son gave her a computer for her eightieth birthday, so she doesn't go out much anymore. The Borden sisters across the street are friendly enough, but they hate kids. Then there's Jeremiah Hamner, your neighbor to the right. His hearing aid doesn't work…"

"Wait a minute." Charlotte interrupted before he could get to the busybodies at the end of the street. "Are you saying I've moved to Geriatric Row?"

"It's you and me, babe."

He'd expected her to laugh, but instead, she walked toward the window to stare into the darkness. "I thought it would be different."

For a moment he thought she might cry. He had a choice: try to comfort her and have her run like a scared rabbit, or see if he could make her laugh.

"What am I?" He twirled her around by the shoulders so she'd have to look him in the eye. "Chopped liver?"

"I meant another woman."

"Will it help if I string a clothesline across the back yard? We can meet daily for a good gossip."

"Say what?"

His brows wiggled. "Is noon good for you? I know some good stuff."

She almost laughed. "I'll just bet you do. But as much as I'd like to stay and listen, it's late, and I have movers coming in the morning."

"A local company?"

She scratched through her purse and pulled out a wad of keys big enough to pass for a weapon. "It's three college guys. I can't afford a company."

The thought of some hunky, bare-chested Romeos flexing their muscles in front of Charlotte wasn't exactly to his liking. "Are you sure it's a good idea?"

"What?"

"You know… college guys," he said, trying not to say what he meant. "Have they done this before? What if they break something, and what about insurance? Are they insured?"

Her chin shot up, and he knew without a doubt he'd hit a sore spot when her eyes flashed. "Excuse me?"

"I don't want you getting ripped off."

"I may look like I fell off the turnip truck," she said, as soon as the girls had finished their goodnights. "But I assure you, I can hire movers without any help."

"What in the... what'd I say?"

She paused at the door, reluctant to leave, or was it his imagination? He wanted to roll back the clocks so she would stay.

"I'm perfectly capable of handling my own affairs."

"You think I'm trying to tell you what to do?"

"Aren't you?"

"No."

"Then why the third degree?"

He wasn't about to admit he'd been slapped by the green-eyed monster. There wasn't a jealous bone in his body. Well—maybe one.

"I was just being neighborly," he said, giving the only reasonable excuse he could think of. "Neighbors look out for each other. Sorry, I didn't mean to pry."

Her frown disappeared and for the first time in years, Jake found himself wanting to be close to another woman in more than just a physical way. Not just any woman, but *this* woman with the green eyes and porcelain skin. He'd noticed when she wiped the table she was still wearing the plain gold wedding band. Taking his ring off had been a heart-wrenching decision to make. It was like losing Betty all over again, and it took three tries before he found the courage to leave it off. Charlotte's ring remained in place. It was possible she couldn't let go of Mitch.

He watched the indecision in her eyes. She remained a closed book, and he couldn't get a grip on his curiosity. So far he knew she worked two jobs, liked pizza, flowers, and chocolate. If she had the big house Bruce had mentioned, why would she move to Robins Lane? It didn't make sense.

Chapter Five

Fear, along with self-doubt, had plagued Charlotte since Mitch's death more than two years ago. There'd been no shortage of well-intended advice. While her parents wanted her to move back home, her in-laws pointed out she had a home at Hidden Hills—with a mortgage. As true as it was, she hadn't needed reminding. Her obligations were nightmares she couldn't shake.

Finances had always been her strong point, but she'd raised no objections when Mitch had offered to handle their bank account after buying his grandfather's estate. A larger home had meant more foster kids, and while it had been a noble gesture in theory, the reality was frustrating; breakfast took twice as long, buying groceries became a weekly three-hour ordeal, the chore of doing laundry went from two loads a day to six, and she'd compared getting everyone ready for school to a marathon. In addition, there'd been afternoon snacks, homework to complete, and supper to prepare.

With Mitch managing the finances, she'd had one-on-one time with their girls, but she'd missed family time with just the four of them. Looking back, she admitted it hadn't been fair to lay all the blame on him. They'd tried to handle more than was humanly possible without help.

He'd wanted the foster kids to have the advantages of a stable home life, something most of them had never had, but with him working long hours to make partner, it had fallen on her to make it happen. She'd known he loved her and his heart was in the right place, but communication between the two of them had become almost nonexistent. It wasn't long until she'd become wiped out both mentally and physically.

Before moving to Hidden Hills, they'd always had time to sit down and discuss the budget. All large purchases had been agreed on ahead of time, and if they couldn't agree, then it was a pass. Things were different after Mitch took over the books, partly because he was too controlling and partly because she was always busy. It wasn't until that hot July morning when she'd stopped for gas and had her credit card rejected that she'd begun to worry.

"No problem," Mitch had assured her when she'd asked about the card. "I just forgot to tell you I lost it. They've issued new numbers, but it'll take a few days for the cards to arrive."

Mitch had his faults like everyone else, but he'd always been honest with her, so she'd had no reason for doubt. Then a few days later the bank had called. They were overdrawn.

"What's going on, Mitch?" She'd confronted him the moment he'd walked through the door. "First the credit card, and now the bank."

"Let it go," he'd replied, sounding more like his father than the man she'd married. "We agreed I would handle our finances—and I'll handle it."

"Don't lie to me, Mitch! We've only been here six

months. Are we broke?"

"No," he'd argued. "We aren't broke, just a little short of cash."

"To me, that's broke!"

"When I get my partnership…"

Unshed tears burned Charlotte's eyes as shame consumed her. The mention of the elusive partnership had set off the worst argument of their married life. A week later Mitch was gone, and their house of cards lay crumpled at her feet. Since then, she'd put herself on a tight budget and was ever so slowly climbing out of debt.

She couldn't afford the luxury of living at Hidden Hills. The decision to move to Robins Lane had been the last of her cost-cutting measures. Money saved on gas would pay the rent, and the house, which was smaller in size, would be easier to manage.

Although the dark hardwood floors needed stripping, a damp mop had sufficed. As for the walls, she'd done the best she could with some old paint found in the attic. The house was solid and she'd felt a special bond the moment she'd walked in. For the first time since Mitch's death, she was able to close her eyes at night and feel safe.

Circumstances had changed her over the past two years. Not in looks, but in perspective. The boxes stacked in every nook and cranny would have been daunting at one time, but not now. She would survive with God's help. He'd already seen her through her darkest days and given her strength when she had none.

"Mama!" Becky shouted from the top landing of the stairs. "Those mover guys put Maggie's bed in my room!"

"See if she'll trade with you."

"I don't like her bed!"

"Then see if she'll switch rooms with you."

"Cool!"

Charlotte doubted the beds were the only mix-up. She hated to admit it, but Jake had been right. Some of her furniture had made the trip without a problem, but other pieces appeared as if she'd bought them at a scratch and dent shop. One of the bedside lamps hadn't survived at all. The old saying "you get what you pay for" was true, but in her case, she'd got what she could afford—the guys were cheap.

Everything she owned had fit into the panel truck except her plants. There wasn't any hurry as long as she got those before the house sold. It had been on the market for over eighteen months without so much as a nibble. She knew it was unrealistic to hope Mrs. Wilson could do any better, but hope was all she had. Time was running out, leaving her with money for only three more payments before the unthinkable happened.

Charlotte forgot her search for a clean cup when a bushy green plant floated past her kitchen window. She checked her reflection in the toaster and ran her fingers through her unruly hair. The pale face staring back was distorted, but there was no denying the dark smudges beneath her eyes. After splashing some water, she grabbed a dishtowel to wipe away the mascara, then realized she wasn't wearing any.

"Hey lady, this thing's heavy. Do you have to take all day?"

The voice was grumpier than she remembered, but the rest of the guy was familiar enough through the screen door. She unhooked the latch. "It's beautiful, Jake."

"You think so?" His lopsided grin let her know what he thought of her taste. "I wanted to get roses, but the girls at work said this was more neighborly, and since I'm not much at picking flowers—except roses."

Charlotte led him around a stack of unopened boxes, trying to keep her attention on the flowers instead of his blue eyes. "This is a Peace Lily, and I love it."

"Then I guess it *is* neighborly. Personally, I like roses."

She found herself wondering how many women he'd bought roses for since his wife passed away. Jake wasn't handsome in the regular sense. His hairline was receding, and his shoulders seemed too wide for his lanky frame, but the man had the most incredible royal blue eyes she'd ever seen. Even his smell had her spirit reaching out for him in a most non-neighborly way.

Why was this happening to her? Why now, with this man? Others had tried to flirt with her, and she'd felt nothing. Now a skinny guy brings her a potted plant, and she swoons like a heroine in an old movie. She cut her eyes away from his before she did something stupid. "I feel like a fraud."

"You do—why?"

"Because I've got all sorts of flowers just waiting for a ride," she admitted, hoping she didn't sound ungrateful.

"One more won't hurt—will it?"

"No, of course not." The smell of his cologne was playing havoc with her nervous system. She inhaled deeply, breathing in his fresh male scent. "There's always room for one more."

He sat the pot on a large box and surveyed the room. "The store's closed tomorrow. We can use the van if you want to."

"You're offering to move my plants?"

"Sure, why not? It might be fun."

It should have been so easy to say yes, but something held her back. If he'd been a woman, she wouldn't have hesitated, but he was a man, and men had ulterior motives, especially the great smelling ones like him.

"What store are we talking about?"

"Bett's."

"The clothing store? You're sure they won't mind?"

"I've used it before." He rummaged through a box on the kitchen counter and turned with a grin, holding up two Alabama coffee mugs. "I knew you were a fan."

Charlotte cleared a place on the table and emptied a couple of chairs, while he poured the coffee. It was the first break she'd had all day.

"So you work in a store." She was surprised at his occupation. The boys complained all week of him spending too much time with his blueprints, and she'd pegged him as being an engineer. "I guess we have more in common than noisy kids."

"Could be." He moved his Peace Lily to the sink and gave it a good soaking. She watched him remove the foil, letting the excess water drain through. For someone who knew nothing about flowers, he seemed to know what he was doing. Afterwards, he unpacked three boxes of dishes, putting them in the cabinets before joining her at the table.

"I'm a checker at Milner's Market," she said, then remembered he'd been in her checkout line. "Of course, you already knew that."

"And do you like it there?" A cookie disappeared into his mouth.

"It's okay."

"But it's not your life's dream?"

Charlotte hugged the warm cup with both hands. Glancing up, she found herself staring into his probing blue eyes, wondering how much she could reveal before he burst out laughing the way her father-in-law had. She wasn't being fair to Jake, and she knew it. Any man who'd offered to meet her at the clothesline for a good gossip deserved the truth.

"I'm also a cosmetologist," she said, noting his puzzled expression. "John Milner offered me a job when our insurance coverage at Mitch's firm ran out. I work part-time at the Beauty Boutique."

"Milner?" Jake dropped into the chair to her right. Leaning back, he reached for another cookie, popping it into his mouth. The teasing light in his blue eyes dimmed. "Is he a special friend?"

She knew what he meant, but decided to take the high road. "Oh, he's special all right, one of the kindest men I've ever met. His wife thinks so too, so you can get your mind out of the gutter."

"I didn't say anything."

"For your information, my husband won a difficult case for Mr. Milner several years ago, and this was his way of thanking him."

"I wasn't prying." His dark blue eyes filled with mischief. "Yes, I was. You seeing anyone on a regular basis?"

"Two girls, two jobs, and a mountain of bills… when am I supposed to have time for a man?" She flipped the tables. "What about you? Any special ladies in your life, right now?"

"Touche'." He laughed, avoiding her question. "How long have you been a beautician?"

Was this a truce or just another tactic for prying into her personal life? She had nothing to hide, but some things were just hard to explain without making Mitch sound like a control freak. "About a year. I was in cosmetology school when Mitch and I married. I went back last year… got my diploma and passed State Boards."

"Good for you." He lifted the coffee mug in salute. "Here's to determination."

She was touched. It had taken a lot of hard work and no one, other than her parents, had cared. To her in-laws, anything short of a university degree was a waste of time.

"Someday I plan to own a string of shops." She waited for him to laugh at her dreams, but he didn't. Instead, he crossed his legs and relaxed, as if he was in for a long visit.

"Who watches the girls?"

"Kimmie Jones," she said, wondering if Jeremy had mentioned sitting to his dad. "She works with me at the shop, but our hours are the same sometimes."

"And then you'll need Jeremy."

He'd said it as a statement—a done deal from which he'd been excluded, and it wasn't what she'd meant by asking the boy. It was time to smooth any feathers she might have ruffled. "Only if it's okay with you."

"It is," he agreed. "Provided his grades stay up. I might as well tell you he's not one for studying."

"I won't ask him on a school night."

He didn't say anything as he pushed his chair away from the table and stood up, as if he was leaving. Had he forgotten about her other plants? She hated mentioning it again, since she'd side-stepped giving him an answer, but...

"About my plants?" She watched him closely. "It's a long ride, almost to Wills' Junction."

At first his expression was blank, as if he'd forgotten what she meant. Then he grinned, looking pleased with himself. "What time do you want to leave tomorrow?"

Chapter Six

The morning sun streaked across the room, shining directly into Charlotte's eyes. She moaned, snuggling deeper under the covers, every joint in her body aching from shifting heavy boxes. Sleep, she needed sleep—restful, mind-numbing sleep.

It was no use. She raised her head at the sound of voices coming from the hall. Her bedroom door flew open and her girls bounced onto her bed. Their giggles put the sun to shame.

"Mama, Mama," Maggie said, patting Charlotte's cheeks. "I sleep all night in my bed, and I didn't get scared!"

She yawned. "Good."

"And Mrs. Parker didn't make any noises at all," Becky added between bounces.

Raking the hair out of her eyes, she raised herself on one elbow. "Becky, Mrs. Parker isn't here anymore. She's in heaven, just like Daddy."

"But Bruce said…"

"Forget what Bruce said. He was just trying to scare you."

"Oh."

"How would you girls like some breakfast?"

They flung themselves into her outstretched arms. "Pancakes!"

"Of course, it's pancakes. Today is Sunday, isn't it?" Hugs from her girls were the best part of the morning. She had started making the special breakfast shortly after Mitch's death as something for them to look forward to.

"Are we going to church?"

"Not today," Charlotte replied, smarting in her shoulders and lower back. She eased into her old housecoat. "I've got too much to do."

"But Grandma says…"

"Grandma wouldn't go either if she was hurting like I am."

"But…"

"We'll find a new church." She followed her girls into the kitchen. "I promise. Just not today."

The hot grill sizzled as the batter hit the metal and spread into perfectly round pancakes. She preferred to ignore the number of calories in each bite. Besides, enough work had gone on these past few days to deserve a treat.

Her spatula stopped in mid-flip when Bruce and Andy walked through the back door and headed straight for the breakfast table. At first, she thought they were there to play, but then Jeremy came in, removing extra plates and silverware from the cabinet. "I'll help you with these," he said, dividing the large stack of pancakes around the table and pouring orange juice for everyone before sitting down.

Charlotte glanced at the door again. Her girls hadn't opened it, and she was positive she'd locked it the night before, even double-checked to be sure. Yesterday had been hectic. Had she invited the boys to breakfast and forgotten? At any rate, they were sitting around her table and her soft heart couldn't send them away. Their plates were almost empty, so she mixed another batch of batter, hoping for a bite before the stack disappeared.

"Where's your dad this morning?" she asked, thinking Jake must have had to go to work after all.

"He's sleeping in."

"What?"

He had some nerve, sleeping while she fed his kids! She had a good mind to send them home hungry. A sharp pain shot through her shoulder, and the bowl slipped. Batter splattered on the counter, adding to her ill humor. She reached for a rag to wipe the spill and bumped into Bruce, holding up his empty plate for a refill. Was there no limit to what these kids could eat?

"Dad's getting old." The boy licked his lips, eyeing the largest cake on the grill. "He needs his rest."

"Him's not got no hair," added the three-year-old, syrup dripping from his chin.

Out of the mouth of babes. Charlotte grinned in spite of herself. They'd left out sneaky; only a sneak would send his kids over for breakfast without asking.

But then, Jake had agreed to move her plants. The lily still sat on the counter where he'd left it. She'd never had such an appropriate gift. Come to think of it, how many people could say they'd been given a toilet?

She thought of his laughing blue eyes when he'd brought it in, and those same eyes turning dark with pain when he'd told her of his wife's death. He was a nice man, one she'd like to know better. She'd felt his pain, and yet he seemed—if not happy, then content with his life.

"Hey, no fair. You got the big one!"

"Aw hush, Maggie." Bruce emptied the syrup bottle

onto his plate. "I'm a guy, and guys need more food. Ain't that right, Charlotte?"

Before she could answer, there was a loud knock at the back door. A hush fell on the room, like the calm before a storm, leaving little doubt as to who was outside. The worried glances bouncing around the table were nothing compared to their dad's when she let him in.

"Have you seen my boys?"

She stepped aside, relief evident in his face when he looked in her kitchen. "Would you like some breakfast?"

"What?"

"Breakfast." The invitation was more for the sake of good manners than anything else. After all, he had promised to move her plants.

He frowned. "You invited my boys for breakfast without clearing it with me first?"

They were standing in the close confines of the utility porch where his wide shoulders took up more than a fair share of space. Claustrophobia threatened, and she tried to make a hasty retreat to the safety of the kitchen.

"You didn't answer me," he said, blocking her way with his arm. "Did you invite them?"

Her eyes zeroed in on his arm. "Well," she said, caught off-guard by the hard strength and the clean male scent. "I can't remember doing it, but they let themselves in and started eating, so I must have."

He jiggled the knob both inside and out. "Let themselves in, huh? Didn't you lock this last night?"

"Of course I did!"

His expression spoke volumes, and Charlotte didn't care for anything it said. She was within a gnat's hair of letting him know what she thought of his bossy attitude, when he went around her into the kitchen, leaving her to

74

follow.

"Okay, son." He held out his palm. "Hand it over."

"But, Dad…"

"Now!"

Bruce reached into his pocket and pulled out a shiny new key, glaring at Charlotte as though it were her fault.

Jake nudged Jeremy's shoulder. "Where's yours?"

Charlotte's jaw dropped when the older boy handed over a second key. She realized their help this past week had been a ploy to set her up. Since when had she become such a pansy as to allow a couple of juvenile delinquents to peg her as an easy mark? "How did you get those?"

She glanced at Jake, but he was looking at his sons. The cold fury in his eyes had the boys dropping their heads, stuffing more pancakes into their mouths. Anything to delay an explanation.

"I give 'em Mama's key."

"You what, Maggie?"

"Give 'em Mama's key. Now we won't get locked out."

His fingers clamped the back of the boys' necks like falcon claws. "Not only have you victimized Charlotte, but you dragged Maggie into it?"

She wouldn't admit it for the world, but she liked watching them squirm. They deserved everything they were likely to get but "death by pancakes" could be national news if she didn't intervene.

"Ah—Jake, you might want to let them swallow. They're turning blue."

The pressure eased, but only slightly. She read his frown to mean, "Keep your nose out of it!"

He had some nerve, blaming her for what his little brats had done. She was the victim, not the problem. "Of all the nerve…"

"I'm sorry," he said, reaching into the cabinet for a cup. "It's not your fault."

"Are you mad, Mommy?" Andy spoke with the wide-eyed innocence of a three-year-old.

She stared at him in horror. Why hadn't she seen this coming? Andy had been underfoot the past week, shadowing her every move. She had sent him to play, but a moment later he'd been back, close enough to touch.

Jake intervened. "I should have warned you. He copies everything Maggie says."

She breathed a sigh of relief. Maybe she was being too sensitive about Andy and not sensitive enough with the older boys. Childish pranks were a fact of life, just like copying an older child was a natural part of growing up. If she ignored Andy, this would all blow over.

Becky's impish grin shot the theory down. "Can Daddy join us for breakfast, too?"

"I didn't come…" With the shoe on the other foot, it was comical to see Jake backpedal.

The older boys watched like hawks, waiting no doubt to see if they'd gotten away with their stunt. It was Jake's place to punish them, and surely he would, but dashing their hopes now would make them sulk, ruining her day. She wasn't having it. "Pull up a chair, Jake. We've got pancakes to eat."

"But…"

"Don't argue with me," she said, shoving the platter into his hands. "It's cooked, and we don't waste food!"

He held the platter close to his nose. Smiling, he savored a big whiff. "Must be pretty bad if you have to force folks to eat it."

She ignored him.

Not since her last family reunion had Charlotte seen food disappear so fast. By the time she'd poured Jake's coffee and refilled her own, the platter was coming back empty. Thankfully, he'd salvaged a small stack for her. Once again she was astonished at what his boys could eat.

She watched the fresh faces around the table, each one beautiful in its own way. The group was quiet for a change. The only noises came from forks clinking against plates and the occasional call for more syrup.

To an outsider, it would look like a real family—except they weren't. They were the remnants of what had once been two happy homes.

Her eyes strayed to the man across the table pouring extra syrup on Maggie's plate, then taking time to cut up Andy's last pancake. Most likely there was a special woman in his life, and she found herself wondering what it would be like to be that woman. His table manners were beautiful, and his relationship with his boys seemed closer than what Mitch had shared with their girls. Jake would probably find his boys a suitable mother someday, but she knew it wouldn't be her. She had her future mapped out, and it didn't include anyone but her girls.

"You're not eating," Jake said, his warm voice breaking into her thoughts. "From the way you're staring, I must have more syrup on my chin than Andy."

Charlotte wasn't fond of being caught staring, and she positively hated blushing. Guilty of both, she reached for her coffee cup. "Sorry, my mind was…"

Jake's eyes darkened, as if he could read her thoughts. They were the eyes of a predatory male. She knew that look, and no matter how tempting the bait, it was best to keep her distance. He blinked, and the hunter was gone, or maybe it had been her imagination all along. Either way, she breathed a sigh of relief.

"Mommy cooks good, huh, Daddy?"

"She sure does," Jake agreed, his attention focused on his three-year-old. "But what did we agree to call Charlotte?"

"Mama Char-it!"

"No," he reminded him. "We agreed to call her Charlotte."

Andy's attention was more focused on his pancakes than his dad. His tiny tongue popped out again, circling his lips to get all the sweet syrup. "Oh yeah, me forgot."

Jake shrugged. "Maybe he'll remember next time?"

She hoped it ended the discussion.

One by one the empty plates were pushed back as each child finished and began to leave the table. His boys seemed to think they'd gotten off scot-free.

"Not so fast," Jake said, his voice leaving no room for arguing. "You guys owe Charlotte an apology."

"We're sorry."

It was a bit too quick for her liking, considering she'd heard more sincerity from the last telemarketer she'd hung up on. But at least it was something.

"And?"

"And we won't do it again?"

"That's right," Jake agreed. "And to make sure you don't forget, I want both of you in her yard picking up limbs while I get the van."

"Aw, Dad," Bruce whined. "All I do around here is work."

"I saw how you worked on the stack of pancakes."

"But, Dad…"

"Get out of here."

She was impressed, so much so she had her girls help

in the yard since the boys couldn't have made the keys without their help.

"But, Dad…"

"What?"

"Does this mean we aren't going to church today?"

Jake glanced at his watch, then at Charlotte. "I'll make you a deal. We'll skip church today and move your plants if you'll agree to visit our church next Sunday."

"You're blackmailing me into church?"

He grinned. "The Lord moves in mysterious ways."

Charlotte craned her neck to see the clock on the wall over his left shoulder. "Sunday School starting in ten minutes has nothing to do with it?"

He pivoted in his seat, a lopsided grin crossing his face. "Didn't know that was there. So, how about it… you going to church with us next week?"

She shook her head. "I've already agreed to go to Annabelle's church next week."

"Annabelle?"

"Smith… from work. She's a member of Cherry Road Baptist. It's supposed to be around here somewhere, but I haven't found it yet."

"Then I guess we can count on you for the next two Sundays at least. Annabelle's our piano player."

Charlotte had a feeling she was going to like the church on Cherry Road, especially if the other members were as nice as the ones she'd already met. If not, God would lead her to the right church.

Bruce slid into the chair next to his dad, his expressive face showing nothing but angelic innocence. "Our Sunday School teacher said God made the Sabbath as a day of rest. I don't think we should be working in the yard today."

"You don't say?"

"Yes, sir, it's what she said."

Jake leaned down until he was eye to eye with his middle son. "Did she also mention it's okay to get the ox out of the ditch?"

The boy frowned. "No, sir. She didn't say nothing about an ox. But I guess we can't leave a dumb animal in a ditch."

"Get out of here." He swatted the boy on the bottom to help him on his way.

She shook her head in disbelief. The man had an odd way of communicating with his kids. "An ox?"

"Hey... it's in there."

"I know. It's just I'd never thought of using it in quite that way."

"You'll learn how to use the stories to your advantage." He shifted his chair under the table and hung the extra keys on her bulletin board. "Do you need any help with the dishes?"

She declined, wanting her plants moved more than she needed a man with soap up past his elbows. With everyone out of the way, cleanup only took a moment. He'd seen her looking her worst, so she rushed around, making sure she'd be presentable when he returned.

There was no doubt she'd been targeted again when she tossed the extra keys into her handbag and disturbed some dry leaves in the top. The purse, a gift from her mother, now held who-knew-what?

The leaves weren't a concern; it was what might be hidden underneath, that made her nervous. The thought of snakes, rats, or spiders made her skin crawl. Was she to expect retaliation every time she disagreed with these boys?

Her queasy stomach had her wishing she'd left off the last pancake when a wad of fat, juicy, red-worms fell from the upturned bag, landing with a thump on the towel she'd placed on the counter.

"Amateurs." She glanced out the window to where the boys were working. "I can deal with these guys."

She gathered the worms into an empty can and sat it on the back step. It was time to put an end to their shenanigans. A damp cloth was all it took to get her purse back in order, and since eavesdropping as a means of survival wasn't a bad idea, she hid behind the door and waited.

"Aw, man!" Bruce saw the worms. "She's no fun. I'll bet she won't even scream when she finds frogs in her car."

Charlotte cringed. Her girls were far from perfect, but these kids were brats. She listened until the eight-year-old cut loose with a string of profanities guaranteed to burn the preacher's ears. His dad would probably be mad when he found out what she planned to do, but she'd heard enough.

"Ohhh!" Maggie cried. "You're swearing. I'm telling Mama!"

Charlotte stepped outside, knowing what it would take to keep her sanity. It worked on her as a kid, and she was betting it would work now.

"Mama!"

"You don't have to tell me, I heard it all."

"Mama, he said—"

"Come on, Bruce." She pinched his shoulder with her knuckles the way his dad had done. "I've heard enough of your foul mouth."

He flinched. "What are you doing?"

"You'll see." She marched him down the hall toward the bathroom.

He grabbed the door facings, locking his arms to keep

from going inside. Not to be outdone, she hooked her leg around the back of his knee to knock him off balance. She clamped him against the sink and rubbed the liquid soap across his lips, her finger slipping inside against his teeth. It was a battle of wills, and she had no intention of losing.

"That's awful," Bruce cried, spewing and spitting soap bubbles into the sink. "You're trying to kill me!"

"No, I'm not. It's my mom's recipe—all natural."

"That stuff's poison," he sobbed. "I'm telling Daddy!"

"Go right ahead."

"You're mean!"

She released Bruce, knowing she'd never catch him again if he made a run for it. "Did it get rid of the swear words, or do we change brands?"

Bruce huffed, spitting for all he was worth. "I hate you!"

Charlotte knew, but there was no way she'd back down. "Did it work?"

His blue eyes grew wide with fear. "I'm telling Daddy!"

"We can always use my granny's lye soap."

The boy rubbed his tongue on the towel until he gagged. She knew how he felt. Her first taste of soap had been about his age. She remembered trying to make herself throw up, so her mother would be sorry for putting the bar in her mouth. It hadn't worked then, and it wasn't working now. Nothing came up, and he finally stopped.

"Well, what do you think?" she said, watching for a reaction in his blue eyes. "Do we try my granny's soap?"

"No!" he said, defeated at last. "It worked. There's no more swear words, honest."

"Are you sure?"

He nodded. "Yes, ma'am, I'm sure."

She crossed her arms, leaning back against the counter to lay out the rules for him and his brother. "So far you kids have had things pretty much your way, but it's about to change. Under no circumstances will I be terrorized. This is our home, and I'm not going anywhere. Now, I'd like to be friends, but I can be your worst nightmare. It's up to you."

The boy's expression fluctuated between bewilderment and total shock. She left the room with her final ultimatum floating in the air. Five minutes passed before he came creeping into the living room where she was sorting books.

"Charlotte?"

She glanced up, relieved at the change in Bruce. The hostility she'd sensed since the first day she'd met him was gone. In its place was the uncertainty of a child wanting more than anything to be loved and accepted. She held out her arms, and he walked into them. The hug was brief, but she understood.

"Would you like to help with these?"

Bruce picked a stack of *Junie B. Jones* books, belonging to Becky, and thumbed through several pages. His lack of interest in the subject matter was obvious.

"I like the *Hardy Boys* and *Harry Potter*." He placed them on the bottom shelf of the bookcase. "Loretta says they're stupid, but they're not. She's stupid."

"Who's Loretta?" she asked, thinking it was a neighborhood girl.

"Just one of the dopey women my dad knows."

Charlotte hid her grin behind a large dictionary. In her opinion, children were much better judges of character than most men. She doubted Jake was an exception, but she wasn't about to air her opinion in front of his son.

"She's probably not so bad once you get to know her,

or your dad wouldn't like her."

He shook his head. "She's nice enough when Dad's around, but she's dumb as a rock."

"Honest?"

"Yeah, like last week," he said. "I asked Loretta who would win the World Series—she said, 'the Crimson Tide.' Now I ask you, is she dumb or what?"

She laughed. "You're right. Seems pretty dumb to me."

Bruce sighed in disgust. "It's been the same with all the women he brings home—dumb as dirt!"

Charlotte laughed. "I can see where it would be a problem, but I hope you don't feel that way about all women. As for me, I played third base for three years in a row, and I ran track my senior year."

"They had sports when you were in school?"

"Watch it, kid!" She cuffed his chin. "I'm also a pretty good fisherman."

"No way!"

"Yes, way." She rummaged through a cardboard box for proof. Her trophy catfish had grown a little dusty over the years, but it was still quite impressive. Smiling, she pulled it out of its hiding place with fanfare. "Ta-da!"

"You caught him?" he asked, eyes wide with wonder.

She winked. "Play your cards right, and I just might show you my fishing hole."

Bruce rubbed the stiff whiskers, measuring their length against his fingers. "Can we go now?"

"Let's see." She glanced at the clock over the mantel. "Eleven-fifteen. It's a twenty mile drive to my house, so if your dad's not much longer getting back, then we should have time."

Bruce sat the fish in the center of the mantel and

readjusted it several times until it was just right. She'd had no idea the boy loved fishing.

"Charlotte," he said in a singsong voice. "You're not half as bad as Loretta."

High praise indeed from this kid.

"You know, Bruce, I chose this house because it was cheaper, and I liked it. But when we discovered you guys next door, well, it's almost perfect."

His head ducked as a pink flush crept into his already rosy cheeks. He cut his eyes toward her, shoving the remaining books into whatever space he could find before bolting for the door. "Wait till I tell the guys we're going fishing!"

"Bruce?"

He stopped. "Yes, ma'am?"

"While we're waiting for your dad, why don't you and your brothers get the frogs out of my car?"

His mouth fell open. "W-o-w! How did you know?"

She stared him straight in the eye, a warning for the future. "I know a lot of things."

Chapter Seven

Jake stopped by to see Ralph and Shelby Watts after picking up the van. Not only were they old friends, but Ralph was also his attorney and would possibly know Charlotte's late husband. He only planned to stay long enough for his boys to finish their job.

"Skipping church? That's not like you," Ralph said when he opened his door, coffee cup in hand. "Come on in—the pot's still hot."

"Maybe just a cup." Jake followed him into the kitchen. The house was quiet now, but he could remember when it had been as noisy as his own, before Ralph's girls went away to college. Now the quietness reminded him of how fast time slips away. "I'm helping a neighbor move some potted plants today."

"I'm assuming it's a woman." Ralph raised his brows. "She must be something to make you miss preaching. What is she, single—divorced?"

"Widow."

"Young—pretty?"

"Both." Jake poured his own coffee. "And she's got two girls."

"Interesting. Is she from around here?"

"Over toward Wills' Junction." The coffee wasn't near as good as what he'd had for breakfast, or maybe it was the company. "She hasn't told me much about herself."

Ralph burst out laughing. "She *must* be hot if she has you working already. Has this woman got a name?"

"McGregor. And get this, she was married to a lawyer. Any of your cronies go by the name?"

Ralph finished his coffee. "McGregor? If his name was Mitch, then you've hit the jackpot."

"What are you talking about?"

"The McGregors of Wills' Junction," his friend replied. "Don't tell me you've lived in north Alabama your entire life and don't know about the family. Judge Tom McGregor? Had two sons—Mitch and Mark? Mitch was a lawyer, died a couple of years ago, and Mark is a pediatrician. I can't believe you haven't heard of them."

"Sure, I've heard of the judge—who hasn't? But are you sure it's the same family? What little I know about Charlotte doesn't seem to fit with what I've heard about him."

"Positive," Ralph said, warming to his story. "Family has old money. Before he died, Mitch inherited his grandfather's estate—huge house with lots of land. I'd say his wife knew exactly who she was marrying."

Jake didn't want to hear this. "Have you ever met Charlotte?"

"No, but I saw her at the Wills' Country Club a couple of times right after they married. I got the impression she didn't fit in—probably used her looks to move up the ladder."

Jake left a few minutes later with conflicting ideas about his new neighbor racing through his mind. Ralph had stirred his curiosity even more. And it hadn't changed the fact he was drawn to the woman like a magnet.

Charlotte had the kids ready to go when he pulled into her driveway. He liked punctuality in a woman. Hopefully, he'd have a lot more answers before the afternoon was over.

The twenty miles from Hillside to Wills' Junction was cut short when she had him turn left about six miles north of the city limit. Another four miles passed before they eased onto a narrow road seeming to lead to nowhere.

"Is this the scenic route?" The thought crossed his mind she was leading him on a wild-goose chase. There hadn't been a mailbox in miles.

She settled the escalating dispute in the back seat before answering. "Afraid not. This is the only way, but we're almost there."

He started to argue when the crumbling pavement came to an end, blocked by a set of ornamental wrought iron gates. Across the top, the name 'Hidden Hills' scrolled in cursive, paying testimony to the artistic skills of a long-ago blacksmith.

"I'll have to open it." She didn't give him time to protest. Instead of taking the key from her purse as he'd expected, she reached up and removed the 's' from the name above the gate, inserting it into the lock.

Jake waited till Charlotte was back in the van before taking his foot off the brake, letting the vehicle roll forward at a snail's pace. Pavement gave way to gravel as God's natural wonders came into view. The dirt road stretching before them was overgrown with grass and weeds, making it appear to be no more than a wide path in a hardwood forest. He could see where the neglect of the present covered the wealth of the past, and it was breathtaking.

As perfect as the place seemed now, he knew it would be even more impressive when the fall colors arrived. Early morning dews and evening sunsets followed by the rising moon of a cold, wintry night would be well worth the drive. While he welcomed the isolation for himself, he only could imagine the fear Charlotte must have felt each time she returned home to this loneliness.

"Would you look at those trees," Jeremy said, his head jutting out the rear window as the breeze ruffled his hair. "They're huge, and get a load of those yellow leaves covering the ground over there. It looks like carpet. Can we camp here, Dad?"

Charlotte glanced over her shoulder. "You're welcome to camp, but you're looking at poison oak."

He sensed the creeping getting on her nerves, but even so, the steep incline leading down to an old wooden bridge called for caution. The kids were glued to the windows, staring at large rocks hanging over the creek bed, some ten feet below the once-covered bridge.

As they left the surprisingly sturdy structure behind, the road curved again, and they topped another hill. His own anticipation surpassed the kids' when he glimpsed a large metal roof in the distance.

The state parks weren't as well kept as the last portion of the drive leading up to the old, two-storied antebellum home. He paused long enough to count the marble columns connecting the wraparound porch to the roof. It was the epitome of the Old South.

Time stood still for a moment. Other than the grass, everything about the house was picture-perfect, as if it was staged for a photo shoot. The only things missing were cotton fields and horse drawn carriages.

"This place is awesome!"

Jake echoed their sentiments. As a kid, he'd heard people talk about the Wills family and their mansion in the woods, but he'd never seen it. Over time, he'd forgotten it even existed. Now he was here in a place where time seemed irrelevant, except for the modern-day version of the Southern Belle, gazing at the home she'd given up. A solemn resolve etched in her delicate profile gave him cause for concern.

The elegance, the beauty, and the lifestyle seemed to suit Charlotte McGregor, yet she was giving it all up for an old house in a middle-class neighborhood with faulty plumbing. It was a puzzle he intended to solve.

He stood back as she unlocked the massive double doors leading into the entrance hall, letting the children enter first. The dim interior burst to life with the flip of a switch, revealing a spotless room. His eyes were drawn to the crystal chandelier, hanging from a sculptured ceiling some twenty feet above. Even more impressive were the two floating staircases, which circled the foyer walls before merging into one on the second-floor landing.

The kids ran wild in all directions, their clear voices echoing with their footsteps on the hand-planed hardwood floors. A low whistle escaped his lips. "This is *some* house you've got here. Mind if I look around?"

"Not at all. It's for sale if you're interested."

"Afraid not." He chuckled at the absurdity of the idea. "A few million bucks for a house doesn't fit my budget too well."

"I know what you mean." She opened a large set of French doors and touched a wall panel. Heavy drapes moved aside, letting in the mid-day sun. The only furniture left in the room was an antique grand piano. "This was the original music room. Not only is it soundproof, but I was told the acoustics are perfect. And, of course, it was built to show off the beautiful grand over by the lovely wall of windows."

"Do I hear a note of sarcasm there?"

"No," she said. "You hear an entire song of sarcasm."

"Sorry you're selling it?"

"I'm just sorry we ever bought it in the first place."

He crossed the room to sit on the piano bench. "Sounds like an interesting story. Do you want to tell me about it?"

She shook her head. "No sense in dumping on you."

He knew a lot of women, but he'd never met one with such an obvious burden who was so determined not to talk. As a gesture, he slid over, making room for her on the piano bench. She ignored him.

"Come on," he said, patting the cushion. "What are friends for? Dump on me all you want."

"It's my problem. I'll handle it."

He wanted to fly into her for being so obstinate, but he opted for changing the subject instead.

"Listen to this." He opened the piano top as if he knew what he was doing. Then flexing his fingers, he attacked the beautiful instrument with the worst rendition of "Jingle Bells" known to man.

Charlotte burst out laughing.

"What?" He pretended a hurt pride. "It took me a year to learn the song."

"It shows," she said, wiping the tears away. "Thanks. I needed that."

Jake reached for her hand and she slid onto the bench beside him. "Do you know it's the first time you've laughed since we've met."

"No, it's not!"

"Afraid so." He nudged her shoulder while searching for a familiar key. "I've been there, Charlotte. I know what you're going through."

A heavy sigh seemed to deflate her resolve. He sensed she wanted to talk, but was quickly proven wrong.

"You know, Jake," she said softly. "I find it hard to believe."

"Try me."

She moved away, but he caught her before she could stand. The kids were nowhere around, so it was a rare moment indeed. "Talk to me, Charlotte."

"You're a glutton for punishment, aren't you?"

"Maybe," he said, encouraged at last. "If you didn't like this house, why did you buy it?"

"I didn't say I didn't like it." She waved her hand at her surroundings. "What's not to like? This house has about anything you can imagine, and it sits in the middle of eighty acres of the most beautiful land in the entire county."

"So the reason for buying?"

"Was to keep it in the family."

"In your family?"

"Not hardly," she replied, as if he should have known better. "Mitch's... actually it was his grandparents' estate on his mother's side."

He frowned. It seemed as if Ralph's source might have been wrong. "If his mother wants to keep it in the family, then why doesn't she live here?"

"Because Ellen likes neighbors, and there aren't any."

He gave up tickling the ivory to use the piano for an arm rest. "Do you mean to tell me, you and the girls have been alone since Mitch died?"

"There was Uncle Eli the caretaker," she said, the look

in her eyes daring him to criticize. "He lived in the cook's quarters."

Jake frowned. "Lived... what happened?"

"He moved in with his daughter. His health is failing, mainly old age."

"How old?"

"Eighty-eight last May."

His anger simmered, just below the surface, at the danger Charlotte and her girls had been in. The stubborn set of her chin affirmed a fight was brewing.

"I can see where he'd be good protection."

"Now who's being sarcastic?"

"Well, you've got to admit..."

"Actually, he used a baseball bat on an intruder a few months after Mitch died."

"Anyone hurt?"

"You mean other than the intruder?"

His jaw dropped. "Yeah, that's what I meant."

"We were fine. But the intruder... not so much so."

"It's just..." He stopped. She was safe now. "Let's get back to the story—so Mitch died and left you with this beautiful house?"

"Uh-huh."

"Then what's the problem? His life insurance should have covered the mortgage."

Charlotte's gaze shot to his, but it was her incredulous laugh which made him pull up short. He didn't need a calculator to know she had big money troubles. No wonder she was worried sick.

"How long have you owned this place?"

"Just six months when Mitch passed away."

Jake chewed his lower lip, wondering if he should have another go at Ralph. His old buddy seemed to have gotten some facts wrong. "So you were married several years before moving here?"

"Yes, why?"

Jake hesitated, relieved at the time frame. "No reason."

"I see," she said, her voice strained. "You thought I'd married Mitch for this house, didn't you?"

"No, I…"

Her head snapped, temper flaring hotter than lightning bolts in a July hailstorm. "You're lying. You think I married him for his money!"

"I didn't say any such thing!"

She shot off the bench as if he were poison. "You didn't 'say' anything, but you implied it!"

"No, I didn't."

"Oh, no? Then why did you automatically assume this house is paid for and I'm selling it to pad my bank account?"

"Stop putting words in my mouth." He scratched his head, trying to recall what he'd said to set her off on such a rampage, but came up blank. Maybe the house held bad memories, and if so, he'd make sure she came alone next time.

"Why would you think such a thing?" She paced back and forth, the fire in her eyes ready to set off the smoke detectors in the next room. "You don't even know me!"

"Now, wait a minute." He forced her back on the bench with a thump. "Let's get something straight. I didn't accuse you of anything."

"Oh, yes you did!"

"What's gotten into you?"

"Nothing, Mr. 'I've Been There'." She drove her point home with a chipped nail against his chest. "For your

94

information, Mitch and I were doing just fine until his grandfather died and left this place mortgaged to the hilt!"

He didn't take kindly to being stabbed in the chest or called a liar to his face, even if it was true. But that was last week—before Charlotte McGregor came along. Now he was willing to put up with a lot more. Why had he listened to Ralph instead of trusting his own instincts? The stabbing stopped when he caught her hand.

"If I said something offensive, then I apologize. I was totally out of line. And you're right, Charlotte—I don't know you, but I intend to."

For a fact, she wasn't listening, and he'd wasted a perfectly good apology. Something was biting her, and he was pretty sure it wasn't him.

"Men are all alike," she said. "You think all we want is your money!"

"I said I'm sorry," he repeated. Minutes passed, and the words hung between them, a glimmer of tears misted her eyes turning them into liquid green pools.

"But most men…"

"I'm not most men."

Her chin quivered, and even though she blinked hard, the thick lashes weren't much of a dam.

He searched frantically for a handkerchief to catch the first wave. "Don't cry."

"I'm not." She hiccupped, ignoring his handkerchief to wipe her face with the back of her hand.

"If you say so." The storm had passed with a couple of swipes under her eyes. His laughter bubbled up when she hiccupped again, and again, and again.

She tensed at his side. "I fail to see the—" *hic* "—humor in being in debt up past my eyeballs!"

"It's not that." He squeezed her in a reassuring hug.

"Feel better?"

She nodded, using his handkerchief to blow her nose.

Unable to resist, Jake tucked a strand of smooth auburn hair behind her left ear and saw the golden hoop dangling from the lobe. He shifted her head to admire the way they moved.

"What are you doing?"

"Just checking to see if steam's still rising."

"You idiot." She was grinning when she shoved his hand away. He figured it was a good sign, but then sadness seemed to wash over her when the memories poured out. "Mitch loved this place more than life itself: the house, the land, and the solitude."

"But I see no reason to bite off more than you can chew."

"Look around. His great-great-grandfather built this house before the Civil War, and the Yankees never found it."

His curiosity was stirred. "How could he hide a house of this size?"

"There aren't any fields, never have been. Julius Wills made his money in railroads. He only cleared enough land to hold the house and barn. The rest of the lumber and everything else they hauled in by wagon. When the war broke out, he painted the house dark green and brown including the windows and roof so they wouldn't reflect in the sun. Then they tore out the bridge, planted fast-growing trees and bushes in the wagon tracks, and moved to town to wait out the war."

"And nobody let it slip about the house being here?"

"Not a soul," she said, warming to the story. "He promised the townspeople if the house survived, he'd bring the railroad to town."

Jake nodded. "Wills' Junction. I wondered about the name. So the old man made good on his word?"

"Exactly. And Mitch gave his word to Grandpa Wills. He'd never let this place leave the family."

Without thinking, Jake reached for her hand, giving it a comforting pat. He understood—about family, loyalty, and a man's word.

"It's a lot of house for a family of four," he said, her hand still resting in his. "Were you planning to have more little girls?"

She relaxed for the first time in ages. "Girls and boys. We were foster parents."

"What about now?"

"They've asked," she replied, regret evident in her tone of voice. "But I had to refuse. It's just too hard on my own."

"If I had a magic wand, I'd wave it to make things right for you," he said, realizing it was the truth.

Desperation tinged her voice. "If you had a magic wand, I'd wrestle you for it and make things right myself."

"Now there's an idea." He wiggled his brows, smiling when her cheeks glowed. A woman as refreshing as Charlotte was a rarity in his world. She reminded him of a soft rose tossed into a river. The current could carry her along, but it couldn't sink her.

"What about your mother-in-law?"

"Ellen doesn't want it," she replied. "And as for Mark, his brother—well, let's just say you couldn't pay him to live here."

"So, if you've bought the Parkers' house, then you must have a buyer lined up." He was beginning to think her problems weren't as bad as she thought. Then again, the upkeep on the mansion would be overwhelming, even for him.

"Not a nibble in the last six months. And it appraises for much more than I'm asking. Are you sure you want to know everything?"

A grim smile tightened the lines around his mouth. It was even worse than she'd let on. "I think I'd be lying if I said no."

She hesitated before taking the plunge. "Now, you've got to remember I've thought long and hard about this." At his nod, she continued, "I'm only renting the Parker house until this one sells. Then I'll buy it, and Mrs. Wilson will make a commission off both properties. It's a good deal."

"Sure," he agreed. "If this one sells."

"It's got to! Just the commission from this one alone will be more than most people make in a year."

"How long are you talking about?"

"Maybe five months?"

"You've had no offers, but you expect her to sell it right off the bat. Have you even thought about being realistic?"

"Something's got to work. I can only afford three more payments."

"What difference will three payments make?"

"If I'm lucky, the bank will let it slide another three months before they foreclose."

Never in his thirty-six years had he met anyone in such desperate need of a lesson in finance. Her logic amazed him.

"Charlotte." He tried to phrase his suggestion so as not to set her off again. "Why not let the bank foreclose now and keep the money?"

"Because I can't! Mitch borrowed thirty thousand

from his parents when we bought this place. If I let the bank foreclose, I'll still owe them money."

"Then why not declare bankruptcy?"

"Because it might sell," she said. "Don't you understand? I need it to sell."

He rubbed her shoulder for comfort. "I can understand, but promise you'll talk to me before you let the bank foreclose."

According to Ralph, the family had money—big money. The father was a judge, the other brother was a doctor, and the mother could be a social butterfly for all he knew. Anger surged through him. Not at the woman sitting beside him, but at the man she'd married. His mind raced ahead. "What about life insurance?"

"Mitch borrowed against it too." Her eyes were as sad as her smile. "I find it hard to believe you've ever been in this kind of mess."

"You're right. I haven't." He closed the distance between them to lay a comforting hand on her shoulder. "And I can't understand how he could do it to you."

She cut him short. "Mitch worked hard, and he was a good husband and father. Dropping dead at thirty-two wasn't part of his plan."

"Oh, come on now—I didn't mean…" More tears ran down her cheeks. His arms enfolded her, letting her cry on his shoulder. Whether they were tears of grief or just frustration, he wasn't sure. She'd finally trusted him enough to confide her troubles. Her tears spent, she tried shoving him away, but he wasn't going anywhere. This was where he belonged.

"I'm sorry, Charlotte," he murmured softly, rubbing her back. "Something will turn up. It always does."

He wanted to take advantage of the situation, but it

wasn't the right time. Reluctantly, he let go when she pulled back to wipe her eyes.

"I keep telling myself that," she said, blowing her nose again on his soppy handkerchief.

"Have you talked to your father-in-law about your situation?"

"No, and I'm not going to." Her shoulders straightened. The momentary lapse in self-control was gone, and her resolve appeared stronger than ever. "I'm a grown woman with two little girls to raise, and with God's help, I'll do it."

Jake remembered what he'd been through. "I admire your spunk, but if it hadn't been for both sets of grandparents helping after Betty died, I couldn't have made it."

"My parents have helped. Mom stayed the first six months after Mitch passed away to take care of us. I would have been lost without her. And it isn't as if his parents have ignored us. They're wonderful to the girls, but I refuse to dump my problems in their laps."

Outside the window, his boys were wrestling, no doubt trying to impress the girls. He pecked on the window, motioning for them to cut it out. Being the oldest, Jeremy had always been the leader and the most dominant. Once an idea settled in his head, it was hard to get it out. Jake wondered if Charlotte's husband had been that way.

"Your in-laws must have known about the heavy debt on the estate. Couldn't they have persuaded your husband not to buy since he obviously couldn't afford…"

"Now wait a minute. I didn't say we couldn't afford it. Had Mitch lived, there would've been some tight years, but we would've made it."

Being a tightwad, he wanted to argue the point, but he

knew better than to say anything else. After all, he didn't know the guy. Then it hit him.

"Your father-in-law persuaded Mitch to buy it, didn't he?"

Her sharp glance indicated more to him than she was willing to admit. She shot to her feet, pacing back and forth. "The fact is, we didn't buy it in the normal sense. Mitch inherited the estate along with its debts and stipulations. He died before we got around to refinancing."

Jake relaxed on the piano bench, intrigued by what she'd said. "Go on."

"I don't know where to begin."

He gestured for her to join him on the bench, pleased she was opening up about herself. "Why not start with his grandpa?"

"That would be Charles Wills. He was Ellen's dad, and he never cared for Tom McGregor. The old man said Tom wanted this house. When Grandpa discovered they were planning to marry, he banned Tom from seeing her. A month later they eloped, making him furious, and even though Ellen was his only child, he practically disowned her."

"Did they ever make up?"

"Eventually, after the boys came along, but his opinion of Tom only got worse."

"Sounds like a bad situation."

"It was. Mitch said his grandpa wanted him and Mark here so they wouldn't spend too much time with their dad."

"Did the old man actually say that?"

Charlotte shook her head. "Not in so many words, but the judge is a workaholic, so they wouldn't have seen him anyway."

"And their mother, where did she fit in?"

"Mitch didn't say."

"At least their grandpa spent time with them."

"They were in grammar school when their dad began to make a name for himself in politics. Grandpa said Tom was dirty, and his grandsons weren't going to be a part of it."

Jake was beginning to like the old man. "So what were the stipulations to his inheritance?"

"Mitch would pay all the debts, without selling off any of the land for five years, and Tom McGregor could never own any part of the estate as long as it's in the family." She answered as if quoting from the will itself.

"So Ellen didn't inherit, but why not Mark?"

She ran her hand over the piano, wiping dust away. "Because Mark told his grandpa he'd sell the place to the highest bidder."

"Does the will say you can't sell it to his mother? It could be in her name and not his."

"Ellen doesn't want it."

"But what if Mitch refused? There's no law saying he had to accept."

"It would have gone into a trust for our girls. No one could have touched it until Maggie reached her twenty-fifth birthday. Grandpa's attorney, William Grant, would have been allowed to sell the land to pay off the debt. I tried to have it put into the trust after Mitch died, but since we had already accepted responsibility for the debt, the attorneys said it couldn't be done."

It sounded strange, but family disputes usually didn't make sense. Why did Ellen not want to keep her parents' estate unless—and there it was, plain as the nose on his face. He had no proof, and it was just speculation on his part, but if the McGregors waited for the foreclosure, they could buy the place for what the bank had against it, and Charlotte would still owe the thirty thousand.

If he was right, it confirmed the tales he'd heard about the judge. He could only pray God would give them wisdom to stop the McGregors. Keeping his suspicions to himself, he pointed Charlotte toward the door, giving her a gentle push. They needed a change of scenery, and he wanted to know firsthand if Hidden Hills was worth fighting for. "You promised a tour, remember?"

* * * *

Although Charlotte no longer called the old mansion home, there was a certain pride in showing it to someone as attentive as Jake. It was nice having a man actually listen to her.

Leaving the music room they entered the formal dining area, where everything was of massive proportions, from the china cabinet measuring ten feet long by eight feet high, to the mahogany table with eighteen matching chairs. A hutch and armoire filled the other end of the room. She hesitated at the sound of the captain's chair scrubbing against the floor when Jake claimed his place at the head of the table. His expression reminded her of a kid in a candy store.

"Miss Charlotte, would you join me as I gaze upon my cotton crop?"

She laughed, shaking her head at his ridiculous Rhett Butler impression. "I've told you, there aren't any cotton fields—never were."

He reared back, gently tweaking an imaginary mustache. "I could go for this Old South stuff. Tell me, woman, what've you done with our young'uns?"

The man was a flirt, and their young'uns, as he'd so aptly put it, were chasing one another throughout the empty rooms. She stopped in her tracks when she heard Bruce refer to the house as a museum. Without their personal belongings, the house was as cold and impersonal as one.

"I'll bet this house has touched a lot of lives over the years," he said, when they were alone again. "Can you imagine the neighbors arriving in their horse-drawn carriages for fancy Christmas parties?"

"I'm afraid I missed the antebellum era." Her hand slid along the length of the china cabinet. Memories of Grandpa and Uncle Eli were connected to the pleasant meals she'd shared in this room. "But I'll never forget my first visit. Grandpa was so proud of his home. He gave me the grand tour, and I loved sitting by the fire, listening to him tell stories about his childhood. With it being so far from town, his greatest fear was it might catch fire."

Jake glanced around the room at the vintage wall paper. "I can understand the concern. This place would be gone before firefighters could get here. And the bridge— there's no way it will hold up a fire truck."

"Grandpa said the lightning rods on the roof were here when he was a boy, but he replaced the electrical wiring throughout the entire house, bringing it up to code. He also installed a sprinkler system on both floors and under the roof."

Jake's eyes were drawn toward the ceiling where twelve inch crown molding circled the room. "Why the roof?"

"He said lightning usually strikes the roof."

"It sounds like the old man was quite a guy," he said,

rising from his chair. "But I want to know how he got the pipes in the first floor ceilings without having to refinish the plaster."

"By removing some boards in the upstairs floor."

Jake eyed the ceiling again. "It makes sense. A sprinkler system sounds expensive. Is there enough water pressure to run it?"

"Not only enough for the house." She led the way to a set of French doors opening into a pool room. "But for six bathrooms—provided you don't flush them all at the same time. Our water comes from an artesian well. Mitch said his grandpa installed the pool so he'd have a second water supply. We have solar panels on the back side of the roof and an automatic generator to pump water from the pool to the sprinklers, if the power is off."

"Why the solar?"

Charlotte laughed. "You wouldn't ask if you'd ever tried to swim in water coming straight from an artesian well. Put your hand in the pool."

Jake did a quick squat and touched the water. "It's warm."

"Exactly. Can you imagine what it would cost to heat this much water with gas or electricity?"

"Are you saying he built all of this just to operate the sprinklers?"

Her gaze traveled around the room before trying to answer his question. The sculptured ceiling with its carved crown moldings matched the other rooms in the house, but the floors were made of marble. Floor-to-ceiling windows doubled as a wall, and when folded accordion-style, they opened the entire room to the outside. It was easy to see why this house had been the love of Grandpa's life.

"I only knew Charles Wills for a few years," she said,

with Jake following her back the way they'd come. She stopped long enough to relock the doors to the pool room to keep the kids safe. "Mitch and I brought the girls to see him a couple of times a week. He was obstinate, opinionated, and his fascination for new technology made him ahead of his time. The girls were crazy about him, and he was like the grandpa I'd never had—I loved him dearly."

"Sounds like I missed out by not knowing him."

"You would've liked him." She knew it was true. As much interest as Jake had shown in the sprinklers and pool, it seemed the library had stolen his heart. The rows of built-in bookcases filled with an odd assortment of reading materials had drawn him like a magnet. He stopped long enough to finger through some of the older editions.

"This was Mitch's home office." In her mind, she pictured the room as it had been before his death. She'd wanted to keep his computer for their girls, but her father-in-law had been adamant, saying it belonged to the firm.

She'd given in, as she had on so many things since joining the McGregor family, just to keep the peace. Those days were gone, or would be as soon as she sold the house and repaid the thirty thousand. Her train of thought was interrupted by Jake holding up one of the books.

"Why are you leaving these behind?"

"Mitch's mother wants them." She wondered why she felt compelled to explain to a stranger, while refusing to acknowledge to herself why she was giving in again. "They belonged to her mother, so by rights they're hers anyway. I'm supposed to call if I get a prospective buyer so she can remove them."

He frowned, but to her relief, he replaced the book without comment and followed her to the next room. She stopped to twiddle her thumbs… taking the girls through the mall was faster than touring the house with Jake. He was forever getting sidetracked when something unique caught his attention.

She gripped his arm, pulling him into the master bedroom, which was empty except for the velvet drapes, and held her finger to her lips. Silence filled the air.

"Listen." The faint sound of scuffling feet and muffled voices echoed from the walls.

His eyes followed the sound around the room, a lazy grin crossed his face. "A hidden passage?"

She nodded. "From here to the library."

The laughter reached his eyes when it became apparent the voices in the wall belonged to Jeremy and Bruce.

"You wouldn't."

"Why shouldn't I?" His soft voice teased her, but the blue eyes sparkled with whatever he had in mind.

She wanted to agree, but… "They said they were sorry."

"Yeah, right!" His quiet laughter made her feel like the most gullible woman in the world. "Let me know when they've pushed your last button."

She opened the closet door and slid the back-wall panel to the left. Out tumbled the boys, spinning her off her feet when they rushed from the hidden passage, gasping for fresh air. Like a flash, they were gone.

Jake's arms locked around her, preventing the loss of her dignity and igniting flames she'd thought were long gone. For such a thin man, he was strong and solid, and the longing she saw in his dark, blue eyes took her breath away. Many moons had passed since she'd felt the intensity of that particular look, and while her mind said run, her feet were frozen to the spot.

Neither spoke when he pulled her close. The warm hands worked their way up her back and set off shock waves of desire so unexpected she gasped. With eyes fixated on his firm lips, her arms locked around his waist, not letting go. His long slender fingers stroked her shoulders and neck, igniting fires along her nervous system. When he touched her cheek and brushed a tendril of hair to the side, her breath caught. He whispered her name and her eyes drifted shut as his lips descended toward her. Somewhere a door slammed, but Charlotte's brain floated in a deep fog as his warm lips became more demanding. She pressed closer, wanting the kiss to last forever.

"Dad! Where are you?"

Jake broke the kiss and stepped back. She staggered. Forever was way too short. The eight-year-old skidded to a halt, colliding with her backside, propelling into the strong arms she'd just left.

"You've got to see this, Dad! It's awesome!"

To her chagrin, the pleasure was short-lived when the boy pulled his dad from the room.

Charlotte touched her moist, swollen lips with her hand as sanity returned. It worried her that she'd responded so completely to a man she hardly knew when her heart still belonged to Mitch. What scared her even more was she wanted it to happen again.

Chapter Eight

Jake went as far as the edge of the woods where the narrow tracks of an old log road were still there, hidden just beneath several layers of pine straw. Knee high saplings, as thick as grass, smothered one another for room to grow. The only sound was squirrels chattering overhead, letting him know he was trespassing in their serene world. He couldn't help but compare the overgrown area with the immaculate front yard. Listening closely he could just make out the sound of running water, probably the creek they'd crossed or maybe the artesian well Charlotte had told him about.

"Come on, Dad." Bruce tugged impatiently on his arm. "We'll never get there if you don't hurry."

"What's the rush?"

"Dad!"

"Hold your horses."

Jake was content with taking in his surroundings, but Bruce wouldn't give up. "There's lots of stuff, Dad. She's got a corral with a wagon, and a tractor, and on the other side of the barn is a real pasture. But the best is down this trail. We found it all by ourselves!"

Jannette Spann

He didn't mind the undergrowth of briars and dead limbs on the old trail half as much as the hungry mosquitoes and gnats circling relentlessly, attacking at will. The need for insect repellent was clear, and he knew he'd have to check the kids for ticks when they got home.

"Bruce, do you know where you're going?"

The boy froze, doing a ninety-degree turn before pointing to his right. "Sure, it's…"

Everything appeared the same to Jake, and if it was confusing for him, it had to be for the boy. Each step they took stirred the damp leaves and caused more mosquitoes to swarm.

"Over here!" The shout came from somewhere to their left, and he recognized the flash of red up in a tree as being Jeremy's shirt. Bruce ran ahead, leaving him to follow.

Jake stopped beneath the giant oak tree, a wide grin crossed his face when his eyes traveled upward. His boys were perched on a platform, a relic from the past. It was probably the only thing remaining of an old tree house.

"Careful," he said, watching Bruce lean over the edge flashing a hundred-watt grin.

"This is great, huh, Dad?"

Jake circled the tree house, paying close attention to the underside of the floor. He could see why his boys were so excited, as he himself was unable to take his eyes off the construction. It appeared safe, since most of the boards had been recently replaced. The platform rested on the bottom limbs of the tree, suspended by metal cables from the higher branches. Their crisscross pattern allowed the round platform to move independently when the wind blew—sort of like a big donut with a tree in the middle. Bark had grown around the ends of the cables, making them a part of the tree, but other than that, the rusty bolts holding the frame were the only clues it had been designed many years ago by someone with engineering skills. It was possible the original structure was as old as the house itself.

His thoughts returned to the master bedroom with its twelve-inch crown molding, where he'd practically thrown Charlotte from his arms. Her soft lips and wounded expression would haunt him for days if he didn't do something about it.

Jeremy swung out from the far side, holding onto the metal cable. "This is awesome... I can even see Charlotte from up here. Oh man—what a rack!"

Her ample curves flashed before Jake's eyes as the younger boy stretched his neck to see for himself.

"Wow! I'll bet it's a twelve point."

A buck... he breathed a sigh of relief.

"Can we go hunting, Dad?"

Jake flexed his shoulders to ease the crick he'd gotten from looking up too long. He was beginning to see how a man could succumb to a place like this, especially if he'd been raised here and knew every nook and cranny.

"It doesn't belong to us, son."

Bruce's feet dangled overhead. "This place is totally awesome. I'll bet you could buy it real cheap, and we could go hunt'n and fish'n all the time."

"Real cheap, huh?"

"Yeah, or maybe we could all live here and..."

"Hold it!" he said, putting an end to the boy's plans before they had a chance to go haywire. "To start with, Charlotte can't sell it cheap... she owes too much. And as for us all living together, we won't even discuss it. Okay?"

Bruce swung his feet, tilting his head to the side. "Don't you like Charlotte?"

111

It caught him off guard, and he wasn't sure he wanted to know where it was going. "Of course, I like her. She's nice."

"I know. You were kissing her, and I bet you want to do it again, too."

Tension mounted in his shoulders and neck. At least he knew what the boy had seen wasn't x-rated. Next time he'd make sure they had some privacy.

"She's our neighbor," he said in hopes of explaining his way out of it. "I was just being neighborly."

Bruce's feet swung back and forth, stirring the warm fall air. "You don't kiss our other neighbors 'cause they're old prunes, but Charlotte's hot. I'll bet she even likes kiss'n."

"Get down, both of you." He hadn't meant to be so gruff. *Lord, give me patience.* If he could just manage to hang on and not let Bruce know he'd hit a touchy spot, then he might have a chance to win Charlotte over before the little rascals could run her off.

Bruce landed with a thump in the leaves near Jake's feet, but Jeremy flipped over the ledge, powering his way through seven chin-ups before touching the ground. The boy was gaining upper body strength now that he'd started lifting weights in gym class. It was another of the many reminders Jeremy was now in his teens. Where had the time gone?

Lost in thought, he didn't realize Charlotte was anywhere around until he heard a low whistle. Her eyes were focused on his legs, or rather on the bloody welts and scratches making them look like he'd been in a cat fight.

"What happened to you?"

"Me?"

Her lips twitched. "Looks like you found the old trail."

"Old trail?"

She motioned toward the way she'd come. "This is the new path. We keep it clean with the lawnmower."

"Wipe the smirk off your face." A dozen or so mosquito bites on his legs were already dealing him misery. The path was in plain sight, but he'd been so fascinated with the tree house, he hadn't even noticed.

Charlotte laughed out loud before walking off, leaving him scratching behind his knee like a dog digging for fleas. By the time he caught up, she'd already made it halfway to the barn.

"I promised to show Bruce my fishing hole," she said. "But it's getting late."

Jake fell into step beside her. "I'm in no hurry if you're not."

She glanced at her watch as if she had somewhere she had to be. Did she have a date? He thought about the kiss, not liking the idea of her responding to another man. "About what happened back at the house…"

"It won't happen again."

His brow shot up in surprise. "What makes you so sure?"

She waited for the boys to pass. "I've got more than enough problems without getting involved."

"Who said anything about getting involved?"

Charlotte's head snapped up. "I've never been a one-night stand, and I'm not about to start now!"

The glare alone was enough for him to know he was skating on thin ice, but the razored edge to her voice was a real eye-opener. After all this, he'd finally met a woman who didn't play silly games.

"So you want to get married again?"

"No."

Jake could see his options dwindling away. All that remained was the Good Neighbor Award, and he'd never been one to settle.

She reached a clearing not far from the backside of the corral fence and pressed two slender fingers against her lower lip. A shrill whistle reverberated throughout the woods. The ear-splitting noise was by far the most unladylike thing he'd ever heard, and certainly something he'd never imagined he would hear coming from a graceful creature like Charlotte.

"What?" she asked, seeing him shake his head in disbelief.

"Nothing."

"You got a better way of getting their attention?"

The response from his boys was instantaneous, with Maggie gingerly pulling a dead briar limb from the hem of her blouse. The kids circled Charlotte as if she was a stick of candy, each wanting their share of attention.

He was the only one to notice when Becky arrived with her arms locked around the toddler riding on her hip. Winking at the girl, he lifted Andy onto his shoulders.

A little seed of doubt popped into his mind as he listened to the kids talking with Charlotte. They seemed to be bonding, and he wasn't sure if it was a good thing. He'd hate to see little hearts get broken.

His boys took to the idea of the creek with the same wild enthusiasm they'd shown for the tree house. It was a kid's dream come true to run free on a place like this, and after seeing it for himself, he had a better understanding of why Mitch had been willing to move heaven and earth to keep it.

Becky ran ahead, ducking into the barn and returning with an old garden hoe for her mother. Then they were off in a single line with Jake and Andy bringing up the rear.

"What's the hoe for?" He raised his voice to be heard.

Charlotte lifted her weapon. "Protection. You never know when a moccasin might appear."

"No self-respecting snake would mess with us. We're making too much racket."

Instead of crossing the yard, she took another cleared path in the trees. It wound through a grove of red maples and poplars, back to the edge of the pasture fence, and then dipped deeper into the woods. Maggie's hard cast brushed against his leg when she dropped back to hold his hand.

"Are we there yet?"

The small palm was as moist as the ringlets curling on her damp forehead. "Tired?"

"Uh-huh," she said, wiping sweat away in a dramatic gesture with her free hand. "It's a long way to the creek, and me and Becky always get tired."

"Becky and I," he corrected.

Maggie frowned. "Are you tired, too?"

"Never mind."

Charlotte raised the hoe like a banner. "Look alert, kids. We're almost there."

Jake was certain they'd been walking in circles when she stopped at a large, familiar rock and pushed back the limbs of a wild evergreen shrub. The only thing separating them from the water was a thicket of mountain laurels and some underbrush. With shrieks of delight, the kids raced to the creek bank where they stopped long enough to remove shoes before jumping into the ankle-deep water. Pea gravel and sand lined the bottom, making an ideal play area for the little ones, and Jake didn't think twice before turning Andy loose. After soaking the girls, Bruce and Jeremy waded upstream to explore the larger rocks around the next bend.

"This is nice." He sat beside her on a thick patch of moss where she was taking in the golden rays of sun filtering through the overhead canopy of leaves. "But why did we take such a long hike to get here when the house is just up the hill?"

She nodded toward her girls splashing and rolling around in the water with Andy. "Do you think I could have kept them out of the creek if they'd known how close it was?"

"I see your point."

They sat in silence, watching their children play. It was peaceful. He liked this woman, and it was more than just her looks. He felt a harmonious accord with her as well as with this place. A soft sigh escaped her lips, and she looked away, as if taking in one last panoramic view of her surroundings.

"Mitch and I used to bring the girls here when they were small. I'm going to miss this place more than I'll ever miss the house."

There was nothing he could say to ease her pain, so he lay back and closed his eyes. The relaxing sound of running water was drowned by squeals and giggles. His boys laughed, but Charlotte's girls giggled—constantly. Soon he was dozing, knowing they'd scream if they got into trouble. An occasional splash of cold water landed on his face, reminding him of where he was.

Charlotte nudged him awake with her elbow. "Look, coming down the creek."

Jake sat up, propping his arm behind her. The wind caught her hair, lifting it gently toward him until he could smell the sweet perfume of her shampoo. It was a short-lived moment as the soft breeze moved on, stirring the wild ferns along the far side of the creek.

He blinked, coming fully awake to see her pointing. Wide grins covered the faces of his older boys when they came wandering into view. Their clothes were plastered to their skin with mud and grass stains, a tribute to the fun they'd had. It was getting late, and someone had to be the bad guy.

"It's time to go."

"But, Dad!"

"You heard me."

"But we ain't found Charlotte's fish'n hole yet," Bruce said, skimming a rock downstream. "There's no fish here, just a bunch of minnows."

She glanced at her watch. "I'm afraid we've spent more time exploring than I'd planned. It's after four, and my fishing hole is actually Mr. Drenfield's pond. If we followed the trail, it'd take a good hour to walk there and back."

"But you promised."

"I said if we had time. What part of the afternoon would you have skipped? The tree house? The trails? Or maybe the creek?"

The boy seemed to consider her question before tossing the last of his rocks on the ground in grudging defeat. His shoulders shrugged. "Guess it's okay. We don't have our fish'n poles no how."

"I'm impressed." Jake grinned at Charlotte's blank expression. "He gave in with just one little sulk. Next time you can be the bad guy."

A few minutes later, they'd hiked along the same pathway up to the yard at the back of the house. The children were barefooted, and he and Charlotte had somehow managed to carry all the shoes.

"This was a good idea," he said, leaning the hoe against the porch. "My boys haven't had this much fun in ages."

"Nor my girls."

"What do we do about Maggie's cast?" He watched her sling the heavy plaster from side to side. "It's bound to be soaked."

She stacked her load of shoes with his. "Not to worry, we're going to see Mark tonight."

"You have a date?"

Her expression gave nothing away when she unlocked the door. "Mark's my brother-in-law and the kid's pediatrician. If you must know, I haven't had a real *date* in a long time, but I do have a specific time I have to meet him."

"And that's supposed to make me feel better?"

Her nose wrinkled. "What do you mean?"

"I don't like competition."

She shook her head. "You never stop trying, do you?"

"Not when it's something I want." He walked on, letting her come to her own conclusion.

****

The sun glistened off the glass greenhouse located near the back porch. Jake's boys ran through the entrance, plundering in the potting materials and grabbing hand tools for a sword fight. Charlotte followed, relieving the boys of their weapons. She soon had everyone focused by pointing to which plants she intended to keep. Jeremy's legs staggered beneath the weight of a large, healthy plant.

"Hey, watch it!" She sprang into action to hold the

door open wide. "You're holding a split-leaf philodendron. I raised it from a sprout."

Jeremy steadied the pot, his young muscles bulging beneath the mud-stained shirt. "How many of these stupid things are we supposed to carry?"

Before she could answer, Jake returned from putting the Areca palm in the van. Pushing the sprawling leaves out of his face, he seemed about as put-out as his son.

"More to the point, have you thought about where you're putting them when we get there?"

The room held a collection of greenery from all over the house. There were several more she'd planned to keep, but clearly he was right. The other house was too small.

"Would you guys like to have a plant?"

Bruce finished his job of watering the flowers by emptying the can on a single Boston fern. "Can I have anything I want?"

"Sure you can," she said, well aware her flowers would probably drown rather than die of neglect.

Jeremy shoved her plant into the van. "Flowers are for sissies. Next you'll be wearing high heels and squat'n."

"Enough!" Jake placed the leaves so they wouldn't break. "Your granddad grows a garden. Is he a sissy?"

"But he grows them outside."

"Makes no difference," he replied. "They're all plants."

Bruce fingered the different types of leaves as if he were shopping. He'd no sooner lifted a large, red impatiens than it dropped, shattering both pot and plant on the tile floor.

"It hissed!"

She froze, leaving Jake to grab a trowel from a nearby table. As a weapon against a snake it wasn't much, but they'd left the hoe outside. Her breath caught when he slid the fern out of his way, the trowel in his hand held like a dagger.

He lay the weapon aside when a tabby cat, its teeth bared, hissed louder. The angry feline swiped again as if he was the enemy. Charlotte laughed. She'd forgotten the cat.

"Cucumber!"

Maggie darted around him and picked up the hissing beast. The racket became a contented purr as the cat responded to her gentle touch. "Mama, Cucumber's got bumps on his belly."

Jake lifted the cat by his nape. It was quite obvious to both adults, Cucumber was a she and she'd had a family. "Yeah, Mama," he teased. "He's got bumps all right."

Ignoring his comment, she shifted the remaining plants out of the way, being careful not to disturb the mound of fur balls sleeping under the foliage. The kids swarmed over the kittens, each picking one or two for their own.

"Where did Cucumber find them?" Maggie wanted to know.

He sat the cat on the floor. "I wouldn't answer if I were you."

"Can we take Cucumber home?"

"No way!" The boys protested. "Dad, if they get their cat, then we can bring Ribcage home!"

The noisy argument soared with each kid trying to outdo the others. He tried to restore the peace by raising his voice but got nowhere, so she let loose with an earsplitting whistle. "Okay!" She had their attention. "Now, who's Ribcage?"

Bruce won out as spokesman. "He's our dog and we had to take him to Granddad's, 'cause he barked too much. But if they can have their cat, then we can have our dog!"

"Cats are nice." Maggie's prima donna attitude sprang to life. "They don't make no noise, so there!"

"Not so," Jeremy shot back. "You're just stupid!"

"Am not!"

"Are too!"

"You don't know…"

Charlotte glared at Jake. "You can jump in anytime now."

He'd perched on the edge of the table, unconcerned their kids were about to slug it out. "You're doing just fine."

Her growl was reminiscent of the cat. Why did she have to be the referee? It was his boys raising a ruckus.

The old cat was just a stray, but her girls had been heartbroken when it disappeared less than a month ago. She hated to hurt them again, but they were going to have to leave her behind.

"Everyone, put the kittens back. I'm sorry, girls, but Cucumber is a barnyard cat. She'd be lost in town, and she might get run over."

Tears sprang to Becky's eyes. "But who'll feed her?"

She glanced at Jake for help, but he was deliberately looking at the ceiling, mischief dancing in his blue eyes and a smug expression on his face. "Cucumber's been taking care of herself for quite awhile now. Mama cats eat rats and mice."

Maggie gagged, turning a pale shade of green when she stared at the cat. "Oh, gross… it's nasty."

"But, Mama.," Becky said, swallowing her tears. "Her kittens are too little. What will they eat if we don't feed them?"

Charlotte wasn't sure if the snicker came from Jeremy or Jake, but she chose to take the high road and ignore it.

She picked up the cat and held her so the younger kids could get a better look.

"Remember the bumps you felt on the cat's belly?" she asked, a thread of sympathy going out to Cucumber as little fingers rubbed across her stomach. "Each kitten has a favorite place to suck. Watch what happens when I put her on the table."

The cat shivered, quickly inspecting her babies before lying on her side. The kittens immediately started tumbling over each other as they snuggled in for their feeding. Charlotte felt rather proud of herself. She walked away, leaving the cat with her audience.

"Your cat's got to feel violated," Jake said for her ears alone.

She grinned. "So next time *you* give the anatomy lesson."

* * * *

Andy and the girls had fallen asleep before they'd reached the gate, but Jeremy and Bruce captured Charlotte's attention with questions ranging from camping and fishing, to tree houses and how many horses the barn would hold. By the time they'd reached Robins Lane, their imaginations had escalated to the point of being world-class fishermen, and Hidden Hills had a bunkhouse with herds of cattle grazing the pastures.

It was hard to remember the last time his boys had gotten along so well, and he owed it all to Charlotte. She'd treated them with the same respect she gave everyone else, and they'd responded in a positive way.

Chapter Nine

"So what time do I need to be at your house?"

"Right after school, if you can," Charlotte replied, thankful Kimmie was free in the afternoons to sit with Becky and Maggie.

"No problem," said the sixteen-year-old. "But Mom says I have to be home no later than nine on a school night."

Reader Elementary was only three blocks away, so her girls could walk home with Bruce and Jeremy in the afternoons, giving Kimmie time to drive across town from the high school.

She tidied her workstation and swept the hair clippings from her last customer into a plastic dustpan before stopping for lunch. It was one of Norma Martin's rules when she'd hired on—never leave a mess. Lately her life was full of messes, but she was determined to clean them up, one at a time.

The cell phone in Charlotte's pocket vibrated while she poured their drinks, sweet tea for herself and a diet soda for her boss. She took out the phone and glanced at the name—Tom McGregor. This was his third time to call in a week. Laying the phone on the table, it vibrated sporadically, while she ate a banana sandwich.

Norma finished her burger and tossed the wrapper into the trash. "You gonna answer it?"

"Nope."

"Think he'll give up?"

She popped the final tidbit of sandwich into her mouth. "It's what I'm hoping."

"Fat chance," Norma said. "It's a pity his ethics don't match his looks, 'cause he's a fine-looking man for his age... reminds me of a gray fox every time I see him."

Charlotte sipped her tea. "He's a fox all right... gave me a month to come up with the money I owe him or he'll put a lien on the property."

Norma picked up the phone when it vibrated again, a sure sign it was getting on her nerves. "Joe's Bait Shop." Click. "That should get rid of him. Do you have the money?"

"No, and I won't have it six months from now either, unless the house sells."

Norma pushed her chair from the table, signaling the end of her break. "You finish your lunch, honey. It's time for me to get started again."

After squeezing the last of the curling solution onto the colorful rods wrapping Wylene Franklin's thinning gray hair, she held the older lady's arm, easing her underneath the dryer. Satisfied the woman would be okay, she set the timer. "How did it go last night? Did you have help with the plants?"

"Uh-huh." Charlotte finished her drink while listing the number of procedures she'd done in the log book. "Jake complained of a hernia, but I think he was joking."

"And who's Jake?"

"My next-door neighbor."

"Sounds like a nice guy if he was willing to move those pots."

"Seems to be." Charlotte realized too late she shouldn't have mentioned Jake. Her boss was a notorious snoop.

"Aha!"

"Aha, what?"

"You're sweet on the guy."

She finished eating and pulled off her smock, tossing it into the dirty clothes hamper with the wet towels. "That's absurd. He's just being neighborly."

"It's one way of looking at it, I guess," Norma said, not willing to let it rest. "Tell me, is there a Mrs. Jake next-door, or do you have a clean playing field? A lot of wives wouldn't be much competition, what with your looks and all."

"Norma!" She was shocked her boss would say such a thing. "You know I don't fool around with married men."

"There's your problem, honey. You don't fool around at all."

Why argue the point when Norma was right? "He's a widower."

Her boss paused in the middle of cleaning a hairbrush. "How old is this guy?"

She had a sudden urge to run, but it wouldn't do any good. Hillside was a small town. All Norma had to do was ask Mrs. Franklin to name the widowers on Robins Lane, and she'd have Jake's family history in no time.

Up ending her purse on the counter, she made a frantic attempt to find her keys. "I'm not sure, but his oldest son is thirteen. I guess he's somewhere in his mid-thirties."

"Mmm." Her boss licked her lips. "He's at a ripe age. Money in the bank and fire in the…"

"Norma!"

"Don't act so shocked. You can't tell me you haven't wondered about him."

"I'm not telling you anything." She found her keys. "I've got to go."

"Wimp out if you must," came the smart-aleck reply. "But this conversation isn't over by a long shot."

She shoved everything back into her purse. There was nothing her boss liked better than trying to get a rise out of her. "I'm out of here, and believe me, this conversation is definitely over!"

Norma's laugh followed her out the door. Friends like her boss and Annabelle Smith, her co-worker at the market, were hard to come by. But unlike Annabelle, Norma wasn't the sort of person she could confide in. As a beautician, talking was part of the job, and Norma's gift of gab was even better than her styling skills. Her boss wasn't known for keeping secrets.

Charlotte almost made it to her car before noticing Tom McGregor's silver convertible pulling up beside her.

"I'm tired of having to hunt you down."

"So why bother?" she snapped, irritated with herself for not getting to her car a couple of minutes earlier. She could have driven off, pretending not to have seen him.

The judge stepped out of his car, carrying a manila envelope. "You've had thirty days. Have you got my money?"

"No, I don't." Mitch had said the money was a gift, and she believed him. The last time she'd checked, gifts weren't meant to be repaid, but in this case, she'd be willing to return the money, just to prove the judge wrong about her.

He held out the envelope. "This is a promissory note. Since you're determined to sell the house, I'll hold off on the lawsuit until then, but you're going to have to sign this."

Charlotte unlocked the car and tossed her purse across to the passenger seat. Her anger simmered just below the surface, but she kept her cool. "I'm not signing a promissory or anything else."

"Suit yourself," he said. "But don't say I didn't warn you. If you lose the house to the bank, I'll still get my money, even if it means taking you to court."

"Like that's supposed to surprise me? Look, Judge, I've changed realtors, so maybe they'll show the house more than the last one."

"Changing companies was completely unnecessary. Cummins Realty is a reputable firm."

She stood her ground. "Reputable, maybe, but they weren't getting the job done."

Judge McGregor crossed his arms, tapping the envelope on his hip. His opinion of her ability to choose a firm, on her own, was evident in his sneer. "Which one have you gone with this time?"

"Wilson Realty."

He shook his head, a sure indication of his disapproval. "You make nothing but bad decisions."

"Just which ones are you talking about?"

"Selling the estate, for starters," he said. "It's been in Ellen's family over a hundred years, and now you're willing to let any Tom-Dick-or-Harry with a checkbook move in."

"We've been over this before," Charlotte said, tired of the same old argument. "I'm not discussing it anymore."

"What about my granddaughters? You've taken them

out of their private school and enrolled them in the public system. Just what kind of education do you think they'll get? And what can you possibly gain by moving to your rundown house in a slum neighborhood?"

"It's a good neighborhood."

"I've told you before, girl. You've got to look successful to be successful."

"You let me worry about my decisions." She slid behind the steering wheel and tried to slam the door, but the judge grabbed the handle. His face reflected the fury of the moment.

"You'll never amount to a thing. Someday Mitch's girls will see what you've deprived them of, and believe me, they won't thank you for it."

Using all the strength she had, Charlotte jerked the door out of his hands and put the car in gear. She glanced up at the rearview mirror and saw Tom McGregor slam his fist against the door of his new convertible when she drove off. Jake had promised things would work out, but with the judge around, she didn't see it happening.

* * * *

Business at Milner's was slow and didn't improve as the afternoon wore on. With no stock to put up, Ray, the assistant manager, sent everyone home except Charlotte and a bag boy. She glanced at the clock above the office door for what seemed like the hundredth time in the last hour. Only when the final two customers of the night began making their way to her register, did the clock start ticking again.

At half-past eight, the bag boy clocked out. She quickly balanced her register, giving the money to Ray to lock in the safe. The second part of the workday had only been a seven hour shift, but her weekend of lifting and tugging made it seem more like twelve.

She paused at the time-clock long enough to check the schedule before leaving. Her next day off wasn't until Sunday, which meant she'd be closing again Saturday night, and it created a problem with the sitter. She couldn't ask Kimmie to give up her date, and the girls were already spending Friday night with Mitch's parents.

The overhead lights went off, leaving the bulbs at the back of the store to provide enough illumination for security. She froze when a man's long shadow fell across the work schedule.

"What's wrong, Charlotte?" Ray leaned his arm against the wall above the time clock and laughed as if they were sharing a private joke. "You got a problem with the schedule, or were you waiting so we could go to your mansion together?"

She'd never particularly liked the assistant manager, but this was the first time he'd actually made her skin crawl. He brushed against her when he swiped his card, and she moved out of his way. "You're married, Ray."

"My wife won't care." He caught her hair at the back of her head, narrowing the distance between them. "Besides, she's out of town."

She snatched the hair free, trying to step back again, but his other hand caught her neck, jerking her up tight against his body. His hot breath fanned against her face. She could scream, but they were alone—nobody would hear. Fighting the rising panic, she found her inner strength and shoved hard… causing him to stagger. "If she doesn't care, then something's wrong with your marriage. You might want to work on it."

"Why, you conceited little…"

Not waiting for his angry retort, Charlotte ran outside before he could grab her again. The safety of her car had never felt so good, and she was almost home before realizing she'd left the parking lot. Her hands still trembled when she crossed the tracks on Dove Street. She couldn't let the girls see her upset again; they'd witnessed enough meltdowns at Hidden Hills. It took a moment to steady herself enough to roll the window down so the cool night air might calm her nerves.

It wasn't the first time she and the assistant manager had closed the store alone, but she knew it would be the last. She needed her job, especially the insurance, but she wasn't stupid.

As a precaution, she circled the block a couple of times and pulled the car around to the back of the house, where it couldn't be seen from the street. She killed the switch and sat with the window down to listen for the sound of another car, but the night seemed quiet except for the tree frogs and a stray cat singing in the alley. On a night like this, it was a relief not having to return to Hidden Hills.

Her nerves were still on edge when she left the safety of the car. Shadows caused the darkness to close in until she neared the single light over the back door. Breathing deeply, she focused on the shiniest key on the chain before inserting it into the lock—it didn't work. She swallowed the rising panic and stepped back to look at her surroundings.

"I know it's the right house," she said, for the sake of hearing her own voice. "There's Kimmie's car, and the awful hedge…"

"Do you always talk to yourself?"

Charlotte screamed, but nothing came out. Her head cried *run*, only her feet weren't listening. The fight instinct tried to kick in, but all she could do was whimper like a scared pup.

"Are you okay?" Jake came out of the shadows. "I didn't mean to scare you."

She slugged him with her purse. "Jake! I nearly had a heart attack, thanks to you!"

"I said I was sorry," he replied, rubbing his arm. "No need to beat me to death."

"Oh, I didn't hurt you."

"Did too! Your bag weighs a ton."

Charlotte took a deep breath, clutching her chest to slow her heart rate. "What are you doing out here, pouncing on me in the middle of the night?"

"It's only nine o'clock. I'd hardly call it the middle of the night."

Her knees crumpled, and she eased down on the top step to keep from falling. "You would if you were as tired as I am."

Jake sat beside her. "Bad day?"

"Parts of it."

"I'd ask if you want to talk about it, but I already know the answer."

"Uh-huh." She maneuvered her hot feet out of the work shoes, followed by her socks. Her toes wiggled on the cold cement. "Mmm. Feels good."

Jake caught her ankles, swirling her around so her feet landed on his knee. "I'll be neighborly and rub the pain away."

She would have objected, but he began kneading the balls of her feet, and the protest died instantly. Goose bumps raced up her spine when his thumbs pressed against her arches and rubbed backward toward the heels.

He sniffed, holding her ankles at arm's length with one

hand. "Shoo-wee, your feet stink!"

"Oh, shut up and rub. You volunteered for the job."

"Well, yeah… but I didn't know these dogs were allergic to soap and water."

She jerked her feet. "If you're going to gripe…"

"Be still," he said, resuming his job. "My fingers are already dirty."

The large, callused hands moved gently, giving her the sensation of melting chocolate, dripping slowly down the steps like syrup on hot fudge cake. Each toe got its share of attention, including the little pig that went to market.

She imagined his hands on her aching back. "I'll bet you were a masseur in your younger days."

He stopped. "You think I'm old?"

"Of course not." She tried to gauge his reaction in the dim light.

He chuckled. "Just saying I'm past my prime?"

Bright light flooded the steps when Kimmie opened the door, saving Charlotte from replying. "I thought I heard voices."

"Are my girls asleep?"

"Fed, bathed, and out for the night."

"Did they give you any trouble?"

"Nothing I couldn't handle, and I left your supper in the oven to keep warm."

To Charlotte's surprise, Jake slid closer to her side, giving the sitter a clear pathway down the steps. Unfortunately, it wasn't enough to keep the girl's book bag from bouncing off his head.

"Goodnight, Kimmie," he said, rubbing his new bump. "Say hello to your dad for me."

The girl's car sprang to life, and she reversed out of the yard in a spray of gravel. The dust settled, leaving the night quiet again, except for Charlotte's growling stomach, which reminded her of the time. "Want some supper?"

"No, I ate about an hour ago." He relaxed against the steps. His arm had somehow managed to wrap around her waist, while his fingers did a gentle tap dance against her ribs. It was much too close for her peace of mind, but he seemed not to notice. "Mom dropped off a chicken casserole. Not much meat, but you should have tasted it… best she's ever made."

"You don't say? I cooked the same thing." Charlotte stood, gathering her shoes and socks, while putting what she hoped was a safe distance between them. It was time to put this day to rest.

Jake reached into his pocket as he unfolded his lanky frame. "I almost forgot to give you these."

"More keys? Why would I need those? The ones I've got won't even work."

A sheepish grin tugged at his mouth. "I sort of changed your locks after I got home tonight."

Her eyes flashed. "You did what?"

"Now wait," he said. "I know it sounds a bit high-handed, but I thought it was the least I could do under the circumstances."

A day she thought couldn't get any worse—just had. "What is it with your family and keys?"

"I knew you'd be hopping mad, but Jeremy gave your key to one of his buddies to make the copies. You could have a dozen keys floating around out there."

"Oh, my stars!" The implications of what could have happened sank into her tired brain. "What's up with your boys? Why are they out to get me?"

"They like you."

"Like me?"

"Sure."

Charlotte dodged a moth headed for the porch light and sure death. "I'd hate to imagine what they'd do if they disliked me!"

Using the utmost care, he placed the new keys in her open palm then closed her fingers around them. "You're holding the only keys to these locks, so guard them with your life."

"You can count on it."

The suicidal moth bounced off the light a couple of times before floating to the ground, its landing made softer by a cool breeze rising from the south. Using her free hand, she raised her hair to feel the wind on her neck and sensed Jake had moved closer. The tiny laugh lines feathering his eyes and the black stubble on his face reminded her it'd been a long day for him also. A warm, almost forgotten longing skittered through her body. He was waiting, and all she had to do was meet him halfway, but she couldn't do it.

"Good night, Jake."

The longing mirrored in his royal blue eyes faded along with his smile, banking his desire for the moment. He released her hand. "Night, Charlotte."

She mentally straightened her spine, shoving aside the regret she felt for turning him down. The plans for her future were set, and they didn't include him... or did they? His arms reached out, and she felt herself leaning toward his lean body. Struggling never entered her mind when she gave in to his warm kiss. Control slid away as before, and she found herself clinging to him like a safe harbor in a violent storm. Being in his arms felt right, and as much as she wanted his kisses to continue, it was way too soon to get serious. It had to stop. Using every ounce of willpower she had, she pushed herself away.

"We can't do this."

"Why not?" He frowned, reluctant to let go.

"It's not right."

"Of course it's right. We both feel it."

"No."

"Don't lie to me, Charlotte. A minute ago you were all over me. You know you want me."

"I want a lot of things I can't have, so I'll just have to add you to my list."

Jake stepped back to fold his arms across his chest, his longing still evident in the dim light. "This is crazy, and you know it. We're both adults."

Without a word, she retreated to the top step. Maybe she was being unfair, but it made no difference. She wasn't sure of what he was offering, and he most likely didn't know either. "It's not going to happen."

"You're right," he said, man enough to admit defeat. "We hardly know each other. I'm not going to rush you, but if you change your mind, let me know."

His words hung in the air long after he'd disappeared through the overgrown hedges separating their yards. She didn't trust herself, so she could only pray he was a man of his word.

****

Charlotte made it a point to avoid Jake the rest of the week, which wasn't hard, considering how late he got home. Out of sight didn't necessarily mean out of mind. She found it hard to concentrate at work, mostly because she figured his late nights were due to dumb-as-dirt Loretta.

While she was avoiding Jake, Ray seemed to be

avoiding her, and rightly so. She'd made a point of talking to John Milner the following morning, and he'd assured her there'd be no more problems with the assistant manager.

When Thursday evening arrived, she was still tallying her bills in her head and trying to solve her Saturday night dilemma. Jeremy was fine for mornings and afternoons, but he wasn't old enough for nights. Without a sitter, she had no choice but to miss the shift and let something slide.

Straightening shelves was a no-brainer, and by the time she reached her decision, she'd worked her way from canned goods to cereals. She jumped when Annabelle tapped her on the shoulder.

Her co-worker held up her watch. "You'll have to cover the register. It's time for me to go."

"So soon?"

"Yeah, I've had all the fun I need for one day."

"You call this fun?"

Annabelle laughed, and straightened a cereal box Charlotte had missed. "It is, compared to my husband's weekend, if I have to work Saturday morning. My sister and her kids are spending Friday night with us before heading to Disney World."

"I'll trade," Charlotte said. "If you don't mind working Saturday night?"

"Fine with me," Annabelle agreed. "One to nine?"

Her friend was an angel. The McGregors would drop Becky and Maggie off around eleven, and she'd pay Jeremy to watch them until she could get home. She whispered a prayer of thanks on her way to the register and added an earnest amen when she discovered Ray was gone, and she would be closing with Mr. Milner.

The rest of the day was busy, making it late when Charlotte arrived home, too tired to eat, but still curious enough to see if there was any soup left. To her dismay, only one small bowl, covered in aluminum foil, remained in the oven.

For the life of her, she couldn't imagine how one skinny teenager could eat so much. Before the ninety-pound weakling began sitting with her girls, it wasn't uncommon to have enough leftovers for an extra meal and some scraps for the cat. Now it seemed, regardless of what she cooked, only one serving remained for her supper. The week wasn't over, but her cabinets were almost bare. At this rate, she'd have to rethink her entire budget, and she didn't know where the extra money would come from.

Chapter Ten

When Friday afternoon rolled around, there was a courtesy call from the girls' grandmother, saying she had picked them up at school. As always, Ellen was punctual. Unless her itinerary changed, the girls would dress for a boring dinner in the formal dining room with both grandparents, followed by an unexciting bedtime story and lights out. To ease her conscience, Charlotte told herself the girls needed to spend more time with the McGregors.

With only herself to please, she opted for a relaxing bath and sandwich, provided there was something out of which to make one. She stirred a cup of hot cocoa, while the rising steam transformed the bathroom into her personal sauna.

The soothing sound of violins filled the air, and with her hair bunched into a make-shift mop atop her head using an old scarf, she was set. A night of pampering would be perfect… except for the constant pounding at the door.

"Okay, okay. I'm coming!" Irritated at the interruption, she shut off the tap before water reached the overflow valve. It didn't sound as if they would leave, so she shoved the chain lock into place and opened the door a crack. "Oh, it's you."

"Let's not show too much enthusiasm," Jake said, pulling on the screen only to discover it too was locked.

Charlotte closed the wooden door and removed the chain before opening it again. "I thought you were someone else."

"Someone even less welcome than me?"

She'd felt uneasy about Ray, but as far as she knew, he still thought she lived at Hidden Hills. She flipped the latch on the screen and stepped back so Jake could enter.

"Where are the boys?"

"You should know by now my boys don't knock."

She laughed. "True, so where are they?"

"With Betty's parents. You aren't the only one needing a break."

She understood completely. While debating on the amount of hospitality she should offer, he filled the coffeepot with fresh water and a filter, then added grounds and flipped the switch.

"Want some coffee?" she said.

A pink flush inched up his neck when he realized what he'd done. "I… this house is so much like mine, I sometimes forget I'm not at home."

"It is homey," she agreed, then added as an afterthought. "You're welcome to wash the pile of dishes if you'd like."

He declined. "Seems a little too much like home."

"I like this house. It's cozy, and I feel safe here."

"Speaking of safe, you were trembling like a leaf when you got home the other night. Do you want to talk about it?"

She shook her head. "No, it's all taken care of. Will Jeremy be home in time to watch the girls tomorrow?"

"When there's money involved, you can depend on him."

She pulled two chairs from the table, sitting on one and propping her feet on the other, leaving Jake to find his own. "You shouldn't talk about your boys like that. They're good kids, and you know it."

He pulled the chair from under her feet and proceeded to make himself comfortable by stretching his legs under the table. His slow mischievous grin mimicked her earlier words. "There're out to get me!"

Not to be outdone, she hooked her toes on the edge of his seat. "Those days are in the past. Bruce and I had a long talk, and I think we'll get along just fine now."

His blue eyes danced with laughter. "Okay. Find out the hard way, but don't say I didn't warn you."

After the coffee finished brewing, Charlotte took the opener from the drawer and reached for the last can in the cabinet. Tuna wasn't what she wanted, but it was all she had, so there was no reason not to enjoy it with her coffee. "Have you eaten?"

When he didn't reply, she thought he was ignoring her, but his attention was focused on the overhead cabinets. Leaving his chair behind, it took a total of three steps with his long legs to reach her side.

The doors swung open, and he dropped a confused gaze to her. "What happened to all the food I saw in there last weekend?"

"We ate it."

"All of it?"

Charlotte chose to ignore him. She drained the tuna, confident Jake was the nosiest man she'd ever met. After adding mayonnaise and pickles, she reached into the bread box her dad built for her last birthday.

140

"Good grief, woman! Y'all eat like an army over here."

Anger gushed through Charlotte like an artesian well. Her elbow flew back, catching him in his midsection, and she realized her mistake when the air whooshed from his lungs. Being on a diet was one thing, but she was hungry and broke.

"For your information, I haven't eaten enough this week to keep a cat alive, so don't talk about what I eat. Didn't your mama teach you any manners?"

"Yeah." He rubbed his midsection. "But she didn't warn me about elbows."

Frowning, she slapped mayonnaise on the last of her bread. She wasn't sure why she was feeding him. Truth be told, she wanted to wring his neck and didn't know why.

Jake propped against the counter a safe distance from her arm. "Guess I should be glad you're slapping bread instead of my face. What's wrong?"

She laughed in spite of herself. "Would you shut up? I'm trying to stay mad at you."

"Now why would you want to be mad at me?" His slow grin made her weak in the knees. The man had no idea how appealing he was, or did he? She'd bet money he was clueless.

"I'm not mad," she said. "It's just…"

"Because your cabinets are empty, and mine are full?"

"Now why would I care about your cabinets?"

"Well, I don't know," he said. "But you were fine until a moment ago. If it helps, I've been working late at the new store so Mom's been bringing our supper."

First his mother feeds him, and now here she was, strapping on the feedbag as if he was incapable of opening a can. She couldn't remember the last time someone had actually cooked for her. "Lucky you… what store?"

"We're opening in the Four Corner's Mall."

The knife clinked in the mayonnaise jar and Charlotte held it up to the light. Empty. She chunked the dirty knife into the sink and slid the jar into the plastic bread bag with the tuna can before tossing everything in the garbage.

"Oh yeah, the kids told me you own Bett's. It's a nice store. I can see why no one cared when we used the van."

"Does it bother you?"

"Of course not," she said. "You've been nosey enough about me. I'm just curious as to why you've never mentioned it."

Jake bit a hunk out of his sandwich and began chewing at a snail's pace. It was easy enough to see what he was up to. She'd seen his boys pull the same stunt with pancakes. The entire family were master procrastinators.

Charlotte grinned. "Oh, stop your dawdling. It's not important. Besides, a good lie is hard to conjure up on the spur of the moment."

He swallowed. "Now, would I lie to you?"

She slid him his coffee. "Probably. But what difference does it make if you own a store? We all have to work."

He didn't seem to mind she was out of milk. "This is good. We don't usually eat as well as we have this week."

"Oh?" She decided to humor him. It was as plain as the nose on her face he wasn't going to elaborate on his job. Not to worry, she could always ask Norma.

"Mom's a terrific cook." He devoured the rest of his sandwich in a couple of bites. "Monday night she made a chicken casserole. Then there was chili, beef stew, and last night we had homemade vegetable soup with cornbread."

About halfway down his dream list, a nasty suspicion popped into Charlotte's brain. "I've cooked the exact things this week... and in the same order, too!"

Jake's cup hit the table so hard it splashed coffee over the rim. "Say what?"

"You heard me." The tuna tasted like sawdust in her mouth. "I realize we have twin houses, and our situations are somewhat alike, but this is getting weird."

He reached for his cell phone and punched in a couple of numbers. His long legs had him near the back door, too far away for her to eavesdrop before anyone answered, but the telltale hand on the back of his neck was a sure sign he wasn't happy. She'd seen the same gesture the day they'd met, when his boys had nearly killed Becky. The man had been furious then, and didn't appear much calmer now. After the phone snapped off, he came back to the table and sat down with a thud, his mouth tightening into a grim line.

"What was that about?" she asked, not sure she wanted to know.

He released a longsuffering sigh. "They did it again."

She frowned. "Did what?"

A mixture of remorse and disappointment appeared in his eyes when he leaned forward, resting his elbows on his knees. "I owe you an apology, and I honestly don't know how we'll ever make it up to you."

"You aren't making any sense."

As before, his hand went to the back of his neck. "I was talking to my mother."

"So?" she said, not liking where this was going.

"She didn't cook for us this week."

Charlotte thought of the saltine crackers she'd called lunch most of the week. "I've been feeding the whole gang, haven't I?"

He nodded. "I'm afraid so."

"I've been had again?"

"Appears to be the case."

143

"But… we had a deal."

His large hands covered hers, and the gentle squeeze reminded her of the last time they'd been together. "I'm sorry," he said. "But I'll be glad to repay you."

There was no mistaking his sincerity, but she drew the line when he reached for his wallet. "I don't want your money."

"I'd feel better."

"Well, you'll just have to feel bad," she said, her appetite a thing of the past. "I'm not upset with your kids for eating my food. If I'd known they were hungry, I would've gladly given them anything they wanted. It's just, we had a deal and…"

"Jeremy and Bruce know you're working two jobs to make ends meet. My boys aren't helpless. They can thaw a frozen dinner."

"Frozen dinners?" Sympathy for the poor kids melted away her anger. "You make them eat frozen dinners?"

"Not all the time," he said, in his own defense. "Just when I'm late."

"And how often are you late?"

Jake cupped his mug with both hands. "About as often as you, I'd say."

She couldn't disagree with him. Her hours were ridiculous. It wasn't fair to her girls, even though she'd taken them to the shop some during their summer break. Her job at Milner's would be history, if she didn't need the health insurance.

"I can't do anything about my hours," she said, resigned to the fact. "Not until I sell the house."

"And neither can I, until the new store opens."

* * * *

The neighborly thing would have been for Jake to go home early and let Charlotte get some sleep, but his feet couldn't seem to get pointed in the right direction. After finishing their sandwiches, he'd poured more coffee and carried the cups to the living room, where they'd shared the couch and watched the late movie, until she began to nod off.

He waited for the chain to slip into place on her back door before making his way through the overgrown hedge. It was eleven-thirty.

The house was too quiet with the boys gone, even more so after the lights went out next door. He usually enjoyed the peaceful nights when the kids slept at the grandparents, but not tonight. His restlessness had nothing to do with his boys and everything to do with Charlotte.

She'd mentioned their twin houses, but it wasn't his stairs he'd wanted to climb or his bed he'd wanted to slide into. It had seemed the most natural thing in the world for them to climb the stairs together, but he knew it was his fantasy, not hers.

The wedding band remained on her left hand, and until she removed it on her own, he would have to be patient. His promise, the one he'd made on her back steps the night she'd been shaking like a leaf, came to mind. Her soft, pliant body had conformed to his, a perfect match until she'd gotten cold feet. He wouldn't rush, but he made another promise, this one to himself, to spend every minute possible getting to know her.

He pulled up the covers and closed his eyes, willing sleep to come, but it was no use as the night kept repeating itself over and over. "I can't do anything about my hours," she'd said, and it was probably true. The woman was in over her head, and his boys weren't helping matters.

Sleep finally came as half-formed ideas floated through his consciousness. He awoke the following morning with the urge to see Hidden Hills again. Something about the place had bugged him for the last few days.

Chapter Eleven

Jake phoned Charlotte with the pretense of checking on the cat, and she agreed to drop off the key on her way to work. By eight o'clock, he'd finished his excuses for not showing up at the store and was on his way to satisfy his curiosity.

Everything at the entrance was the same, except for the fresh coat of black paint on the wrought iron gate. While willing to admit they were more impressive than before, why waste money she didn't have?

His truck stirred up a thin plume of dust when driving deeper into the thick woods toward the hairpin turn. He'd started down the steep slope when he noticed a white jeep with Alabama Land Surveyors on the side door, blocking his entrance onto the narrow bridge. The postcard scene was marred by a man in dirty fatigues adjusting a transit in the middle of the road. Jake pulled up next to the truck, switching off the motor to wait.

The surveyor finished jotting his figures on a small notepad, then turned back to his equipment. Jake sensed a bit of irritation in the guy's demeanor, as if he didn't appreciate being interrupted.

"I'll be out of your way in a jiff," the man said.

"No hurry." He was glad for once his curiosity was working. Rounding the front of the truck, he held out his hand.

The surveyor's handshake was firm. "I'm Conner Sparks."

"Jake Weatherman," he replied. "Peaceful job you've got."

The man removed his cap and wiped the sweat away with his forearm. "Yeah, kind of hot though. You buying the place?"

Jake slid his hands into his pockets and gazed around as if seeing the area for the first time. "No, I'm just here to look it over. The owner seems to think I might be interested in making an offer."

Sparks crammed his damp hair under his cap and spit a wad of tobacco juice into the dust-covered, Black-eyed Susans beside the road.

"I don't see why the judge is in such an all-fired hurry for me to finish the survey, if you haven't even seen it yet. From the way he talked, it was me holding up the sale."

"I wouldn't know anything about that."

More juice splattered the ground. "I've a good mind to stop work and go fish'n when I get over to Sam Drenfield's place."

Jake frowned. "Are the forty lines located there?"

Sparks spit again. "You talking about the corner markers?"

"Yeah, I guess that's what they're called," Jake said, not caring if the man thought he was ignorant, as long as it kept him talking. He wanted to know why the judge, and not Charlotte, was having it surveyed.

Sparks raked his nasty finger inside his jaw and slung a

black wad of tobacco into the grass. "Naw," he said, biting off a fresh plug. "The judge stays in a tizzy... wants both places done yesterday."

"I get antsy myself sometimes," Jake admitted, trying to imagine Maggie's reaction to this tobacco-spitting stranger in his dirty fatigues. "What judge are we talking about? I was under the impression a Mrs. McGregor was the owner."

"Oh, she is," he agreed. "But Tom McGregor is her father-in-law. If I didn't know better, I'd say he was doing this to help her out."

"I've heard of him." He contemplated what the surveyor said. "If he's the one I have to deal with to get this place... I'm not sure it's worth it."

Sparks laughed. "I do a lot of work for the judge. Believe me, there's bad blood between those two."

He could like this guy. "Guess it wouldn't hurt to look. Mind if I ease around and go up to the house?"

The surveyor eyed the distance between his transit and the nearest tree, a reminder to Jake that he was there first and he wasn't moving. "Help yourself. The old house is something to see."

Hidden Hills mansion was as impressive as Jake recalled, only this time he'd steeled himself to its grandeur. Taking his time, he walked around the house, checking the foundation for cracks and signs of termite damage and found none. He'd need a carpenter to check underneath, but it wouldn't be a problem since the crawlspace appeared to give a good four-foot head clearance in the back, dropping to three at the front.

Jake wasn't sure why he was taking such an interest in the house, other than his overactive curiosity. Returning to the truck, he tore a page from one of Jeremy's notebooks lying in the floorboard and carried it inside. The elegance of the large entry hall had the same impact as before. He'd been able to see only part of the house then, but now he had time to study the layout of the rooms. His diagram was hastily drawn, noting things like heating and cooling, bathroom locations, and the availability of hot water. The house seemed to have most of the newfangled conveniences, including a satellite dish out back, yet it still retained the character of the Civil War period.

To keep the house as a private residence would take a healthy bank account, and as much as he'd like to help Charlotte, there was no way he'd gamble away the security he'd worked so hard to build. There had to be another way to save the house. He just needed to find it.

There was no sign of Conner Sparks when he crossed the creek on the way out. The white jeep was gone, along with any evidence the place had ever been surveyed.

The boys were in the backyard playing football when he arrived home. From the look of things, he'd just missed seeing the younger boys tackle Jeremy. When the huddle broke, he blew his horn and the game came to an abrupt end. It did his heart good for them to gather around the moment he stepped out of the cab.

"Hurry up, Dad. Granny dropped us off over an hour ago."

Jake lifted Andy to his hip. "Why didn't you let yourselves in?"

"'Cause we didn't have a key," Bruce replied, the ball rocking back and forth in his hands.

He quickly unlocked the door, stepping back while they wrestled their way in. Jeremy went straight to the refrigerator and poured milk to go with the snack cakes Bruce tore open. Their ravenous appetites gave him an easy opening. "Where's the extra key?"

"We lost it."

Walking over to the answering machine, he checked for the message his mother had left earlier in the week... blank. "Well, do you think God could be punishing you boys for what you did to Charlotte?"

The older boys eyed each other. "We didn't do nothing."

"You didn't copy her keys? Or you didn't eat supper over there every night this week without asking?"

Bruce began edging toward the door. "That's crazy. Where'd you hear such a dumb thing?"

Their saintly innocence was getting old. "Knock it off. You two have done some rotten things before, but this takes the cake. Charlotte's gone out of her way to be nice to you."

"Nice!" Bruce cried, full of righteous indignation. "She made me mop her 'ole floor, and then she put soap in my mouth!"

Jake eyed his eight-year-old. Soap? He could only imagine what the boy had done. "I want some explanations."

Jeremy slumped against the refrigerator. "We didn't think Charlotte would mind. We were hungry, and she always cooks lots of food."

"That's not the point," Jake said, disappointed they'd taken her kindness for granted. "You should have asked, or better yet, waited for her to ask you."

Bruce munched on a raisin cake. "But what if she forgot to ask?"

"Son." Jake rubbed his forehead where the pain had set in. "If she didn't ask, then maybe it's because she wasn't cooking for you."

"But you ate it too." Bruce crammed the rest of his cake into his mouth. "How come it's okay for you to eat, but not us?"

"I didn't say it was okay…"

"But if she cooks too much, won't it just be thrown out if somebody don't eat it?"

"Sit down, both of you." Jake motioned toward the kitchen table where they'd had many discussions. "Guys— Charlotte has worked two jobs for over a year, and she's exhausted when she comes home at night. She cooks a couple of meals at a time so she won't have to cook every day."

The boys were quiet as his words sank in. It was evident from their expressions this hadn't crossed their minds. Jeremy frowned, gnawing on a piece of beef jerky. "Does this mean we ate all of her food?"

"We didn't know," Bruce admitted, contrite for once.

He had their attention and it was time for their lesson. "I know you didn't, but it happened, and now we need to replace her groceries. I think since you guys did the crime, it's only fair you pay."

Bruce's mouth fell open. "But groceries costs money!"

"Yeah, Dad… lots of it!"

"Exactly," Jake agreed. "I think twenty dollars from each of you should make a good start."

"But Andy ate, too!"

"Your brother didn't know any better, so I'm paying for the rest of the grocery bill."

"But, Dad—twenty bucks? It'll wipe me out!"

Jake reached for the phone. "Sounds fair to me. Eating Charlotte's groceries behind her back is the same as stealing from her. Now get your money while I talk Grandma into shopping."

* * * *

Charlotte inserted her key in the new lock, her thoughts returning to the night when Jake had been waiting in the shrubs. He could have turned a deaf ear when he'd heard about the extra keys, but instead he'd spent his own money to replace her locks. She remembered other things about the night that should be forgotten, like his arms holding her close, and the feel of his lips on hers.

Maggie squirmed, holding her knees together. "Hurry, Mama, I gotta use the bathroom."

"And I'm thirsty," added Becky.

Charlotte shifted the small bag of groceries in her arm to open the door. She'd bought only the basics. Hopefully, it was enough to feed them until payday. When reaching for the refrigerator door, she noticed the pantry by the stove. The shelves were filled with staples of flour, shortening, cooking oil, and potatoes. There were boxes of macaroni and cheese, crackers, peanut butter, and an assortment of cereals and oatmeal. Canned vegetables, sauces, and juices filled the bottom shelf, and when she opened the refrigerator, there wasn't room for the half-gallon of milk she'd bought.

A wave of gratitude washed over her. It had to be Jake's handy work. No one else knew they were starving. She'd refused his money, so he'd bought her groceries instead. His kindness warmed her heart, and she thanked God again for moving her to this house.

She heard the back door open and then the quiet voice of the man she'd come to rely on.

"I only replaced what we ate."

He was lying, and they both knew it. She couldn't remember the last time she'd had so much food under her roof. Taking a deep breath, she wiped the tears of gratitude from her eyes.

"You sure know how to apologize."

With his hands buried deep in his pockets, Jake moved closer to her side. "My mama taught me."

"Then tell her I said thank you."

His eyes held hers, and a warm familiar sensation flowed through her body. She knew she was falling for the guy, but there wasn't a lot she could do about it, since her heart refused to listen to her head.

"I'll be glad to," he promised, then turned to go. "If my boys pull anymore stunts, just let me know."

Chapter Twelve

"Hurry, Mama." Maggie buckled her black, second-hand shoes as fast as her little fingers would work. "We'll be late for church."

Charlotte closed the mascara with a snap and applied a thin layer of her only lipstick before making one last turn in front of the mirror. She hated walking into a new church for the first time. To make things worse, if Jake's boys were still mad for being caught red-handed in their last escapade, there was no telling what they might do to get even.

"You look pretty, Mama." Becky's sweet expression did more for her self-esteem than the compliment. The girls were excited about going to church.

Maggie clicked the patent leather heels together like Dorothy in the Wizard of Oz. "I'm ready."

Church was only three blocks away, but Charlotte decided to take her car for the sole purpose of having an excuse not to ride home with Jake, if he offered. She'd yet to see a church without its tongue-wagging gossipers, and she didn't intend to be linked to him.

Following her girls to the third pew on the right, they sat down, hopefully not taking anyone's favorite seat. Annabelle's fingers danced over the keys as the music filled the sanctuary, calming her nerves. This was what she'd been missing—God's house and His people.

She relaxed on the padded pew, noticing the material worn from years of use by faithful believers. The wooden beams overhead were darkened with age, and the floors gleamed where colorful streaks of light poured through the stained-glass windows. The church, just like the house on Robins Lane, seemed to welcome her with open arms. Talking quietly to the lady in front of her, the peaceful tranquility shattered when Andy bounced onto the pew beside her.

"Hi, Mama Char-it!" His excitement echoed throughout the entire sanctuary. Laughter from the other congregation members proved his clear, sweet voice had been heard loud and clear.

Of all the pews in the church, she'd managed to sit with the one family with whom she'd hoped not to get her name linked. She tried to pretend the red glow of her cheeks was normal, but then Annabelle nodded from the piano, confirming she'd inadvertently started the tongue-wagging. There was no one to blame but herself.

The elderly preacher walked up to the pulpit with a slight stoop in his shoulders. She wondered if he was carrying a burden as heavy as her own. His thick, white hair matched his bushy eyebrows, and when he began to read, "Now faith is the substance of things hoped for, the evidence of things not seen," it was as if he was speaking directly to her.

Looking back, she realized she'd been living on nothing but hope since Mitch's death. Had her faith begun to waver? She knew all things happened for a reason, and God's grace would handle any situation, but had she been so busy lately she'd failed to ask for His guidance?

Time had flown since making the decision to move to

Robins Lane. Her girls were happier, she was actually sleeping at night, and her problems didn't seem to be consuming every moment of her life as they had at Hidden Hills. She listened intently as the sermon continued. By the end of the service, she was sure the pastor's stoop was osteoporosis-related. This godly man possessed a contentment that could only come from walking with the Lord

"If you've got a burden, give it to God."

Charlotte experienced contentment from the reading of God's word. Her problems were far from being over and she might not like the outcome, but she knew in her heart God's will would be done.

She spent several minutes visiting with members of the congregation before going outside where Jake waited to walk her to the car. "I heard Andy, and I'm sorry."

"Don't worry about it." She waved his apology aside. "I can handle the gossip if you can."

He rubbed the back of his neck. "Yeah, well… Mrs. Franklin may be hard of hearing, but she perked up when she heard Andy's comment."

"Tell me it's not Wylene Franklin."

Laughter shook his chest. "The same. Do you know her?"

Her head dropped. "She's a customer at the shop. I'll never live it down."

"Other than being embarrassed, what did you think of the service?"

She relaxed against the car, not caring if she created more gossip. "I'm not sure if I've ever enjoyed a sermon more. Do you realize how lucky you are to have a pastor like him? I know he was preaching to everyone, but I felt like his message was directed straight at me."

"He's good at that. Today's sermon focused on hope and assurance, but just wait until he's slinging the fire and brimstone. I've limped away many a day with stomped toes, plus he's burnt my britches a few times, too."

"I can believe it." She was glad she'd felt welcomed by the congregation.

"Do you think you'll be back?"

He seemed to have forgotten he'd practically blackmailed her into coming again. She glanced over his shoulder at the white steeple perched high on the roof of the old building and nodded. "You can count on it."

Jake nodded and walked away, the boys following close behind. Andy waved. "Bye, Mama Char-it."

****

Excitement coursed through Charlotte's veins the following Saturday, when Mr. Milner told her she could leave early. Her paycheck would be short, but she had plenty of groceries, so they wouldn't starve. It also meant she could spend time with Jake, maybe.

Ordinarily, she would have worried about Hidden Hills or her father-in-law while waiting at the crossing on Dove Street for the slowest train of the week to pass, but not today. She'd decided to do nothing at all.

It was Jeremy's first time to sit with her girls, and even though no one had called to tattle, she was still a bit surprised to find him stretched out in a hammock, with Maggie and Andy playing together in the nearby sandbox. He seemed to have everything under control, but best of all, his dad's truck was in the drive.

She unplugged his earphones. "Where's Becky?"

He sat up, fully alert. "You're home early."

158

"Just a bit." Since he'd been willing to work all day, she went ahead and paid him the full amount. "The train caught me, or I would have been home ages ago."

"Yeah, it's a bummer," he said, coming out of the swaying hammock. "I'll get Becky. She and Bruce are messing with the computer, and Dad's taking a nap."

"Don't bother. If your dad's napping, then they can't be getting into too much trouble."

"My exact thoughts." Jeremy had started up the steps to the house, but then he stopped and came back with a look of concern in his eyes. "Uh—Charlotte?"

"Is something wrong?"

"No, but… I was just wondering. Do you have time to cut my hair? Dad says we're to ask first, in case you're too tired."

Raking her fingers through his dark locks, she couldn't help comparing the thick texture to his dad's receding hairline. "Just give me a minute to change into some sweats."

"Hey, Red, your mom's home!"

Maggie stomped across the yard, pulling Andy along with her good arm. "That's not my name, Jeremy, and you know it!"

He ruffled her curls, making wild ringlets bounce around her head. "You look like a clown!"

Her tongue shot out. "My hair is beautiful—so there!"

"Cut it out, you two," Charlotte said, making her way through the hedgerow. Jeremy was constantly teasing Maggie. One thing for sure, it was never dull when these two were together.

"What happened to Red's hair?" he asked, following her inside.

The pile of hair in the floor was proof of her hectic

morning. "She fell asleep with gum in her mouth. I had to cut off several inches."

When Charlotte returned from changing clothes, the floor had been swept clean, and Jeremy sat straddling the stool with the plastic cape slung around his shoulders. "Maggie cleaned up the floor for you."

She reached for her comb and scissors. "I'm surprised she bothered. Cleaning isn't her favorite chore."

"Your kid's weird. She took the hair with her."

Jeremy bombarded her with non-stop questions about girls while she clipped. No names were mentioned, but she knew he had a huge crush on Kimmie Jones at the moment. His new hairstyle drew attention to his dark eyes, making him look older than thirteen. She had a feeling his girl troubles were just beginning.

The back door flew open and slammed against the clothes dryer, leaving a small dent in the white enamel. Becky rushed in, laughing so hard she was gasping for air. "Hurry! You've got to see this!"

"See what?" Charlotte jerked the cape off the boy when he shot out the door. "What have you done?"

She ran to keep up with the kids as they bolted across the yard and into Jake's house. Skidding to a stop in his den, she found him snoring peacefully on the sofa with a wild patch of Maggie's hair plastered all over his head. She froze, her hand flying to her chest while trying to catch her breath. He would most likely erupt like a volcano when he awoke, so she started inching backward, motioning for everyone to clear out, but it was too late.

As if sensing he wasn't alone, Jake sat up, rubbing his eyes to bring the room back into focus. He yawned. "What's up?"

Charlotte glanced at the boys, expecting them to be as

cracked up as Becky, but she realized from their horrified expressions these professional pranksters had never had the nerve to pull such a stunt. Gone were her dreams of a perfect afternoon, shot down by her own flesh and blood. How could Maggie have done such a thing, and to him of all people?

From her vantage point, his head resembled a disheveled porcupine. She cringed, dreading what was to come. "Oh—ah, not much. But, we might have a slight problem."

Jake yawned again, raking his fingers through his hair until he hit a snag. One look at his hands and an angry growl began reverberating deep in his chest. "What have you done to me!?"

"Now, Jake." She backed up for safety. "Let's try to be reasonable about this."

"Reasonable?" He shot off the couch coming toward her holding out his hairy, red palms. "You want me to be reasonable? Just look at this!"

The accusation was aimed at her, and in a way, she felt responsible. The red hair was a dead giveaway. Behind her, the kids exploded with laughter, while she struggled to keep a straight face. It was hopeless, and she was soon laughing too hard to defend herself.

Jake stomped into the bathroom, where he braced his hands on the sink and stared into the mirror. "I'm ruined!"

Charlotte followed, wiping away the steady stream of tears running down her cheeks. He looked ridiculous.

"This isn't funny!" he shouted, making the kids laugh even harder.

Charlotte tried to get a grip. "What happened?"

"You tell me. I took a nap, and now this!"

Ordinarily she would have been outraged he'd think

her capable of such childish behavior, but she couldn't stop laughing. "I'm sorry—but it's funny."

"Oh—you think?" he snapped. "Well, I'm glad you're enjoying this, because I'm not... think you can sober up long enough to get it out?"

With a gentle push, she moved him out of her way and tore off a wad of toilet paper to dry her eyes. He seemed not to notice when she blew her nose and flushed the soggy tissue before closing the toilet lid. "Sit down so I can see what we're up against."

Jake squirmed, reaching up to scratch.

"Be still, you big baby." She didn't bother to hide her grin. "I think she used an entire bottle of glue. How could you possibly sleep through this plaster job?"

"I was tired, okay?" he said, pulling at the homemade toupee. "We've had some problems with the new store, and I've not been sleeping much at night."

She hadn't slept so well herself, but it was her problem, not his. She took a closer look at his hair. "If this is school glue, it should wash right out. Is there anything else Maggie could have gotten into?"

He thought for a moment. "There's other glues in my shop, but Maggie wouldn't do this."

"Oh, believe it," she said, with certainty. "Who else around here has this particular shade of red... other than yourself?"

He snarled. "Real funny."

She grabbed towels, a comb, some shampoo, and a hand mirror before heading for the kitchen sink. Drinking a glass of water, she waited while Jake lathered his hair and rinsed. Unfortunately, when the towel came off, the red hair stayed on. His scrubbing proved to be a lost cause.

"We know it wasn't school glue," she said, the comb

hitting a snag. "A solvent is the only thing strong enough to dissolve this."

"You're not using the stuff on my head!"

"Then you'll have to sit still while I peel it off piece by piece," she replied, her lips twitching.

He squirmed. "Go ahead. It feels like ants crawling on my scalp."

"Don't be so grumpy. It could be worse."

"You wouldn't be Little Miss Perky if you were wearing a mop. Why did she do this?"

Charlotte was at a loss. "Why does a five-year-old do anything?"

Peeling the glue from each individual hair shaft progressed at a snail's pace. He continued to squirm and Charlotte knew it was taking too long when white flakes began popping up, giving a rippled effect to his tender scalp. "You're beginning to look like a baby's bottom with diaper rash."

"It's not funny."

She snickered. "It is from where I'm standing."

"You're getting a malicious satisfaction from this, aren't you?"

She patted his shoulder. "Come over to the sink, and let me rinse."

Jake adjusted the water temperature then ducked his head under the faucet. At first he seemed relaxed, but he tensed when she pressed up against his side, reaching across his wide shoulders to massage his scalp under the running water. He was warm and solid, and somewhere in the back of her mind she knew Maggie had to be punished for what she'd done.

With Jake at her mercy it was hard to concentrate. The lukewarm water continued to flow through her fingers, and for some strange reason, it reminded her of the dream she'd had during the night where he'd held her in his arms, and her problems had drifted away.

Lost in her thoughts, she failed to notice the sink clogging with the remaining hair. Jake forced himself up, trying to get out of her grasp, but not before she'd accidentally slammed his head against the faucet in her attempt to shut off the water.

His hand shot to the new bump. "What the..."

Charlotte threw a bath towel over his head to hide her embarrassment. What was she thinking? Her silly daydreams had almost knocked the man out. "Sit down, and I'll see what's left."

Following her orders, Jake towel-dried his hair. Her face glowed when she caught his reflection in the hand-held mirror. He winked. "Why so serious? I thought you were enjoying this."

"But I didn't mean to drown you."

"I know."

That was the problem. He knew too much. Concern darkened her green eyes. "This doesn't look good at all."

"How bad is it?" he asked, still communicating through the mirror.

"The glue is gone, but your scalp has a nasty burn. I'm calling Mark to see if he'll come by to look at it."

Jake started to protest, but she cut him short. "I know he's a pediatrician, but it's him or a trip to the emergency room."

"I have a doctor."

"But does he make house calls?" His angry expression was all the answer she needed. "I thought not... I'm calling Mark."

After Charlotte hung up the phone, she went in search

of Jake to let him know her brother-in-law was on his way. She found him in front of the bathroom mirror again, his skin a bright lobster-red. The remaining hair resembled the bristles on an old scrub brush.

"I look like a clown."

"Oh, I wouldn't say a clown, exactly." She stood at the doorway. Knowing the condition of his scalp, her conscience kicked in, making her feel bad for laughing. It was the first time she'd seen him out of sorts, proving someone as easy going as Jake could have a bad day. "I'm sorry Maggie did this to you."

He spared her a quick glance. "And?"

"And, I'm sorry I laughed."

A cynical smile touched his mouth. "You'd be more believable if you weren't about to bust a gut." He shook his head. "You've got a warped sense of humor."

Amusement gleamed in her eyes, but she didn't laugh.

"Do you know what Monday is?"

She shrugged. "The first workday of the week?"

"Smart aleck." His expression snarled at her from the mirror. "It's the ribbon cutting ceremony at our new men's store at Four Corners. The local paper's sending a photographer. I can't show up like this."

Placing her hands on his shoulders, she moved in for a closer look at the deep frown creasing his forehead. It made him two-toned. His downhearted expression was almost comical. "Maybe it'll be better by then."

The words hung between them. "Yeah—right," he finally said. "Did you talk to your brother-in-law?"

"He's having dinner at his parents, but he'll stop by my house first."

"I hope he's not as big a snob as his mother."

Charlotte threw up her hands. "Whatever!"

165

"You weren't here when she dropped off the girls!"

She turned with a vengeance. "Now you listen to me. Mark happens to be an excellent doctor, so *be nice!*"

He was fast on her heels going out the door. "Okay, I'll be nice. Losing my hair was bad enough—now I look like a freak."

She stopped. "You're not a freak. I'll grant, you look a bit ridiculous right now, but it's not permanent."

"Thanks!"

"What is it with men? You lose a little hair, and you're automatically dog meat?"

He followed her into her kitchen and went straight for the coffeepot like he always did. "We're not like that."

"Sure you are. It's as if the only thing a man's got is his hair, and when it's gone—poof, there's nothing left."

Jake drained the pot, lifting the cup toward her with a questioning glance. He waited for her to decline before taking a sip. "Did you take the soap out of that box before you climbed on?"

"I'm not preaching," she said, amazed he could drink cold, day-old coffee. "I'm just stating a fact."

"What about women?"

"We're not half as vain as men. You'd be surprised how many men get facelifts."

He opened the microwave to heat his coffee. "So wrinkles don't bother you?"

Charlotte fought the urge to check her complexion in a mirror. Besides drinking plenty of water and avoiding too much sun exposure, she had a stringent cleansing routine she practiced faithfully. "I don't have wrinkles."

"Sure you do." He put his hands on each side of her face. His thumbs slid upwards, slowly gliding over her cheekbones. "Cute little tiny ones—right here."

166

Gazing into his royal blue eyes, Charlotte leaned forward, forgetting about his promise not to rush, but unfortunately, he hadn't. Instead of taking what she offered, his lips brushed her cheek as if marking the spot.

"It's just crow's feet." Flustered he was making her wait, her eyes drifted shut when his lips moved to her other cheek. They were alone. The kids were back at his house, and she had the freedom to lose herself in his passionate kisses without being interrupted. Her arms circled his waist, drawing him closer as he tilted her face up to his. She waited.

"Charlotte." He whispered her name, caressing the temples with his thumbs. His lips danced across her brow.

"Mmm."

"I'll bet you color it, don't you?"

"What?" Her mind concentrated more on his misplaced kisses than what he was saying.

"Your hair... I'll bet you color it."

She pushed him away. "You're checking my roots!"

His laughter was better than a bucket of cold water at restoring her senses. She raked her fingers through her disheveled hair and tried to cover her discomfort. Just as before, she was putty in his hands. The distinctive purr of Mark's antique sports car pulling into her drive saved her from further embarrassment. She hurried to the door.

Her brother-in-law bolted up the steps and pointed over his shoulder at her old hatchback. "Why don't you get a decent car?"

"It is decent."

He stood in the doorway, comparing the two cars. "It's a pile of junk."

Charlotte laughed. Her car had been a shared joke with Mark since the beginning, mainly because it was a sore spot with his parents. "Don't talk about my car—you'll hurt its feelings."

"If it had any feelings, they rusted and fell off years ago!"

His kiss was accompanied by a good-natured hug, which Charlotte gladly accepted. "Hey, gorgeous... how's my girls?"

"One's doing fine, but the other's in trouble up to her cute little bottom!"

"I see." He noticed Jake for the first time. "You must be her victim."

Jake introduced himself. "I'm afraid so. It's nice of you to come out of your way."

Mark wasted no time moving him into the bright light near the kitchen window. After looking at his scalp and feeling the textured stubble, he winked at Charlotte and scribbled on the prescription pad he'd taken from his back pocket. "This should take care of the problem. It does wonders for a baby's bottom."

She did her best not to grin when Jake cut his worried eyes her way. "Am I going to lose the rest of my hair, doctor?"

Mark laid a reassuring hand on his shoulder. "No, I don't think any permanent damage has been done. You were just sensitive to the glue. The worst part will be the itching when your scalp begins to heal, but this cream should help, and even replace some of the oils in your hair."

Unconsciously, she began scratching her head, and Jake caught her hand.

"Do it again, and so help me I'll paddle your backside."

She quickly locked her fingers together to keep them

busy, although the thought of Jake's hands on her backside was quite appealing. "Sorry."

Mark burst out laughing. "I'm leaving that problem with you. Mom's serving the main course about now, and if I don't get there soon, she'll feed mine to the dogs."

"I'll call your office for the bill."

Mark shook his head. "Since your condition is due to my niece's mischief, it just wouldn't seem fair."

"I appreciate it."

"Your head needs to be checked in a couple of days. You can see your own doctor, if you'd like, or come by my office."

Charlotte quickly intervened. "Maggie has an appointment Tuesday after school for you to look at her arm. Can he come then?"

She glanced at Jake in time to see his relief when Mark said, "You won't need to register, just come into the examining room with Maggie."

Chapter Thirteen

The itchy scalp had dealt him misery all morning even though he'd already used half a tube of medicine. He stretched his shoulders and neck to get the kinks out. There wouldn't have been any kinks had he not wasted the last hour searching for discrepancies in a handful of invoices, because *somebody* had failed to check off the merchandise.

He scratched again, trying to think what he'd done to upset Maggie enough for her to do this to him. Uncapping the ointment, he smeared a large wad across his head and rubbed it in without the aid of a mirror. The cooling sensation brought instant relief, making him grateful to Charlotte's brother-in-law. Mark had not only saved him the embarrassment at the pharmacy by writing the prescription in Andy's name, but he'd convinced her to pick it up.

He leaned forward, resting his elbows on the desk, and recalled the feel of Charlotte's arms, holding him tight. In all fairness, he should have warned her about the town busybodies… a good many belonging to their church.

Not only was his new neighbor beautiful—she had spunk. It took a lot of courage for her to sit in the same pew on her return trip. The two of them were most likely the main topic at several dinner tables around town—him for wearing a cap during preaching and her for running interference when Wylene Franklin demanded he take it off. It meant a lot to him.

Plenty of churches would have welcomed her and the girls with open arms, but he wanted them to worship with his family. If anyone ever needed the loving fellowship of God's people, it was Charlotte. Loneliness had been a big part of her when she'd moved next door, but not anymore.

He needed to be in the store working, but he was tired of everyone staring at his cap. Rocking back in his chair, he stretched his legs again and readjusted the cap to cover as much scalp as possible. The door flew opened and Sara, Betty's mom, rushed in to let him know Judge Tom McGregor was there to see him. His mother-in-law was a sweet person—and his best buyer—but it irritated him to no end when she made a big show over wealthy people and ignored the less fortunate.

"Send him in" had been a waste of words since the man was right behind her. Jake rose, offering his hand. "What can I do for you?"

"I'm here on behalf of my daughter-in-law," the judge said, giving the impression he had her best interest at heart.

Jake wanted to make sure they were on the same page. "Are we talking about Charlotte?"

"Ah… yes. I've been told you're thinking of buying Hidden Hills."

It was a statement, blunt and to the point. Therefore, it needed no answer. Not that he felt like giving one. He waited while the tall, distinguished man slid into the chair directly across from his desk. The judge reminded him of a sleek fox and appeared to be just as cunning. Charlotte's distrust of her father-in-law was understandable, and he was inclined to agree with the late Charles Will's opinion of the man.

The judge crossed his legs and pinched the crease in his wrinkle-free trousers. His perfectly tailored suit, crisp white shirt, and expertly knotted tie went along with his pretentious attitude. On the surface he appeared relaxed, but Jake sensed a rigid control at work. Noting the arrogant tilt of Tom McGregor's head made his hackles rise. He didn't like the judge.

"I'll get right to the point. You see, my daughter-in-law has received a firm offer for her home. It's quite generous, and I can't see her turning it down."

"I see." Jake took a moment to consider this latest turn of events. If he was telling the truth, then Charlotte could get on with her life. "So she's already made her decision to accept the offer?"

"We've discussed the situation, and like I said, it's a generous offer."

Jake nodded, disappointed she hadn't confided in him. "Too bad—it's a nice place."

His business done, the judge stood. "I just thought since I was in the neighborhood, I'd drop by and save you the trouble of making an offer."

He'd heard more believable lies coming from his boys, but common courtesy dictated he see the man out. A firm offer to buy could explain surveying the estate, but there was still the question of Sam Drenfield's property. Was the same person buying both places?

"My boys would have loved the creek. Do you get a chance to do much fishing?"

The judge shook his head. "No, I'm not much of a fisherman. I stay busy most of the time, but I try to fit in a few rounds of golf when I can."

Something didn't feel right, and he refused to let it rest until he knew what it was. He began by calling Charlotte at the Beauty Boutique to see if she'd heard from her realtor, or talked with her father-in-law. She hadn't, which meant Tom McGregor was lying.

Jake had come to rely on his instincts. He'd met Charlotte's in-laws and wasn't impressed. They seemed to want Hidden Hills and the neighboring property bad enough to run off any potential buyers. What he wanted to know was why?

According to Charlotte, Ellen McGregor had refused to live in the country, so what was left? Buy for pennies on the dollar and sell to a buyer they already had lined up? Maybe, but there was always the possibility they wanted it for a business venture of their own. The house was in excellent shape, and a lot of people were opening their older homes to the public as bed and breakfasts.

Lunch had been the only thing on his mind when the judge had dropped in. Now he wasn't hungry anymore— just curious. It only took a second to search the net for the state tourist bureau. "And there it is…"

The arrogance of Tom McGregor made his blood boil. Not waiting for the foreclosure, the cocksure buzzard had gone online, advertising Hidden Hills as a country resort offering fishing, hiking, and horseback riding. Reservations were being taken beginning in March the following spring.

Jake rocked back in his chair, chewing his lip while concentrating on the webpage in front of him. Assuming the foreclosure took place by mid-December, it allowed only three months for renovations. Were the McGregors guessing when her money would run out, or had they accessed her bank account?

Hitting the send button, it only took a moment to email a copy of the Hidden Hills webpage to Ralph. His lawyer would know if what they were doing was legal. Before logging off, he downloaded a copy for his own use. He'd sworn not to get involved in anyone else's business, but circumstances change. There had to be some way to stop the judge from destroying her life.

Sara rushed back into his office, her arms piled with ladies' tee-shirts and a frown on her face meaning trouble. "Just look at this. I ordered first quality, and these aren't fit for the thrift store!"

"So? Send them back."

"I intend to." Her attention focused on the clock above the file cabinet. "If you're taking the neighbor's kid to the doctor this afternoon, you'd better get cracking."

Her bossy attitude irritated him at times, but she was Betty's mother and had been with the store since the beginning. He tugged his cap lower. "Maggie."

"What?"

"Her name is Maggie."

"Well, you'll be mud if you don't hurry."

He ruffled through the folder until he found the invoice for the shirts. "Adjust the account and make sure we don't get struck with the shipping."

"Yes, boss," came the smart-alecky reply from behind her bifocals. "We're taking bets on why you're wearing the silly cap. You can let us know who's right when you feed us, and by the way, the winner gets the day off."

"You don't say?" The dinner had slipped his mind. He was glad she'd reminded him of his promise. Reaching out, he mussed her hair until it stood on end. "See if they take bets on what you've been up to."

Sara swung a shirt at him, but her short arms missed their mark. "You're as bad as our boys. No wonder they're brats!"

Jake laughed going out the door. His employees could wager all the bets they wanted, but he wasn't taking off the cap. He'd never live it down if he did.

The doctor's office should have been a twenty-minute drive, but he'd forgotten about the road construction. Now he was locked in school traffic, crawling at a snail's pace with Andy and Maggie in the back seat. It was hard to believe the noisy little chatterbox was as quiet as a mouse.

He glanced in the mirror at the red curls and wondered how someone so precious could be related to the man he'd met earlier in the day. "Did you say something?"

"Uh-huh. I said I'm sorry."

"About what?"

Looking over his shoulder, he saw her chin drop while she concentrated on scratching inside her dirty cast. "I'm sorry I glued your head."

"Why did you do it?" He was surprised she'd finally owned up to it, even though her mother had scrubbed both hair and glue from her hands.

"So you'll be pretty like my daddy."

Talk about an ego buster. He'd seen pictures of her dad on their living room wall. "But why?"

"So you can be our new daddy."

It was high praise for him, but it would probably make Charlotte run for the hills. There was no denying the kids had bonded, fighting one minute and defending each other the next. If things didn't work out, there would be five broken hearts, six if he counted his.

"Why don't we let it be our secret?"

After passing the construction site, the traffic moved more freely, and he was able to reach Wills' Junction before closing time at the clinic. Thankfully, the doctor's parking lot was empty, except for the familiar antique sports car and a red muscle car.

They appeared to be the last patients of the day, but it didn't seem to bother the young nurse in banana-print scrubs. She gave the kids suckers and waited while Maggie stepped on the scales. When her vital signs were taken, the girl showed none of the reluctance his boys would have had in a similar situation.

"Uncle Mark lets Becky and me be last 'cause him and Mama like to talk."

He held Andy's hand and followed Maggie and the nurse into the first room on the right. "They do?"

"Uh-huh." Maggie twisted like a contortionist trying to poke a finger in the top of her cast. "They talk all the time, but me and Becky don't get to listen. I think they tell secrets."

The doctor hung his stethoscope on a hook outside the door. He caught Maggie from behind in a bear hug and swung her around. "How's my girl?"

She giggled. "It itches, Uncle Mark!"

"Of course it does." He heaved her onto the table in an exaggerated show of strength. "My goodness you're heavy. How would you like to lose five pounds in a hurry?"

"Yeah! Mama says Andy can sleep with me when it's gone and she don't have to work and Mr. Jake says okay."

"Is he your new boyfriend?"

"No, silly. You're my boyfriend. This is Andy. He's only three."

Jake kept his toddler out of the way while Mark removed the cast. Not only was he quick, but his nurse kept Maggie talking so there was none of the earsplitting screams he'd expected.

176

"This might hurt a little." Mark lifted her arm in a range of motion exercises. "Good girl. Now, no more playing in the toilet."

She gave him a hug. "I promise, Uncle Mark."

Jake sat Andy on the floor and traded places with Maggie. Sitting there surrounded by cartoon characters, he felt as out of place as Gulliver in Lilliput.

"Lose the cap," Mark said, washing his hands.

He did as he was told, revealing patchy flakes of peeling skin. "Was the cream supposed to take the red out?"

"Usually," replied the doctor. "But yours was almost a second degree burn where the glue was the thickest. This looks a lot better."

Maggie tugged at her uncle's coat. "Can we have a toy?"

"Sure you can. But come back in here when you get it." He returned his attention to Jake. "Tell Charlotte not to worry about Maggie. Her arm's fine."

"Good. Then she only has a house and thirty thousand dollars to keep her awake at night."

The doctor glanced at him while washing his hands again. Reaching for the handle, the towel rack groaned when he cranked out a paper. "What thirty thousand?"

"The amount she owes your dad." Mark's scowl of displeasure had Jake thinking his scalp was worse than he'd let on. "My head?"

"You're head's fine," he replied with a dismissive gesture of his hand. "Charlotte doesn't owe Dad a red cent. The money was part of our inheritance and a tax write-off for him. Mine went for medical equipment, and Mitch spent his on the house."

"Then why did she say…"

Anger emanated from the doctor, causing Jake to wonder what can of worms he'd unwittingly opened. "Because Dad probably told her she did."

"The woman's flat broke with two kids. Why would he insist she pay him back?"

Mark's expression revealed pure disgust. "Because money is money as far as my dad is concerned, and it doesn't matter who he hurts to get it."

"You've lost me."

"Charlotte doesn't deserve another raw deal." Mark shut the faucet off before continuing, his bleak tone was like a dreary winter's day. "She could've had a string of shops by now, but Mitch wanted her to stay home and look after those foster kids. My brother knew how to get his way."

Jake frowned. Charlotte mentioned caring for the foster kids, just not how it came about.

"Don't get me wrong, I love my brother, and helping those kids was a good thing, but he failed to ask her opinion—just told her what they were going to do. Then the same thing happened when he agreed to the terms of Grandpa's estate—even though it meant selling their home."

Jake whistled through his teeth. "I'll bet it raised a ruckus."

"Oh, yeah." Mark dried his hands before hurling the wet paper towel into the trash. "But Mitch talked her into it. Now they're squeezing the life out of her. He's my dad, and I can't stop him—but you can."

"Me?"

The doctor's gaze was steady. "I don't know of anyone else."

He could see where Mark would have trouble defying

his parents, especially since they'd lost their other son. The odds were against Charlotte, and up to this point, he'd been no help at all. What she needed was a miracle.

"I've seen the way you look at each other," Mark said. "You're the only one she'll listen to."

Jake glanced at Maggie and Andy digging in the toy chest in the waiting room. He didn't think they could hear them. "Tell me what I need to know, and I'll do my best."

Mark hesitated, his conscience seeming to battle against a strong familial loyalty. It was commendable, but badly misplaced.

"I can assure you, anything you say goes no farther than this room."

"Fair enough." He removed his lab jacket, indicating his day was over. "I'm not sure how much you know about Charlotte's finances, but you know she's broke, so I'm assuming she's confided in you."

"We've been over a few things."

"Okay. For starters, Dad's going to make an offer to buy the property for what she owes in Wilson's Realty name, prior to the foreclosure. If she won't sell, then he plans to wait until the estate goes into foreclosure. Once Charlotte loses the house, or sells to the business, the terms of the will have been met. There's nothing to stop him from buying it outright in his name."

Jake thought for a moment, recalling an article he'd read after learning of Charlotte's problems. "State law says a notice of foreclosure has to be run in the local paper for three weeks, then the sheriff auctions off the property at the courthouse. If that happens, how can your dad be sure about having the highest bid?"

"I don't know," Mark said. "But I promise, he'll get Grandpa's estate if you don't stop him."

He didn't like what he was hearing. "And he'll still demand the thirty thousand. It sounds like she's sunk, unless the house sells to an outside buyer."

"It's not going to an outsider," Mark added. "Charlotte doesn't know Dad owns Wilson's Realty. I've heard he's telling potential buyers Hidden Hill's has already sold. Like I said, he's determined to get Grandpa's estate."

"I know." Jake recounted his morning visit. "How much money does Charlotte have invested in the place?"

Mark's arms were crossed while he studied the tile floor and did some quick calculations. "Let's see, Mitch sold their first home, borrowed on his life insurance, and cashed in everything they had, plus the money from Dad. I'd say probably upward of three hundred thousand."

Knowing the dollar amount made the seriousness of the situation clearer. It was hard to understand why anyone could hate Charlotte so much. What had she possibly done to make Mitch's parents feel this way, or were they afraid she would remarry and the estate would leave the family?

"I had no idea of the amount. How can he want her to lose so much money? Does the fact she's raising Mitch's kids not mean anything?"

"Like I said, money is money, and there's no love lost between Dad and Charlotte. If his plan works, by this time next year, Hidden Hills will be a country resort. He's got a paving crew ready to asphalt the dirt road as far as the bridge and bulldozers on standby to join Sam Drenfield's fishponds together. We're talking about a ninety-acre lake, fully stocked."

Jake had proof it wouldn't take a year. "Is Drenfield in with your dad?"

Maggie came bouncing into the room, waving a princess crown in the air. "Are we going fishing?"

180

"Not today," Mark said, urging her back toward the toy chest. "Why don't you get Becky something?" He waited until she'd started digging again before he continued. "As far as I know, Sam's holding out for more money."

Jake reached for the webpage in his pocket, then thought better of it. He'd never been much of a poker player, but he knew not to show his cards until he was sure of the hand he'd been dealt. Mark came across as a straight shooter, but this was his father they were talking about.

On their way home, Jake and the kids went by to check on Cucumber and her kittens and put out fresh food. The day of reckoning was getting close for the cats. Their fate rested in the hands of the judge unless he could think of something fast.

Chapter Fourteen

Jake's grim mood brightened considerably when he returned home and saw Charlotte, dressed in cut-offs and an old tee-shirt, materialize from under the hood of her car. A greasy rag swung in one hand and an empty oil bottle in the other. He adjusted his cap, reached back to unbuckle Andy's seat belt, and open the truck doors.

"Hey, neighbor," she called. "How were the check-ups?"

He came around the truck, his eyes never once leaving her grease-smeared face. Charlotte McGregor had to be the prettiest mechanic this side of the Mason-Dixon. Her bright smile made his heart race, and he crossed over to her yard, a fresh spring in his step.

"Maggie's fine, and I'm still bald. How is it with you?"

"Don't ask!" She closed the hood; a solid slam shook the car.

He leaned against her old hatchback, amazed it still ran. "How many miles does she have?"

"More than me, but I'm gaining fast." She wiped the oil from her hands. "They did a good job. It looks nice."

"What does?"

She nodded behind him. "The yard."

He'd been so wrapped up in watching Charlotte he

hadn't noticed the open space separating their houses. Now he stared dumbfounded at the spot where the overgrown hedge had stood undisturbed for the past ten years. It was gone, the ground tilled and raked smooth.

The nerves in the back of his neck tighten into rigid bands. First his scalp—now this! He glared at Charlotte. A fierce anger surged through him when she appeared more concerned with the grease under her nails than anything he was feeling. Her brazen indifference rubbed salt in an open wound. "What happened to my hedge? Betty planted the hedge, and you had no right to get rid of it!"

Her chin shot up. "You think I did it?"

"Who else? You've always hated it!"

The greasy rag slammed against the car. "What did I use, my scissors?"

Jake didn't know why he was accusing Charlotte. He'd seen her sorry excuse for a toolbox with its hammer and handful of bent nails. She didn't own a saw, much less a shovel or rake. An apology might have gone a long way toward saving the day had he given one, but Becky and Bruce rounded the corner coming to a screeching halt at the sight of him.

"I should have known." His anger mounted, disappointed the boy cared so little for his mother's memory. "He's gone too far this time."

"Now, Jake." Charlotte jumped between him and their kids like a human shield. Her hands pushed against his chest, leaving oily fingerprints on his blue dress shirt. "You don't know for sure it was Bruce. Mistakes happen. Someone might have gotten the address wrong."

Grim certainty marked his expression. "Just how many houses on this street are separated by hedgerows?"

His large hands clamped her shoulders, picked her up,

and moved her aside to get to the kids. "Come here!"

Lunging from behind, Charlotte locked both arms around his middle and made him stagger. For a featherweight, she had a solid grip.

"A minute ago you were blaming me!" she cried. "Why don't you try listening for a change?"

"Excuse me, folks," came an amused voice from somewhere behind them. "I hate to break up a good fight, but I have a bill for a Ms. McGregor."

Her arms went limp, and they turned in unison to see a tan, muscular man about their age walking toward them. His green cap and shirt matched the truck parked at the curb, both carrying the Larry's Landscaping Service logo in bright yellow print.

Jake fumed when the man's eyes consumed Charlotte from head to toe, but when the landscaper handed her the invoice and his fingers deliberately brushed against hers—he saw red. The guy wasn't any taller or better looking than himself, he reasoned, just a swift reminder adolescence wasn't the only time testosterone ruled the male brain. He had squatters' rights.

In an effort to reaffirm his claim, Jake slid his arm around Charlotte's shoulder and locked her to his side. He glanced down expecting a fight, but she'd gone pale as a ghost.

"Oh, my…" she began, staring at the total. "I don't have any cash. Will a check do?"

"Give it here!" He snatched the bill from her shaky hand. Women! He'd swear this one didn't have a pot to pee in, but if pride were money she'd be a millionaire. This beat all; he couldn't believe he was paying for the privilege of being victimized, but here he was pulling out his wallet like he had good sense. "I'll pay it!"

He felt a slight tug on his sleeve. "The bill has my name on it," she said, the color returning to her cheeks. "But it wasn't me."

"I know." He glared at the landscaper for being alive. The way he saw it, the man should have been paying more attention to his money and less to Charlotte.

The wallet he returned to his back pocket was as flat as a proverbial pancake, but at least the bill was marked paid-in-full, thereby eliminating any reason Larry's Landscaping might have for a return call. All in all, it was money well spent.

"I'm truly sorry, Jake. Jeremy told me they were spending time on your computer, but I never dreamed they'd do something like this."

Charlotte's remorse-filled eyes made him forget about the money—almost. He propped his hands on his hips and gave a significant nod in the kids' direction. They were huddled together, all five of them, looking as angelic as babes in a cradle, but he knew better. The cap on his head was a constant reminder of what Maggie had done, and now, if he wasn't badly mistaken, he'd seen firsthand what the older girl could do. As for his boys, he wouldn't even go there. "Who's taking responsibility for this mess?"

The quick glance passing between Bruce and Becky was enough to confirm his suspicions. He nodded. "You two—come here."

Bruce took a deep breath, reconciling himself to his fate as Jake knew he would, but Becky's eyes brimmed with unshed tears, and her bottom lip quivered. She sniffed.

"Well? I'm waiting."

"Sor-ree."

"Sorry isn't good enough."

Becky's face crumpled as big crocodile tears streamed

185

down her cheeks.

"Stop crying and answer me!"

"That's enough, Jake!" Charlotte snapped, her protective arms encircling the girl's trembling shoulders. "It's just a bunch of bushes. The yard looks better without them."

"Not just any bushes," he fired back. "They were Betty's, and now they're gone."

"It's not the end of the world."

"You don't understand!"

Charlotte's eyes shot daggers as she gathered her chicks close like a mother hen. "Come on, girls, let's go inside. I can tell when we're not wanted."

Jake glared at her disappearing backside, her parting shot ringing in his ears. The woman was clueless to how badly he wanted her. Following suit, he stormed inside, leaving his eight-year-old with a stunned expression. His boys had come together as a united front, but he knew they wouldn't follow him until he'd had time to cool off.

The jumbled thoughts ran wild as he paced the kitchen floor. He still loved Betty—always would—but she was gone. Accepting it had been hard, but it didn't mean he couldn't keep something she'd nourished with her own hands. Hadn't he done what everyone said, removing her personal things? He'd moved on, even to the point of dating a few times.

His gaze traveled the length of the kitchen to the adjoining den, where reality stabbed him in the heart. He'd been a widower for over three years, yet none of the furniture had been moved throughout the entire house, not even the baby bed, although Andy hadn't slept in it for well over a year. It was as if time had stopped on the day Betty died.

186

A sharp knock intruded his thoughts, and Charlotte barged in without warning, slamming her personal check on the table. "Just for the record, it was Becky—not Bruce, and I take full responsibility for the hedge! Hold this 'til Friday. It won't be the same, but I'll replace every last bush!"

Jake felt like unleavened bread. "It doesn't matter. They're gone."

"What?" Her eyes flashed, and the stubborn set of her jaw meant she hadn't cooled a bit. "It sure mattered a few minutes ago when you scared Becky half to death!"

"Well, it doesn't matter now."

"Why not?"

"It's hard to explain." He wished he'd kept his mouth shut instead of making a fool of himself. "Let's just say my priorities got mixed up, okay? I'd rather just drop it."

A moment passed with neither saying anything. He'd never been good with words, and at times like this it was worse.

Charlotte placed a comforting hand on his shoulder. "Jake, I know what it's like giving up things that tied you to her memory. It tore me apart leaving the home Mitch loved, but then I realized I've got our girls. They're a bigger part of him than anything material could ever be."

He sat like a dummy, knowing she was right. The words he needed to say wouldn't come and the silence grew, creating a wall between them.

She walked to the door, placing her hand on the knob, a sadness he'd never heard before was in her voice. "I'm sorry we hurt you. From now on, we'll stay on our side of the line."

"Charlotte." Jake called her name, but she'd already gone. He'd been so worried about her needing time to put her memories to rest, he'd completely forgotten about his own. All this time, he'd been clinging to the past as if it were a lifeline keeping him afloat. Until today, he'd thought she needed him, but now he knew he needed her even more. In the short time he'd known her, she'd become more than just a friend. Having her next door had given him hope for the future. Now he'd be lucky if she ever spoke to him again.

****

Supper was quiet. The only one making an effort was Jake, and he finally gave up. His apology to Bruce fell on deaf ears, making it clear his boys were on Charlotte's side.

"I'll have to be gone Friday night." Their sulky expressions became even more so. His absence was nothing new.

Jeremy pushed the lumpy potatoes around in his plate. "Are you working?"

"No, it's…"

Bruce's head shot up. "You ain't going out with old dumb Loretta again—she's puke!"

The mention of the woman's name caused an unholy uproar with the other boys. Their feelings for the pretty brunette were plain. Jake raised his hand.

"No," he said, once they'd settled down. "It's a dinner to thank my employees for opening the new store on time."

"Can we go?"

"It's just grown-ups. I hate to leave you guys again, but I promised."

"Are you taking Charlotte?" Bruce said around his mouth full of peas. "She's the prettiest grown-up I know."

Jeremy agreed. "She's off Friday night."

Jake hated to disappoint them again, but her personal check lay torn in half on the counter—a reminder of the afternoon's disaster. "She's not talking to me anymore."

Bruce groaned. "Aw shucks, Dad!"

"It's okay. She's not mad at any of you."

The boy slumped in his chair. "You sure blew it this time!"

Jake didn't need reminding. He knew from their stares of total disgust, dire repercussions were in store if he didn't fix things. Their feelings for Charlotte and her girls couldn't be much clearer.

Chapter Fifteen

Charlotte stared out the window, her mind in turmoil. So far, the to-do list on the cabinet door remained stagnant. She washed her hands, drying them before adding Jake's hedge to the list and marking off the oil she'd put in her car. Life wasn't fair. The bushes would cost a lot more than a quart of oil.

"Remember, baby, it takes hard work to get ahead," her dad had said, when she'd shared her dreams with him. He'd lived by the rule and been fairly successful, but she was bone weary from working two jobs and getting nowhere.

She'd stood in this exact spot at her kitchen window, watching the backhoe rip through the ground. Jake was right—she'd hated the hedge. It had been scraggy and overgrown, but it never crossed her mind he hadn't hired the men.

Tears stung her eyes when she tried to focus on the growing stack of unpaid bills on her table. Until a few minutes ago, she'd been wondering which to pay, but now, thanks to Becky's handiwork, they would all be late. She released her breath in a long, weary sigh and buried her face in her hands. First it was Maggie ruining his hair and now this. Could it get any worse?

"I'm sorry, Mama," Becky said, in a subdued voice. "Don't cry. It'll be all right."

Charlotte peeked through her fingers to see her girls in their pink nighties clutching String and Patch, the old bears she'd found in a thrift store. Maggie wiggled onto her lap while Becky leaned against the chair.

"Mr. Jake was mad, huh, Mama?"

She squeezed them close. "Yes, Becky. I'd say he probably rues the day we moved in."

Maggie giggled. "Yeah, I'm glad we moved here, too."

Even with all that had happened, Charlotte had to agree it was the best decision she'd made in a long time. Their smiling faces provided the proof she needed; the world was right once more.

"It's time you girls were in bed."

After setting the timer on the coffeepot and rechecking the locks, Charlotte followed them upstairs. She was restless and tired—extremely tired—but something made her glance out the window at the house next door. It was dark except for the lamp above the computer where Jake sat staring at the screen.

She quickly shut off the lights so he wouldn't see her if he happened to look up. Spying on her neighbors had never been a hobby, but she couldn't seem to pull away. His wire-framed glasses made him seem more distinguished, until he rocked back in his chair, and the lamp reflected the redness of his scalp. A truckload of guilt washed over her.

Jake had gone out of his way to be a caring neighbor, something she hadn't had in a long time. So how was he repaid? Charlotte moaned when the word torture came to mind. Why in the world had she made a dramatic exit, claiming she would stay on her side of the drive? She stood in the darkness, lost and alone.

A tingling sensation in her lips revived memories of the passionate kisses they'd shared at Hidden Hills, then again in her own back yard. She'd even sensed something in his eyes as he crossed to her yard. But who was she kidding? Other than those few kisses, he'd treated her as he did everyone else.

Forcing herself from the window, she curled up on her empty bed and hugged her knees to her chest. When sleep finally came, it was images of Jake, not Mitch, filling her dreams.

* * * *

Charlotte had no idea when Jake had become so important to her, but he was still on her mind Friday afternoon when she walked to meet the girls. She entered the schoolyard shortly after the last bell and waited at the curb. A sense of pride swelled in her heart when she saw Jeremy, followed by Bruce and her girls, coming down the sidewalk. The protective manner shown by the boys toward Becky and Maggie reminded her of just how lucky she was to have them next door.

Jeremy smiled, his blue eyes shining at the sight of her. At least the boys still liked her. "Where's your car?"

"At home," she replied. "The weather's perfect for a walk."

"Jeremy has a girlfriend!" Becky teased, well out of his reach. "He likes Brandy Harris."

"As if he's got a chance with a cheerleader," Bruce chimed in, dodging a shoulder punch from his older brother.

Maggie frowned at Jeremy. "She better not have red

hair."

He rumpled her flyaway curls into an even bigger mess. "Don't worry, motor-mouth. You're still my little Red."

Jeremy fell into step beside Charlotte when the others ran ahead, chasing golden leaves swirling around in the strong gusty wind. Their laughter floated through the neighborhood, causing the Borden sisters to wave as they passed.

"The storm's building." She pointed to the west where dark clouds were beginning to cover the horizon. The heat of the sun and hot winds would add fierceness to the storms. "I had the television on. We'll be under a tornado watch for most of the night."

Jeremy pointed at the sky where lightning flashed in the distance. "I have to get Andy from daycare."

"Doesn't your dad pick him up?"

"Not since they opened the new store. Besides, Dad's going out tonight."

The guilt Charlotte had been harboring for destroying the man's precious hedges fell away. In its place came a burning anger for dumping so much responsibility on the boy.

As for his dating, it was none of her business. He wasn't attracted to her, or he would have found time to ask her out, and he hadn't. She'd been foolish to hope they might someday have a future together.

* * * *

Jake tried to call off the dinner because of the weather, but Sara claimed it was too late to cancel the reservations. One thing for sure, he couldn't leave his boys alone on a night with such threatening weather moving in. It was only a quarter 'til six, but the storm clouds blocked all traces of the sun.

Seeing Charlotte's car in the drive should have given him the option of leaving the kids with her rather than taking them to his parents, but not after their fight. She had every right to be mad.

He changed into khakis and a lightweight pullover. "Get ready, guys?"

"Why?"

"You're going to Grandma's."

"Do we have to?"

"You'd rather stay home by yourselves in a storm?" he asked, well aware of their fears.

"No, but—"

"Those are your choices. Pick one."

Jeremy shivered when lightning lit the room. "We can stay with Charlotte. Like you said, she's mad at you—not us."

Liking the third option better than the ones he'd offered, the younger boys bolted for the back door. "You're awesome, thanks, Dad!"

Jake shook his head. "Hold it. I'm not asking her."

Their disappointment tore at his conscience, and he knew he'd lost the battle when their sad eyes locked on him. They deserved better. Moments later, he was knocking on Charlotte's door, a feeling of impending doom making his hands sweat. He wasn't sure if it was habit or good manners, but she allowed him in.

Her arms crossed defensively, and he could tell she wasn't ready to forgive or forget. "What do you want?"

Since property lines work in both directions, it was the welcome he'd expected. "I've come to apologize for being a first-class jerk."

"Go to your room, girls," Charlotte said, her voice stern.

"Aw, Mama."

"Now!"

Jake searched for words while her gaze raked him from head to toe without missing a thing. "Nice outfit."

He'd forgotten what he had on. The navy sweater was a bit dressier than what he usually wore, but it surprised him when she noticed. "I'm going out."

She motioned toward the door. "So go."

Her terse reply was a slap in the face. She had every right to be mad, and he knew it. Regardless of what his boys wanted, there was no way he could ask her to watch them until they'd ironed out their differences.

He took a nervous step forward. "Charlotte, we need to settle this now."

"You're late." She walked passed him to rest her hand on the open door, a clear indication he wasn't welcome.

"Not until…"

"Since the weather's bad, tell the boys to call if they need me. I'll be here."

Her offer surprised him, but it reaffirmed what he already knew—she was mad at him, not his boys. She'd assumed he was leaving the boys alone on a stormy night, and she was right—sort of. It spoke volumes of what she thought of him. He had fences to mend, but she'd made it plain it wasn't going to be anytime soon.

* * * *

It hadn't surprised Charlotte when Jake's boys called before his truck reached the end of the street. Although no official warnings had been issued, the storms were getting closer. She could smell the rain in the air when she went next door to see what was keeping them.

"Grab your jackets, and let's go!" A strong blast of wind pushed her further into Jake's kitchen than she'd intended to go, but it didn't matter since he wasn't there. She glanced at the counter where a three liter bottle lay on its side, the liquid having soaked into the peanut butter and banana sandwiches before running down the cabinet to the tile floor. Open bags of chips and cookies, along with banana peelings and half empty glasses of milk littered the table.

"Hurry up," Charlotte urged. "I've got supper—let's go!"

Her blood boiled at Jake for leaving his boys to eat cold sandwiches while he wined and dined his airheaded bimbo. She snatched an open mayonnaise jar and shoved it into the refrigerator, not seeing the tuna casserole on the top shelf.

The boys were gone when the phone rang. She grabbed it out of habit—then wished she hadn't.

"Is Jake there? He should have been here ages ago, and he hasn't..."

Charlotte froze. The sultry voice hurt far more than she'd ever thought possible. Until then, Loretta had only been a name. A dumb-as-dirt joke shared with the boys. It took a deafening clap of thunder to jar her back to reality.

"He's on his way!" She shouted, finding pleasure in slamming down the phone. A lightning bolt struck close enough to feel the heat, and her granny's voice repeating "one Mississippi, two Mississippi" darted through her mind. On the third Mississippi, she shot across the freshly plowed dirt between the two yards, red mud caking her white sneakers. The only bright spot in her otherwise dreary night came in knowing Jake was coming home to a well-deserved pigsty.

* * * *

The Silver Spur wasn't the classiest restaurant in town, but it always lived up to its reputation. Their steaks were tender, the salads fresh, and the service excellent. Even thunder rattling the tin roof couldn't dampen the lively atmosphere inside the renovated feed store.

Jake's cap was the hot topic, as he knew it would be. He went along with the good natured ribbing, but his heart wasn't in it. Charlotte was on his mind, instead of by his side where she belonged. Using his cell phone, he called her only to hang up when he heard his boys in the background. She'd sounded harassed and he'd hear about it when he got home, but for now his boys were safe. During dinner he listened to the latest gossip and made a point of thanking each employee individually for their hard work.

The evening was over before he noticed Ralph and Shelby sitting at a corner table. It wasn't unusual to find the tall, vivacious blonde on his friend's case, this time for inviting his entire family for Thanksgiving dinner without first clearing it with her. The nagging was nothing new, so it mostly went over Jake's head—all except the part about not having enough room.

Jake pictured the dining room at Hidden Hills as an idea sprang to mind. It could be a good business venture, providing he could get everyone to agree. Borrowing a chair from a nearby table, he attached himself to the unsuspecting couple.

* * * *

His house was in total darkness when he returned home, making the light next door was a welcome sight. As late as it was, knocking on Charlotte's door wasn't nearly as hard as it had been earlier. Her disposition probably wouldn't have improved, but he didn't care. Like it or not, he was determined to make her listen, even if she was waiting with a noose for his neck. It couldn't wait, so he took a deep breath, and knocked.

"All right, already," he heard as she opened the door. "If you wake those kids, I'll—"

"I only knocked once."

"More like hammered."

Jake slid into the room and closed the door with a decisive click. At first glance, he'd assumed she'd been asleep on the couch, but then he realized work and worry had brought on her disheveled appearance. "Why's it so quiet in here?"

Charlotte retrieved the mop bucket from her back porch before answering. "Because they finally ran out of anything to fight about and went to sleep."

He'd been afraid of this. "I'll have a word with them in the morning. Any punches thrown?"

"Not from your boys," she said, moving the chairs out of the way. "Although, Andy forgot he was potty-trained and pooped his pants."

Jake cringed. No wonder she'd been so ticked when she let him in. He jumped, dodging the damp mop when it swiped toward him, barely missing his feet. "Do you have to do this now?"

"I do, unless I want to be invaded by ants in the morning. Maggie spilt her milk, and you're standing in what's left of Andy's chili."

He moved to the side, but still near enough to enjoy her swaying backside and heavy breathing. The mop stopped, and he caught her reflection in the window. Her eyes narrowed, and he got the full effect of the ramrod straight back. "What are you staring at?"

Sparks in her eyes reminded him of a firecracker, ready to explode, and he knew it was time to lose the grin and start mending fences. "We need to settle some things."

"Come back tomorrow," she said, the mop flying past his feet in a wide circle. "It's late."

Jake pursed his lips. "Yeah, right—then you'll be headed to one of those jobs!"

Anger flashed in her smoldering green eyes. "You may find it hard to believe, but if I don't go to those jobs—they won't pay me!"

"Oh, for crying out loud." He jerked the mop from her hand. "Sit down, and I'll finish this!"

He had her in his sights when she hooked a leg over a nearby chair. Even in sweats, with her hair falling out of a scarf, she was gorgeous. She stretched, pointing to an area near the sink with undisguised satisfaction. "You missed a spot."

"I said I'd finish it," he replied, his mouth twisted to one side. "Never said anything about getting it clean."

"Then why bother?"

Jake was beginning to ask himself the same thing. So what if he'd been an idiot, and she'd had a horrible night? Her nasty attitude was enough to turn any man off. "It could be you're important to me."

Her eyes narrowed. "So I'm important, am I? Then I suppose that's why I spent the night refereeing five kids, while you were out carousing with your woman!"

"For your information, I don't drink," he said, blindsided by her attack. "And what woman?"

"The one calling your house right after you left."

The corners of his mouth tilted upward. "Real soft, sweet voice—like honey oozing through the phone?"

Her eyes sparkled. "That's the one!"

Jake laughed. "You were talking to the boys' grandmother."

"Oh."

He stood, tossing the mop handle back and forth, the floor forgotten. "No wonder you're so bent out of shape. Somebody's been stewing all night. You're jealous!"

"Now why would I be jealous?" She stood, holding the back of the chair.

"Because you like me more than you'll admit." He moved in closer. A shot of adrenaline raced through his veins at the possibility of Charlotte caring for him. Keeping his hands to himself for fear of scaring her off had taken its toll. The time had come for her to listen.

"Not so fast." He caught Charlotte and she leaned into him, her arms circling his waist. The reflection in her eyes was the same yearning he'd felt since the first time he saw her. Smiling, he finished closing the distance between them. Her soft lips met his in a warm, hungry kiss, their bodies a perfect match.

Jake couldn't remember falling in love with Betty. They'd grown up as best friends, been high school sweethearts, and just seemed to know they were meant for each other. With Charlotte it was different—*she* was different. Although he'd only known her for a short time, he knew he couldn't lose her. Was this what being in love for the second time was like?

He was floating on air, knowing without a doubt she

was the only woman he'd ever want. "Marry me," he whispered, not realizing what he'd said until he saw the shock in her eyes.

"Are you serious? We don't even know each other!"

Jake stroked the hair from her forehead and kissed her again. "We've got the rest of our lives to get acquainted."

He could feel her gentle fingers stroking his chest through the pullover. She leaned closer, his breathing matching hers. "But aren't we supposed to get to know each other before marriage? The courts are full of people who jumped the gun."

Jake relished her closeness, knowing he'd won her trust, if not her heart. "It's just something to think about."

"When I have nothing else to do?"

Closing his eyes, he kissed the top of her head again. The fragrance of honeysuckle filled his nostrils, reminding him of their time together at Hidden Hills when they'd relaxed on the creek bank and watched their kids play.

"Charlotte?" he said, relaxing his hold so he could gauge her reaction. "Were you kissing Mitch—or me?"

She frowned as if he'd lost his mind. "Mitch is dead."

"You know what I mean." He worried her answer would break his heart.

Her fingers traced the woven pattern of his sweater again, her eyes darkening with concern. "I could ask you the same thing about Betty."

"You could," he agreed, breathing a sigh of relief. "But there's no need."

"Same here—I'm ready to move on."

His hands sank into the soft, silky curls surrounding her face, before molding her to his heart. He kissed her soft lips again, worrying if in the morning light, when their kids were being kids, she might come to her senses.

He held her tighter. There were things he'd meant to say, important things, but he couldn't remember what they were.

Chapter Sixteen

The late October sun was an orange globe on the horizon when Charlotte headed west toward Robins Lane. Along with broken branches, last night's storm had brought clear blue skies and cool, crisp air. It seemed as if, by one violent act of nature, fall had arrived.

Mrs. Jones, Kimmie's mom, had graciously allowed Becky and Maggie to spend the day with her after Ellen McGregor canceled their Saturday shopping spree at the last moment. From things Mitch had said, Ellen's maternal instincts were no better now than when he was a boy.

A haze of smoke hovered over a small pile of limbs in Mr. Hamner's yard when she pulled into her drive. Riding shotgun beside her was a plastic bag filled with milk and eggs, and in the back seat, the girls sang a new song they'd learned from Mrs. Jones. She eased the car around back where this morning's overgrown grass now held the playhouse Mitch had built. Lights shone in the heart-shaped windows as the evening shadows stretched across the yard. Only one person was thoughtful enough to spend his Saturday disassembling a playhouse, hauling it twenty miles, and then putting it back together again.

"Look, girls!"

Maggie bounced out of the car before she could set

the parking brake. Moments later, her girls met Bruce and Andy at the playhouse door, and excited voices became angry shouts. It seemed as if they were in for another skirmish of last night's free-for-all. Ignoring the others, Jeremy lifted the handful of groceries from the passenger seat without being told and headed for her kitchen.

Charlotte stood by the car, swallowing the lump in her throat, when Jake came around to meet her, his silly grin melted her heart. She shoved the keys into her purse and tossed it on the hood to get it out of her way. A moment later, she had Jake's face sandwiched between her hands, peppering him with kisses. "Thank you!"

He took her in his arms as he'd done the night before. "My pleasure."

She'd spent the day wondering if last night had been a dream, but she knew this was real... their kids were fighting.

"Dad..."

"Mama..."

Charlotte stared in amazement when Jake held up his hands, stopping the argument before it became another slugging match. "Listen, boys, I'm siding with the girls on this one. It belongs to them."

Becky's tongue popped out. "Yeah, so there!"

"Rebecca!" Charlotte said. "I've heard enough. Everyone shares the playhouse, or their swings are off-limits."

Becky glared at the boys, reminding her of Mitch when things didn't go his way. "I'm talking about their computer and bicycles, too!"

"But, Mama! It's not fair!"

Charlotte waited. "I think it is."

Grudgingly, the older girl backed down, but just like her dad, there was always a stipulation. "Okay—but they better not mess it up."

She took a deep breath. "Sounds fair to me. Whoever messes it up has to clean it."

Still arguing among themselves, the kids headed toward the playhouse. Their fights were getting more frequent, and keeping them apart had only led to constant whining from her girls. Jake's hand rested on her shoulder, a reminder she wasn't alone.

"What's wrong?" He massaged the tired muscles, pulling her back against him. "This was supposed to make you happy."

She relaxed at his warm touch, wondering if he realized how much he was intertwining their lives. "It does, but you wasted your entire day moving the playhouse."

"We enjoyed it," he said, his gentle squeeze telling her she was making a mountain out of a molehill. "I'm impressed with the way it's built. Mitch had it bolted together at the corners and after we lifted the roof, the walls came apart in four separate pieces. Putting it back together was a snap."

"I don't recall it having electricity."

A mischievous gleam entered his eyes. "Must be battery lights."

"Must be," she agreed.

"There's a water hose they can use."

He was spoiling her girls. "I'm not so sure…"

"Dad!" Jeremy yelled from her back porch. "You gotta see this… hurry!"

"Oh no, not again!" Charlotte grabbed her purse and took off after Jake. Other than last night's calamity, peace had lasted for three whole days. She skidded to a halt, colliding with his backside in her utility room. "Oh, my goodness."

Jake stood in rising water. "I'll check your washer. It must be a busted hose." He rushed over and turned off the faucet behind the machine, but the water continued to flow.

Charlotte watched a wad of lint floating her way. "That's coming from my dryer."

She dumped the dirty clothes hamper to make a dam at the kitchen door. This repair job couldn't wait, except— she couldn't afford a repairman. A moment later the water slowed, then stopped, and Jeremy came in dangling the three-year-old under his arm. "Okay, squirt, tell her what you did."

Andy squealed, proud as punch. "Me wash you house!"

"You what?" she cried, wringing a saturated towel over the mop bucket.

Jeremy shifted his little brother in his arms. "Sorry Charlotte. Somebody left the water running, and Andy stuck the hose in your dryer vent."

"Andy," she cried in frustration. "Just look at the mess you've made!" His lips began to quiver at her harsh tone, making her feel like a rat. "It's okay, honey. Go upstairs with Jeremy and get some more towels."

Jake reached for the mop. "This is getting old."

"What—mopping?" The sight of his pants rolled up past his knees helped restore her humor. "You're getting good."

"No," he replied. "These disasters. They're getting out of hand."

She shrugged. At least she wasn't lonely anymore. "It's called parenting. We live and learn, don't we?"

"If we're lucky."

They worked in silence, each lost in their own

thoughts. "Jeremy put your mail on the table."

She loaded the last of the towels into the machine, set the dial, and poured the detergent before his comment registered. "How did he get in my house?"

"I thought you…"

She shook her head. "Wait a minute—how did he get into my post office box?"

Seeing the disappointment in Jake's eyes made her realize he'd reached the end of his rope. Something had to be done. "Spare the rod and spoil the child" was close at hand.

"Let it go," she said.

"Are you sure?"

"I can handle it." Charlotte wasn't quite sure how to back up her words. His warm hand on her shoulder kept her from walking away, and his blue eyes held a world of understanding.

A gentle smile lifted the corners of his mouth. "I know you can. They'll listen to you, but this other problem of yours… there's a solution if you're willing to listen."

She wanted to stand her ground and remind him it was her problem, not his, but she couldn't. Time was running out. "I'm listening."

"Okay. Just for the record, Hidden Hills isn't going to sell."

"You don't know. I still have a few weeks before they'll start the foreclosure. Anything can happen."

He shook his head. "It won't. Mark told me his dad owns Wilson Realty."

"No, it can't be," Charlotte said, panic rising in her throat. "I checked. It's always been a family business. The Wilsons started it over twenty years ago."

"Mrs. Wilson got in a financial bind, probably from

making deals like the one she made with you. She overextended her credit, and your father-in-law took over her company."

Her forehead dropped against his chest; a coldness she'd never felt engulfed her heart. The world she'd worked so hard to preserve crumbled into a million pieces. It was over. All the scrimping and saving had been for nothing. Through her dazed senses, she felt Jake's strong hands stroking her shoulders, but it was no use, the trembling wouldn't stop.

"Talk to me," he said. "I can't help if I don't know what's going on."

Charlotte couldn't believe the concern in his eyes. He had every right to say "I told you so", but instead he still wanted to help. Why hadn't she listened to him that day at Hidden Hills? Now her worst fears were coming true.

"The silver devil is going to sue me."

"For thirty thousand?"

She chewed her lip to keep the tears at bay. "He swore he'd bankrupt me."

Jake's blue eyes clouded with a determination she'd never seen before, except in Bruce when he was plotting revenge. He pulled her chair from the table and waited while she sat, then continued to the counter where he made a fresh pot of coffee. While it brewed, he reached into the cabinets for cups and a bag of cookies. "He doesn't have to win."

"Yeah, right, and pigs fly. You don't know the guy."

His confident expression made her do a double-take.

"As a matter of fact, I've got a plan."

"You're serious?"

"I can't actually take credit. It's more like we're stealing it from your father-in-law—a resort with swimming, fishing, hiking, and horseback riding."

Anger consumed her at what she was hearing. "It wasn't his plan—it was mine. The old goat stole it from me! But it wasn't for a resort. It was a bed and breakfast. Mitch's dad convinced him there wasn't a snowball's chance of making it work, because I had no connections."

"Well, we're stealing it back," Jake said. "And believe me, it'll work. I'm sure of it."

"I don't have a dime to my name! Just how am I supposed to work this miracle?"

"*We...*" Jake pulled a webpage from his pocket. "...take the original idea and make it work."

She raised her hands to stop him. "There's no way I'll be stuck at Hidden Hills by myself again."

"Now wait," he said. "Remember last night when I said I wanted your key to check for storm damage out there?"

She nodded, remembering other things he'd said as well.

"It was just half true. I carried some friends to see the place this morning and get their opinion. Shelby's always had her heart set on running a bed and breakfast, and Ralph thinks the house is perfect."

She felt hope for the first time in months, but it didn't last. "It sounds good, but even if they want to buy, the judge will find a way to hold up the sale until I lose it."

He planted his hands on her shoulders, giving a little tug. "They don't want to buy. How would you like to be business partners?"

She had to refocus. It wasn't a matter of trust, but in her state of mind, he was moving too fast to keep up. "Partners in what? I'm broke! How can I afford to go into business?"

"You've already got upward of more than three hundred thousand invested. After we run the figures, I'll match whatever Ralph and Shelby invest, so you and I will always have controlling interest. They'll live there and draw a salary for running the place."

"But you don't have the kind of money we'll need." It wasn't right for him to get in over his head, trying to help her. She'd been down that road and it was a bumpy ride.

"You don't know what I've got."

"No, but..."

His confident stance reinforced what she'd already come to realize. He wasn't like Mitch. She was worrying for nothing.

"You mentioned fishing?" she said. "There aren't enough fish in the creek to pay you to bait a hook, much less entice fishermen. I was bragging to impress Bruce."

Jake laughed at her confession. "Ralph and I talked with your neighbor, Sam Drenfield. He's willing to lease his ponds, plus three hundred additional acres for hunting, with the option to buy if our venture pays off. It's worth a lot to the old man to see the judge get his fingers burned. Seems you aren't the only one he's trying to put the squeeze on."

Her eyes were drawn to the image of the house when she unfolded the paper. It showed Hidden Hills at its best with the azaleas in full bloom, and the lawn freshly mown. "I don't understand. Why did you make a picture and scan it?"

"Look closer. It's his web page. Your father-in-law has even had the road paved as far as the bridge." He pointed to the paper in her hand. "I found it after he paid a little visit to discourage me from making an offer. You need to give the guy credit—he's got *some* nerve."

"But…"

"Did Bruce ever mention he's been in trouble for hacking?"

She scratched her head, trying to keep up. "What's Bruce got to do with anything?"

"I had him visit the site…"

"Visit or hack?"

He shrugged, the corner of his mouth tilting upward. "Call it what you will, but anyway, the resort's scheduled to open this coming March with eighty-percent bookings through July. We've got a list of the reservations."

Charlotte was glad Jake cared enough to have gone to so much trouble, but those tiny seeds of doubt kept sprouting up. "The real estate contract I signed with Wilson's Realty is for a year. He's not going to let me out of it."

"Doesn't matter." Jake assured her. "Even if he comes up with a buyer, you don't have to sell."

"But the money I owe him?"

"Pay with some of the capital I put in."

"But it'll cost a fortune to get the house ready for paying guests."

"You're wrong there." He went to the sink and got the pot for a refill. "Want some coffee?"

After the cups were filled, he sat and began munching on another cookie. "As I was saying, five of the guest rooms have private baths. The windows are tight and the roof doesn't leak. We couldn't find any termite damage or sewage problems and…"

Charlotte pressed her fingers against his lips in an effort to slow him down. She was sure he didn't have a clue as to the upkeep of the house. "I know, we lived there—remember? Grandpa Wills took care of those things when he installed the pool. He also replaced the plumbing and wiring, but it was eight years ago. Most of the house has been closed off, so you can only be sure one of the three heat pumps work."

He removed her fingers, kissing each one before lowering her hand. "Everything works, even the gas logs in the fireplaces—we tried them today."

"But the water?" She was determined to make him aware of the headache involved in the running of the house.

"Now there's our biggest problem," he admitted, not at all as concerned as she thought he should be. "But Ralph's checking into it. The current well won't be adequate, so we'll need a water tank and possibly a filter."

Charlotte shook her head. "You're wrong. There's a second artesian well. It will supply more water than we'll ever need. Mitch had them tested for purity before we moved in, and it's cleaner than any water system in the state. Instead of spending money on a tank and filter, all we'll need is to run a line to the second well like the one we've already got. We'll be able to split the pool and private bathrooms away from the main line."

He grinned. "You said *we*."

"No, I didn't."

"Yes, you did." He pinned her with his gaze. "You've given this project some serious thought, haven't you?"

"It was a long time ago. Becky was about six months old."

"Think you can draw up some more plans?"

Memories she'd forgotten came flooding back. "A couple of days after Mitch's funeral, the judge came by the house, demanding I return Mitch's computer to the firm. He knew, even back then I'd lose the house. All he had to do was wait."

"So he used your plans?"

"I don't see how he could. The plans were transferred to a disk the night before, and the files deleted. It's here somewhere, and we can print a spreadsheet, but the estimates are outdated and most suppliers on the list may not be in business anymore."

He nudged her with his elbow. "I like you—always willing to admit when I'm right."

"Smart aleck." Charlotte knew he was being sarcastic, but she was willing to give credit where it was due. "Yes, Jake. You're right. I do think it's a good plan."

Along with the house, he and Ralph had checked the barn and farm equipment, but had decided those improvements would have to wait. His enthusiasm was contagious, and his thoroughness led her to believe he'd also spent a lot of thought on the project.

"Since you've kept the plans, it should save us a lot of work."

"Jake?"

"Am I boring you?"

"Never," she said, her full attention focused on him. "Why are you doing this?"

A strange expression crossed his face, as if she'd hurt him, or maybe it was just her imagination. Like his proposal, she wasn't sure if he was serious. Last night's kisses made her hope for things she shouldn't.

"It's a good business venture. Plus, I like helping a friend when I can." His thumb stroked her chin, and her breath caught when he smiled. "Then there's the fact I can't stand your father-in-law."

None of his reasons were exactly what she wanted to hear, but they were honest. "Let's not call him my father-in-law."

"Whatever you say, but let me know what you decide. Ralph can draw up the contract, and you'll need to have a lawyer you trust read it before signing."

"Do you trust him?" From the expression in his eyes, she was expecting a raking over for being naive again.

"I do, but you're still taking it to another attorney."

Charlotte knew plenty of lawyers, but only a few names came to mind she actually trusted. One thing for sure, it wouldn't be anyone from Mitch's old firm.

"What time do you get off next Saturday?" Jake asked her, catching Andy when he ran by with a water gun in his hand.

"About three, why?"

He planted a quick kiss on her lips before wrestling his toddler toward the back door. "Ralph and Shelby want to meet you and discuss a partnership. I'll see when they can be here."

"Here?" she said, catching his sleeve. "Look at this place—it's a wreck! I can't have anyone over."

Jake glanced around. "Looks fine to me."

"It's filthy."

He shrugged. "So clean it up."

"I'm working all week, and this house isn't self-cleaning!"

He laughed. "Calm down. We'll meet at my house. Shelby would be shocked if it were anywhere near as clean as this."

* * * *

Charlotte agonized all week over what to wear on Saturday. It was a business meeting, but the kids would be there so it was informal. When the time arrived, the only thing concerning her were the nerves settling into a burning sensation in the pit of her stomach. The last time she'd arrived unannounced at Jake's house, she'd slammed her check on his counter and stormed out before he could explain why he was so angry. A lot had happened since then.

Meeting his friends would have made her nervous anytime, but this wasn't just any meeting. The partnership depended on the four of them being able to get along. What if their personalities didn't click? A new worry crossed her mind. Ralph and Shelby Watts might not be as interested in Hidden Hills as he'd led her to believe. Was she supposed to sell them on the idea?

The gnawing sensation in her stomach felt like a full-blown ulcer when she raised her hand to knock on Jake's door. Bruce jerked it open, and the fresh scent of pine was thick enough to cut with a butter knife. She glanced around, seeing the others sitting at the table, and the pride in their expressions let her know they'd worked as a team.

"I hope you're happy," Bruce said. "We've worked all day 'cause Dad said this house *had better be clean* when you got here."

Jeremy slid a piece of gum to each of the younger kids. "I figured he meant for us to be clean, too, so we took baths at your house—sorry about the wet towels."

Her heart swelled. It was as if they understood the importance of this night. "You kids did a good job. I'm proud of you."

"Don't tell Dad. He'll expect us to do it all the time." Bruce's aversion to housework was public knowledge. She hooked her arm around his neck and ruffled his hair with her knuckles. "You'd better watch it, or I'll tell him you cleaned it all by yourself."

Becky smacked her gum. "Can we go home and play now?"

"Go ahead, but come back when Jake gets here."

Charlotte paused from picking up gum wrappers when a tall, slim blonde, dressed in jeans and a red tee-shirt, appeared at the door. She held it open and counted heads as the kids filed out. "Where's everybody going?"

"Next door," Bruce replied. "So our house won't get dirty."

The woman stuck her head in the kitchen. "Not bad—it's the first time I've ever seen it clean."

"Me too," Charlotte agreed, wondering where the stranger had come from.

"Reminds me of when Betty was alive," the woman continued, closing the door. "But even then, there were toys everywhere."

This couldn't possibly be the "dumb as dirt" Loretta. She seemed too intelligent.

"I'm Shelby Watts and you must be Charlotte." The woman's warm manner put her at ease. "Jake told me the boys would either be here or at your house, so I came on over. He and Ralph have gone to the Pizza Plate to get supper."

Charlotte breathed a sigh of relief. If Ralph was as down to earth as his wife, then the partnership could actually work. It had been a long time since she'd felt so excited about her finances.

* * * *

"This spreadsheet—when did you say you worked it up?" It was the first time Ralph had glanced up from the

216

computer since he'd put in the disk. She'd kept the plans for sentimental reasons, like old family portraits of her dead relatives, never dreaming they might someday be used.

"Seven years ago." She tried to hide her nervousness. "We'll have to make adjustments for inflation, but the basic plan should work."

His focus remained on the spreadsheet. After several minutes of serious concentration, he squared his shoulders. "I'm impressed. You're not only beautiful—you've got a good business head on your shoulders."

Shelby's jaw dropped. "I can't believe you'd say such a thing."

Charlotte's face glowed. Married men had made passes at her since she was in her teens, but never in front of their wives. This partnership didn't stand a chance.

"What?" Ralph said. "I'm just stating the obvious."

"We know," Shelby replied. "But look at her face. You're embarrassing her."

Charlotte saw the quick exchange of a nod between the men and realized Ralph's intentions were to make her blush. He'd succeeded.

Shelby waved the men aside. "Don't pay any attention to them."

"You're not much older than our girls." Ralph laughed, putting her at ease. "So don't get upset if I treat you like a kid sometimes."

Charlotte glanced at Jake, but he wasn't paying attention. Ralph Watts moved with an air of authority, and she'd felt slightly intimidated by his quiet confidence from the moment he'd walked in. Like his wife, he had an unusual way of breaking the ice.

"Now," he continued, concentrating once more on the

computer screen. "Tell me why you budgeted so much for linens."

Feeling more comfortable, Charlotte slid her chair closer to the handsome, middle-aged man. "This was to be a topnotch bed and breakfast. Guests would've expected their sheets to be changed daily, and since all linens were to have the Hidden Hills logo embroidered in a corner, we had to allow for stealing. I thought it would be necessary to keep a large supply. You'll also notice the extra china and silverware."

Ralph frowned. "What kind of clientele were you expecting—the county inmates?"

"Income level has nothing to do with taking souvenirs. Some of your nicest guests will pick up a small item and think nothing of it. We'd planned for ladies' groups, retirees, and people just wanting to get away for a quiet weekend."

"Then we shouldn't embroider anything."

Charlotte refused to give in on that point. "A lot of people consider it advertising, instead of stealing. I'm a pretty good seamstress, so if we invest in a smart sewing machine, then I'll do the monograming myself and save hiring it done."

"Mmm." Ralph conceded. "We do need the advertising."

Their discussions ranged from liability insurance to toilet paper and everything in between before the evening was over. Even the kids took turns in voicing their ideas and opinions at the supper table.

After saying goodnight to Ralph and Shelby, Jake cradled her back against his broad chest. His arms rested comfortably around her shoulders, and she reached up to kiss his cheek.

"Thank you."

"For what?"

She sighed. "For finding the right people. Shelby's nice, and talking to Ralph is like being with my dad."

"Ralph's not old."

"He's mature and settled—just like my dad," she said, feeling Jake's lips against her hair.

"His saying you're beautiful had nothing to do with it?" he said. "For the record, I think you're beautiful, too."

"You do?" she said, turning in his arms, to hold him close. "But you've never said anything."

He frowned. "Why would I need to say anything? You've got a mirror."

Her head dropped against his chest. Jake was clueless at romance. Had he asked her to marry him? She wasn't sure anymore.

"Tell me something." The curious tone of his voice got her attention. "If Ralph is right, and you've got a head for business—which I'm assuming you do since the seven-year-old spread sheet is yours—what's with the dumb decisions about Hidden Hills?"

Charlotte eased out his arms, returning to the table where Ralph had left some notes of the updates needing to be checked. Jake had been quiet during the evening, only commenting after he'd been asked a direct question. Now she knew why.

"Seven years ago my life was safe—or so I'd thought. Mitch had a good job with a steady income, and we were financially secure. I loved being a stay-at-home mom after Becky was born—but I got lonely. Then one day, Mitch suggested I spend some time with his grandpa, so I did."

"Go on," he said.

Memories of the old man made her smile. "Charles

Wills was quite a character, telling me things about the family even Mitch didn't know. Things like, one of his great-uncles being a sheriff in Texas at the turn of the century, and the guy's wife, the town dentist—stuff like you'd only read in books."

"Anyway," she continued, "spending our days at Hidden Hills was good for me. Grandpa believed in staying busy. The worksheet I did was for him, not me. His changes to the house were finished, and he needed another business venture. We spent most of the winter planning menus and listing everything we could possibly need to run the house. The problem was he'd borrowed more money than he'd realized, so our plans had to be put on hold. He started having health problems shortly afterward and lost interest."

"It sounds like you loved the old man."

"I did. He was the grandpa I'd never had."

Chapter Seventeen

The following week kept Charlotte busier than usual, since she had to revise the figures on her original spreadsheet. She'd either underestimated the cost of things, or prices had soared in seven years. Having finished the changes Ralph had requested, she found time to relax at her kitchen table and enjoy a fresh cup of coffee. It wasn't unpaid bills occupying her thoughts today, but the conversation she'd had with Shelby about refurnishing Hidden Hills.

Three years ago, when she and Mitch had moved in, the house had been entirely stocked with beautiful antiques. Instead of taking a chance on the children ruining anything, she had moved the downstairs furnishings up to the second floor into rooms they never used. She'd felt more at home living with their own furniture.

"Why so serious?"

"Just thinking about all I need to do." She watched Jake drain the pot and sit it in the sink. It was the first time he'd visited all week, and she'd missed him.

He downed a swig of coffee and sauntered over to her side. "Ralph and I have been working on plans for adding the second waterline you were talking about. We'll save money by laying the pipe ourselves, so we're renting a trencher for the weekend."

"I thought he was drawing up the contracts."

He nodded. "Our Ralph is a man of many talents."

"Would one of those talents be using a trencher?"

"No, that's my talent. I intend for him to use the shovel."

Charlotte stood up, meaning to take a sip of his coffee, but noticed the cup was almost empty. "While you men are doing the grunt work, my girls and I will be shopping with Shelby…want more coffee?"

"No, this is plenty."

She moved into the circle of his arms. His inviting blue eyes weren't to be ignored, but neither was Maggie's persistent tugging at her shirt hem.

"Mama, there's a cowboy at the door!"

Maggie's comment reminded her of the phone call she'd received earlier at work. Some guy with a Texas drawl saying something about mineral rights and e-mails, but she'd been too busy to talk. Leaving Jake to follow, Charlotte entered the living room and saw Maggie standing with her hands propped on her hips, talking through the screen door to a slim, middle-aged man.

"Mrs. McGregor?" There was a brief moment when she swore his handlebar mustache winked at her, but it was a quirk in his jaw. She put a hand over Maggie's mouth, in fear of what she might say.

"Yes, may I help you?"

"I'm Dennis Waters, of Samuel Jones and Associates," he replied. "We spoke earlier."

"Come in, please." Charlotte welcomed the stranger into her home. She wouldn't have let him in at Hidden Hills, but with six other people in the house, how could she not feel safe?

When Jake and the lanky Texan in cowboy boots struck up a conversation like old friends, she decided it had to be a man-thing. At any rate, it gave her a chance to empty the room of curious kids.

She sat on the couch beside Jake, and watched as the man removed a stack of papers from an old briefcase. His weather-worn face and steady, gray eyes would have made her nervous had she been alone.

"Like I tried to explain on the phone, e-mails are fine, but I'm old fashioned. I like doing business face to face."

She frowned. "What are we talking about?"

"Our phone call."

"I don't know anything about e-mails…"

He shuffled through the remaining pages in the case before finding the two he was looking for. "Isn't this your husband's e-mail address?"

Her blood boiled when she read the date, August 19, the day she'd told her in-laws she was looking for a smaller house. "I didn't send this."

"Of course not," Mr. Waters assured her. "It was sent by your father-in-law. I believe it's the one where he explains you were touring the Greek Islands at the time. He goes on to say, although he had your power of attorney, it would be better if we waited until December when you'd be back in the states, so you could handle your own affairs."

Charlotte felt the pressure of Jake's hand on hers, taking it as a warning to keep her mouth shut. She didn't know this man, and she trusted Jake's instincts when it came to reading people. After all, he'd pegged Mitch's parents fast enough. "What brings you back so soon?"

His mustache wiggled. "Antsy investors. I signed the last of the other landowners yesterday afternoon. Then I swung by the courthouse to see Judge McGregor again about signing for you, but I missed him. The judge's secretary told me I'd find you at Milner's today. I hope my calling hasn't caused any problems."

"No," she assured him. "I'm glad you did. Now, what's this about my mineral rights?"

She listened as he explained from the beginning about his company, the investors, her mineral rights, and the fact her back forty had been designated as one of the most likely drill sites in the area. Since all of Grandpa Will's land was located in four different sections, if they were to hit gas or oil on any part of it, she would have more money than she'd had in her entire life. The new onslaught of information was overwhelming.

Charlotte failed miserably at hiding the tears of relief stinging her eyes as she watched the taillights of Mr. Waters' rental car disappear from sight. "Do you realize how close I came to losing everything? I mean, if you hadn't tried so hard to help me, and Mr. Waters had waited until December to get those papers signed—the judge would have got it all."

She felt the steadying warmth when his arm circled her shoulder. "Didn't I tell you everything would work out?"

"Like you knew?"

Jake laughed. "There's one thing I do know. The judge is going to croak when you let him know he's lost."

"I've a good mind to go over there and punch the old goat's lights out!" She could picture Tom McGregor's arrogant face.

"Let's not be so hasty," Jake said, ready to offer an alternative. "Doesn't the judge have friends at the bank in Wills' Junction?"

"Yes," she said. "But what's it got to do with

anything."

"How much do you have in your account there?"

Charlotte shrugged. "About fifty cents. I made a payment on Hidden Hills last week."

The quiet rocked on for a moment. "Why not let him think he's beaten you, say… until the day before your next payment is due? It should give your attorney time to study the contracts."

"I know now why your boys are such brats. You're a good teacher."

His laughter was contagious. "Nonsense, it's hereditary—comes from their mother."

* * * *

The negotiations on the partnership went without a hitch. Charlotte knew she had Jake to thank. He'd picked the right people. Best of all, they'd agreed to keep things quiet until she'd confronted Tom McGregor.

Charlotte debated on going to the judge's office or to his house, finally deciding on the latter for one simple fact. If they had a yelling match, it would be in private. He'd waited thirty-five years for Charles Wills to die and leave the estate to Ellen, and another three had passed since then. She hated confrontations, but this one was unavoidable and it wouldn't be pretty. Nervous fingers clutched the purse she carried, fearful the check might disappear if she relaxed her hold.

The stark elegance of the McGregor house was worlds apart from anything she'd ever want to call home, but it suited their lifestyle. With her head held high, she followed Ellen through the wide entrance hall past hand-painted portraits of their ancestors—Wills' men on the left,

McGregors' on the right.

Charlotte had been in their home on numerous occasions with Mitch, but she'd never felt welcome. Ellen led her into the den, where the judge sat reading the daily news. He glanced up, then folded the paper, clearly unhappy with the intrusion.

"I was planning to give you a call after dinner," he said, laying the paper aside. "We ran into your agent today. It seems Wilson Realty has agreed to buy Hidden Hills. Now I know their price is well below what you're asking, but it'll just about cover the loan. The market's soft in your price range, so I'm advising you to take it."

"No—I'm not losing everything Mitch and I put into the place."

His entire manner shifted before her eyes, becoming sharp and fierce, as if ready to attack. The intense hatred would have been daunting, had she not faced it before.

"Don't be crazy, girl. At least you'll be out from under the mortgage. You had nothing when you married into this family, and you'll take nothing out. I'll see to it."

Charlotte held her tongue. She'd expected him to place an offer after the foreclosure, but there was a chance of someone else bidding higher. This was practically foolproof. No one would think twice if she sold to Wilson Realty, not even Mr. Grant, since it wasn't public knowledge the judge owned it. His next step would be to put Hidden Hills in his name. "No thanks, I've decided to keep it."

"What's this?" he said, taking the check from her outstretched hand and reading the amount.

"It's the money you gave Mitch before we bought the house."

His jaw snapped. "Where's the interest?"

She'd been in the family long enough to expect the unexpected. Her gaze remained steady in the face of his attack.

"There is no interest," she said, steeling her voice to remain calm. "Just as there's no proof it was a loan and not a gift."

"You owed the money!"

"And I paid it!" she shot back, relieved she was no longer tied to Mitch's family.

The check shook in his hand. "So help me, if this bounces I'll have you under the jail!" he threatened, as if she was a common criminal. "I know for a fact you don't have this kind of money."

Her chin shot up. "Take another look at the bank's name. You don't have a snitch on their payroll, so you don't know *what* I've got!"

"You watch what you're implying, girl!" he said, nostrils flaring. "You've not got Mitch to protect you."

"Neither do you, old man!"

"I should—"

"Does the name Samuel Jones and Associates mean anything to you?"

At the mention of the Texas firm, Ellen joined her husband on the sofa. Charlotte knew it was a ploy to give the judge time to regroup. "I don't recall…"

"You should," Charlotte informed him, still fed-up with all she'd learned. "I have copies of the e-mails you sent from Mitch's computer. Thought you'd get your hands on Hidden Hills before they got around to leasing the mineral rights, didn't you? You lied about me being out of the country and having my power of attorney—so they wouldn't try to contact me."

"I don't know what you're talking about."

"Yes, you do!" She was more than ready to leave, but first it was time to finish wiping the pompous smirk from his face. "But like I said, Hidden Hills is mine, and I'm keeping it."

"There's a contract…"

"But I can, and will, turn down any offer."

"You're talking lunacy. There's no guarantee they'll find gas or oil. Do you honestly think you can pay off the debt with what you get from leasing the mineral rights?"

"Of course not," she said. "So I've decided to turn it into a resort."

Anger, making his face glow a dark crimson against his white hair, was no surprise. She'd been the cause of it countless times, but she was a little dismayed when his forehead splotched, and the veins in his neck popped like a frog on a lily pad. The thought of him stroking had never crossed her mind.

"It takes capital!" he hissed, actually shaking. "The world is full of get-rich schemes not even warranting a line of credit. You might as well get it out of your head, missy."

His attitude hadn't changed one bit since he'd learned of her plans to open a beauty salon. But this time, it didn't matter. With God's help, she'd faced the fears of raising her girls alone, and now, with the additional help of Jake and his friends, her biggest liability had a chance to become her most valuable asset.

Having finished all she'd come to do, Charlotte crossed to the door, then stopped. "You know, Judge, it seems as if everything you've tried to do to me was meant for evil, but God's used it for good. I'm sorry you hate me so much."

"Mitch should never have married you," he said, seething. "My boy was going places!"

She was a gnat's hair from unloading her full contempt for him, when a strange calmness descended on her shoulders like a cooling blanket. In an instant, she saw the judge, not as the greedy, corrupt man she knew him to be, but as a lost sinner who'd gone through the agony of losing a son without God's strength to lean on. For the first time in her life, she felt compassion for the man.

"Mitch went to the best place of all. He's in Heaven."

"How do you know?"

"Because we discussed our faith before we married. Mitch told me he'd given his heart to the Lord when he was a junior in college."

The judge squirmed. "About the time he started talking his silly nonsense about saving those kids."

Tom McGregor needed someone to witness to him, but he hadn't listened to Mitch so there was no way he'd listen to her, not even if he was standing at hell's gate. She'd made it to the end of the hallway when she felt a light touch on her arm.

"Mitch would have been proud of you in there," Ellen said, glancing back toward the den. "He never had the courage to confront his father, but I sensed he wanted to many times."

Charlotte blinked. Not in her wildest dreams had she ever expected an ally in Mitch's mother. "Thank you?"

Ellen laughed. "I've never wanted anything to do with the house—mercy me, I grew up there. All of those floors! To this day I won't touch a mop!"

"Mitch said his grandpa was tough, but fair."

"Sure," she agreed. "If you were a boy. With me he was just tough… Charlotte, I want you to know your money will go into college funds for the girls."

Charlotte had a new respect for the woman. Living

with a man like the judge had to be difficult.

"You know," Ellen continued when they reached the door, "I used to go to church when our boys were little. Maybe it's time I got started back. And who knows, if Tom gets tired of being alone, he might even go with me."

Chapter Eighteen

Charlotte scanned the appointment log for the third time, trying to squeeze another perm in before the holidays. Norma had been able to fit Annabelle Jones in for a quick cut, but the following week was already booked solid. "Where has the time gone?"

Annabelle laughed. "You think it's flying now, just wait until you're my age."

"It's just nerves talking." Norma never missed a snip with her trusty scissors on Annabelle's brown locks. "Jake has invited Charlotte to his folks' for Thanksgiving dinner, and she's terrified of meeting the family."

Charlotte couldn't deny it. Her first meeting with Mitch's family had been a total disaster, and in the back of her mind lurked the fear Jake's family wouldn't like her either.

"They're good people," Annabelle said. "You'll fit in."

Norma chuckled, measuring the length of the woman's bangs. "Yeah, but it's different when you're on parade as the future daughter-in-law."

Annabelle squealed, springing from the chair. "He proposed? Fantastic! Have you set the date? And a shower—we have to plan a shower."

Charlotte's mouth flew open. "No, it's…"

"It's about time, is what it is. These two have been dancing around each other since the middle of summer," Norma added, ignoring Charlotte's protest. "Seeing them together every Sunday—if we didn't know better, I'd say they were already married."

"Now, it's not what you think!" Charlotte insisted, a bit too vehemently for her own good. "We're together because…"

"Tell me you're not sleeping with him." Annabelle appeared more than a little upset at the possibility.

"Of course she's not," Norma replied. "Are you?"

"No!" Charlotte wasn't sure how she'd gone from a blushing bride to a floozy in less than a minute. "He hasn't asked—I mean, actually he did ask, but…"

"Explain yourself, young lady. Just what's he up to?"

"He asked me to marry him, but he wasn't serious."

"How do you know he wasn't serious?"

"I just know, okay?" Charlotte wished she'd kept her mouth shut. Other than Jake, the two women in front of her were her closest friends. But she couldn't explain what she didn't know.

Norma wasn't having it. "Neither of you have looked at another soul since you met. Don't wait for a man to lay his heart out. Look at how he treats you, how he makes you feel. There's more to love than fancy words. Why do you think he's worked so hard to turn your house into a legitimate business?"

"Because it's…"

"I'll tell you why." Norma persisted, determined to make her point. "He's head-over-heels in love—that's why! Now, what's your problem?"

"It's not like we're being buttinskis," Annabelle added, softening the tone with her voice of reason. "We're just concerned."

"Speak for yourself," Norma continued. "The guy's a catch, and she needs to reel him in."

"Maybe so, but it's her decision. Just make sure you love him."

Norma wasn't to be deterred. "Charlotte, honey, I've seen men crawl into liquor bottles after losing their wives, but not Jake. They say his Bible and God's strength are what pulled him through. You've got a good man there. Don't let him get away."

The difference in Norma's outlook since accepting Jesus as her Savior last month was amazing. Her boss's conversion made her realize it was time to move her church home to Cherry Road. Her relationship with Jake, and where it was going, had been the holdup. Since giving her problem to the Lord, she knew the peace of having a church home.

Glancing at the street, she saw the blinker flash on Jake's truck and ran for the door. "I'll make a deal with you. If he gets around to asking, and it's a big if, we'll make sure the kids get to spend our entire honeymoon with the two of you."

"No way!" Norma cried. "Your bunch may look angelic sitting in a church pew, but we know what they're really like."

* * * *

Jake pulled into the parking lot of the Beauty Boutique just as Charlotte came out the door laughing. It was the welcome he'd needed to brighten his day.

"Thanks for giving me a ride." Sliding into the seat beside him, she fastened her seatbelt and waved at the staring faces in the shop's window. "Bill ordered a fuel pump for my car, but it won't be here until tomorrow around noon."

"No problem." He inhaled the clean, sweet smell of honeysuckle. She always smelled fresh and clean, regardless of what she was doing.

"If it's not too much of a bother, can I get a ride to Milner's in the morning?"

"No problem," he repeated, concentrating on pulling into traffic before glancing her way again.

Charlotte changed radio stations until the soothing sounds of violins filled the air. "You sure are agreeable today. What gives?"

"I'm always agreeable. You just haven't noticed."

She rattled on non-stop about the problems with her car, not once realizing he'd been waiting for just such an opportunity. The traffic was light when they entered Broad Street, headed toward Birch. Up ahead, past the video store, the Silver Spur's parking lot began to fill with hungry patrons. This time Jake wasn't worried about standing in line. He'd called, right after Charlotte had asked for a ride home, and booked a corner table.

"Why are we stopping here?"

"As of right now, you're kidnapped."

"Like someone would pay a ransom for me?"

"I would."

Charlotte laughed. "But you're my kidnapper."

"I suppose I'll have to release you after dinner, won't I?" The truck barely squeezed into the parking spot. "Besides, the kids would miss you."

"Works for me." She flipped the visor down to inspect her makeup in the mirror. For a woman straight out of the beauty shop, she was wasting valuable time trying to improve perfection. "Speaking of kids, are they meeting us here?"

He killed the switch and relaxed his arm on the steering wheel. "I've taken care of our little problem."

She replaced the lip gloss in her purse, and reached for the door. "I hope Kimmie remembers to wash their faces before bringing them."

Jake rested his free hand on the back of her neck. "Charlotte, I didn't kidnap the whole bunch—just you." He had to fight the urge to take her in his arms when a slow grin tilted the corners of her pink lips. Her eyes glowed.

"You mean, this is like a real date?"

He nodded, trying to keep a straight face. "If doubling Kimmie's price and having six extra-large pizzas delivered, so I could be alone with you..."

"Six?"

"Oh yeah." He nodded. "They drove a hard bargain."

She toyed with the door handle. A slight blush tinted her smooth skin. "You *must* want to be alone with me."

Jake lifted her chin with a gentle touch, forcing her to look into his eyes. "You have no idea," he said, before tasting the lips he'd been longing for. Her response was exactly what he'd hoped, considering the truck was in the parking lot of the busiest restaurant in town.

A loud slap on the hood followed by "Atta-boy!" interrupted the kiss. Of all people, it was Ralph and Shelby who'd been witness to his lack of control. "Don't worry, we're meeting clients, so we can't intrude on your evening."

He waved his eternal gratitude. It was his first chance to be alone with Charlotte, and he intended to make the most of it. The vibrating phone in his pocket proved to be another interruption, but glancing at the number, he knew it had to be answered.

"What's up, Kimmie? Out of pizzas already?"

"There's marshmallows, and fire, and the curtains. Andy's burned and—you gotta come home!"

Jake froze at the panic in her voice. She sounded like gibberish, talking a mile a minute. Fear gripped his heart when he heard smoke detectors in the background.

"Kimmie, slow down—I can't understand you."

"Just. Come. Home!"

"Kimmie!"

The phone died.

"What's wrong?" Charlotte refastened her seatbelt when he put the truck in gear and spun out of the parking lot.

"I'm not sure, but I have a feeling it's not good."

"Do I hear sirens?"

He lowered the windows, and realized the sound was up ahead. The truck shot forward, running stop signs as if they weren't there.

Charlotte's eyes widened in panic. "It's a fire truck. Oh, no! Kimmie's call?"

"Now don't panic." The nerves in the back of his neck were ready to snap. "It may be nothing."

"Nothing? You don't call the fire department for nothing!"

Kimmie's frantic cry of "Andy's burned" had pierced his heart. Thinking of his baby in pain was too much to bear. The restaurant wasn't more than a mile from home, but it seemed to take forever to get there. He could hear Charlotte's prayers before they ever reached Robins Lane.

The fire engine parked in front of her house with the lights flashing confirmed his worst fears. Why had he thought they could have a night alone without a disaster happening?

He whipped into his drive and saw the firemen returning to their truck, rolling the hoses as they went. A strong stench of smoke hung in the air, but the only damage to her house appeared to be the kitchen window. The Borden sisters, from down the street, were standing on the curb watching the children, while a paramedic wrapped Andy's hand in white gauze. Relief soared in his heart when he did a quick head count and everyone was there.

"Oh, thank God!" Charlotte offered a prayer of praise and then was surrounded by kids the moment the passenger door opened, everyone telling a different version of what had happened as she lifted Andy from Jeremy's arms, wiping his tears away. " You poor baby!"

"Is everybody okay?" Jake tried to hug everyone at the same time, including Kimmie. He shook like a leaf but couldn't stop.

"I'm so sorry, sir," she said. "The paramedic said Andy's fingers aren't bad—but, it shouldn't have happened."

With Andy in his arms, he checked the bandaged hand and glanced around for Jeremy and Bruce. He found them climbing like monkeys on top of the fire truck, as if nothing had happened. Their fears from the fire, replaced momentarily by the resiliency of youth, would probably return in the form of nightmares.

"Sitting with boys should be the same as watching girls," Kimmie said, babbling from nervousness. "I had no idea they would do something like this."

Jake froze. "What happened?"

"They caught the curtains on fire!"

What was he thinking, asking this skinny, little, sixteen-year-old girl to control his boys, when it was a

237

constant battle for himself. This was by far the worst thing they'd ever done, and he'd had enough.

"Get over here—now!"

"Aw, Dad." Bruce dropped to the ground. "The fireman said we could check out the fire engine. We even get to wear their hats."

"You boys are in big trouble."

Jeremy frowned. "But the chief said we could…"

"Forget about the truck! I want to know what happened here today."

Kimmie stepped between the boys, her hands on their shoulders. "They didn't do it. It was my fault."

Jake pinned her with his gaze. "You wouldn't lie for them, would you?"

"No, sir. But it wasn't them. We were watching a movie when Maggie and Andy left the room—I didn't even know they were gone."

"The fire—Kimmie! Who started the fire?"

"Andy."

Jake blinked. "Andy?"

"Yes, sir. He and Maggie."

"Were they playing with matches?"

"No, sir. They were stuffing marshmallows in the toaster, and when the flames started, Maggie said she threw a towel over it. It must have started smoking again, because she threw it into the sink and missed."

"Ms. McGregor?" The fire chief walked up behind them. "There's some smoke damage in the kitchen, but other than the curtains and the window, everything appears to be okay."

Charlotte held onto her girls. "Thank you. Those lace curtains came from the thrift store, so it's no great loss."

"Lace, huh?" The fireman walked away. "No wonder

they burned so fast."

"Maggie." Jake lifted her with his free arm so he'd have the full attention of both kids involved. He hugged them close. "Want to tell me what happened?"

"No, sir." Maggie shook her head, red curls flying. "Are you mad, Mr. Jake?"

He walked away from the others in hopes of getting the truth without an audience. "I'm not mad. Your mom and I just want to make sure it doesn't happen again. You could have been hurt bad. Do you understand?"

Andy held up his bandaged hand. "Hurts!"

"I know," he agreed. "Marshmallows catch fire when they get too hot. Did you see the fire?"

"Uh-huh, marshmallows burn big!" Maggie's head bobbed. "There was fire, and I throwed the toaster in the sink, but it hit the window, and the window busted. And there was more fire, and Andy cried, but I didn't cry—'cause I'm big. Then the fire truck come and…"

"You were a brave girl, throwing the toaster in the sink," he said. "Did you get burned?"

The little arms circled his neck again in a tight hug, her body trembling against his chest. "Not me, but Andy did 'cause he's little."

Jeremy asked to take Andy over to see the fire truck, but Jake held on to Maggie until her heart rate calmed. It wasn't the evening he'd planned, but at least they were together, and the kids were safe. Six pizzas should feed everyone. But first, they had to call Mrs. Wilson and see about getting rid of the smoke damage and replacing the window.

* * * *

Less than a week later, the house was back to normal. Charlotte couldn't say the same for herself. The fire had been small, but she kept thinking it could have happened at the other house. The outcome would have been a lot worse.

Hidden Hills had beautifully decorated rooms throughout the old mansion when Grandpa had been alive—every piece of furniture gleamed from years of hand polishing. As much as she'd loved the antiques, she'd had to be logical. The day Mitch passed away she'd had less than twenty dollars to her name, a funeral to pay for, and no source of income. She hadn't held a job since the girls were born, and Mitch had borrowed against his life insurance policy. Selling the furniture from the second floor had seemed like her only option, never dreaming she would someday be able to buy any of it back—but today was the day.

Taking her time, she sat at the table and removed the lid from the oval hat box. It somehow seemed wrong to be probing into the Wills' family history without Grandpa's permission, but she knew in her heart he wouldn't mind. She began searching the pictures for any glimpse of the pricey antiques.

"Whatcha doing?"

Moving the photos aside, Maggie snuggled in her lap. "I'm looking at the furniture in these old pictures."

"Don't you 'spose to look at the people?"

"Most of the time, but I'm trying to find Grandpa's furniture in here."

Maggie looked inside the hatbox. "Grandpa's stuff won't fit in there."

Charlotte glanced up when Jake came in, carrying Andy in his arms. The baby's fingers were now wrapped in farm animal Band-Aids. "What's going on?"

"Mama thinks Grandpa's in here." Maggie pointed to the box, then jumped down to catch Andy by his good hand. "Come on, let's draw pictures."

"Becky left her coat at the house," Jake said, tossing a pink jacket on the table. "I thought she might need it in the morning."

"Thanks." Charlotte replaced all but a handful of pictures she thought might be helpful when they began scrounging the antique shops.

"Have any luck?" He followed his nose to the pot of soup simmering on her stove and removed the lid. "Mmm, this smells good."

"It's just vegetable." Charlotte closed the hatbox before following him to the soup to give it a final stir. "Have you had supper?"

"No, but…"

Bumping him aside with her hip, she bent to open the oven door. He sighed after inhaling the smell of fresh-baked cornbread. She enjoyed having someone appreciate her cooking.

"Why don't you guys eat supper with us? I've got plenty."

"Are you sure?"

Charlotte refused to take no for an answer. After all he'd done, it was time she did something in return.

"Would you mind getting the bowls and silverware? I'll get the glasses, and we'll be ready to eat."

Charlotte watched the smiling faces as Jake ladled soup into the bowls and passed them around the table. The difference between now and the first time they'd shared a home-cooked meal seemed like a lifetime ago. She remembered thinking Jake would someday find a mother for his boys, but it wouldn't be her. Now she couldn't imagine anyone ever loving them more than she did. Their lives were intertwined like a real family, but she knew they weren't, and might never be. It didn't stop her from dreaming though. Annabelle had asked if she loved Jake, and at the time, she wasn't sure—now she was.

The closeness Jake shared with his boys warmed Charlotte's heart. She liked to think had Mitch lived, her girls would have found the same closeness in a relationship with him.

Chapter Nineteen

Jake relaxed in his recliner to watch the nightly news before going to bed. There wasn't any reason to be in a hurry—he wouldn't sleep anyway. Charlotte was on his mind. He loved her, and it didn't matter a hill-of-beans if they'd only known each other a few months. His proposal had popped out of his mouth before he'd known it was there, but he'd meant every word of it.

He glanced up when his boys came down the stairs, dressed in pajamas. The clock chimed ten. "What are you guys doing up?"

"We need to talk." Bruce led the way to the kitchen. It was past their bed time, and they should have been asleep. The solemn expressions made him wonder what was on their minds.

"Dad," Jeremy said, as soon as they'd seated themselves at the table. "We're calling a family meeting."

"You're what?" Jake eased out of his recliner. He was the one in charge of family meetings, and it usually meant trouble for someone. There hadn't been a complaint from the neighbors since Charlotte and her girls moved in.

"Come on, Dad," Bruce said. "This is important."

Jake clicked off the TV. Regardless of what they'd done, it was late, and tomorrow was a school day. The neighbors seemed happy, and he'd had no letters from school, so it could only mean one thing. They'd done something to Charlotte. It must have been bad for them to confess before he heard it from her. He took his usual seat at the end of the table. "What did you do?"

Bruce cut his eyes toward Jeremy, as if waiting for a cue.

"Well—spit it out."

"We've decided it's time you married Charlotte."

Jake's jaw dropped. "You've what?"

The boy pulled a paper from his pocket, smoothed the wrinkles, and then slid it across the table. "I've listed all the women you know, and Charlotte's the best of the bunch. We've talked it over, and it's time you married her."

"Just like that?"

He nodded. "Yes, sir."

"Is that why we're having this meeting?"

"Yes, sir."

Jake stood. Getting married wasn't something he'd planned to discuss with his boys anytime soon. He saw Bruce nudge Andy with his bare foot.

"Sit down, Daddy. Me like Mama Char'it!"

His eyes narrowed. "What did *you* say?"

"Please?"

"That's more like it." He eased back into his chair. The whole thing was more rehearsed than their school plays.

Jeremy took the lead. "You see, Dad, we heard Uncle Ralph tell Charlotte she's beautiful. Now it got us to thinking, if an old geezer like him made a pass at her— what's to stop some young, good-looking guy?"

Bruce reached over, and patted his arm. "Do you get what we're saying, Dad?"

Jake bit his tongue. Unfortunately, he knew exactly

what they were saying. As a kid, he'd thought his dad was ancient. "To clear the record, Uncle Ralph didn't make a pass at her. He and Aunt Shelby are happy together."

"What about the landscaping guy? He looked like he could eat her up. Even the guys at school say she's hot, and some of them are seniors. I'm telling you, Dad. You'd better do something."

"Seniors, huh? Exactly what am I supposed to do?"

Bruce shoved back from the table, his hands flying in the air. "You tell her y'all are getting married!"

Jake chuckled. "Son, you don't just tell someone she's going to marry you."

"You don't?"

He shook his head in wry amusement. "No, you don't. First of all, we need to get to know each other."

"But you know Charlotte. She lives next door."

"That's not…"

"Honestly, Dad. How did you ever marry Mom without our help?"

"I managed."

"Well, I don't see how."

"Why don't you let me handle this in my own way?"

Jeremy threw up his hands in disgust. "But, Dad, somebody's gonna grab her while you're trying to get to first base."

"What do you know about first base?"

"First, second, or third," he replied. "It makes no difference in your case. What you need is a homerun."

Bruce shot out of his chair. "We're not talking about baseball—we're talking about making Charlotte our mama!"

Jake folded his arms across his chest. His steady gaze was meant to remind his meddling sons of who was in charge. "Do you boys know why Charlotte and I were together the day of the fire?"

"'Cause her car was tore up?"

"Have you guys said anything about this to Charlotte?"

"Not yet, but…"

"Then—don't!" Jake said. "This is between Charlotte and me. If we get to know each other and decide it's the right thing to do, then we'll talk about getting married. Understand?"

"Yes, sir, but…"

Jake stood, indicating the meeting was over. "No buts, and remember what I said. This is between her and me. Do I make myself clear?"

"Yes, sir."

It was probably a good thing his boys had called the meeting; now he knew for sure how they felt about Charlotte. When reaching for the light switch, he noticed the lone piece of paper on the table. Curiosity got the best of him, and he picked up the list—Charlotte, Loretta, hooker.

He glanced out the window toward the upstairs bedroom. Her house remained in total darkness, except for what appeared to be a bedside lamp. It was late, but he needed to hear her voice before calling it a night. Taking his cell phone out, he scrolled to her name and touched the screen.

"Hello."

"Hi, Charlotte," Jake said, relaxing at the sound of her voice. "Did I wake you?"

"No. I was reading my Bible."

"I won't keep you then. Just wondering if you'd like to finish our date?"

She laughed. "Do you think it's safe?"

"I'm willing to chance it if you are."

"Okay. When do you have in mind?"

"Let's do this right," he said, a smile finding its way into his heart. "How about Saturday night? And I'll find a sitter."

"Suits me—goodnight, Jake."

* * * *

Everything was set. The kids would be staying with Ralph and Shelby, and since their girls were home from college for the weekend, it should be a fun night for everyone.

He wanted their date to be special and not rushed. Hadn't he always believed everything happened for a reason? His and Charlotte's kids had bonded into a tighter family unit than some siblings sharing the same blood. All he had to do was convince her they belonged together.

Saturday nights at the Silver Spur were busier than what it would have been earlier in the week. He'd talked to Bart, the owner, about arranging a quiet table. As soon as they arrived, he and Charlotte were seated in a back corner, where strategically located plants separated them from the other diners. Soft music muffled the conversations going on around them, adding to their seclusion.

The waiter arrived to take their orders, returning a few minutes later with their iced teas and a small tray of flaky rolls. Instead of returning to the kitchen or checking on his other tables, Jake noticed the boy hovering nearby with his attention focused solely on Charlotte.

"You don't remember me, do you?"

Jake watched Charlotte smile in recognition. "You're

247

one of my movers. How's college?"

The guy seemed to gloat in the attention of a beautiful woman. "I've changed majors since I last saw you, and I must say you're looking awesome."

"Ahem!" Jake glared at the boy, pulling rank.

"Oh, yes, sir," the kid stammered. "I'll check on your order."

It was his personal opinion their waiter could find his own woman. This one was taken.

"Why were you so rude to the poor boy?"

"I wasn't rude," he replied. "Just hungry."

"You aren't that hungry."

Charlotte was right, but he wasn't going to admit to his jealousy. "I can pick a fight if I want to."

"But you won't," she teased, captivating him with her smile. "Because?"

He took her hand in his. "Because I'm having dinner with the most beautiful woman in the world, and I've waited for this night since the day we met."

"Wow. Talk about a line. Have you got any more?"

Jake laughed, feeling as foolish as a school kid. "I didn't know I had the one."

Charlotte rested her elbows on the table. "It's been a while since I've heard a high-caliber come-on."

"I find that hard to believe."

"It's true," she said. "And my ego thanks you."

"I can call our waiter back and let him drool over you."

"Don't bother." Charlotte motioned toward the other end of the room. "He's flirting with a pretty blonde at the moment. She looks a lot like Shelby."

"Speaking of our mutual partner," Jake said, glad to change the subject. "How was the shopping trip? Did you find what you were looking for?"

A smile curved the corners of her mouth. "Not everything."

Just as he'd thought, the women had spent more time talking than buying furniture for Hidden Hills. At least they'd hit it off. "There's no rush, as long as we're ready for the first guest in the spring."

"Shelby is amazing." Charlotte's eyes glowed with admiration. "We shopped the antique store where I'd sold Grandpa's more pricey pieces. Not only did we get most of those back, but Shelby found several other items. They could have been made for the house."

Jake's gaze narrowed. "It's too expensive to decorate the house with antiques."

"I agree, but Shelby explained our customers would be paying good money to experience the antebellum era, so we need as much furniture from the time period as possible."

"Okay, but keep her within budget."

Charlotte blinked. "Me?"

"Yes—you," he said, determined to make his point. "Shelby knows antiques, but she's been known to get carried away with credit cards. It's my card you've got, so try to steer her toward reproductions when you can."

"Guess I have to be the level-headed one."

"Exactly," he replied, as their food arrived. "It's one of the things I like about you."

"One of the things?"

Jake chose to ignore her question. A noisy restaurant wasn't where he intended to list her attributes. But, on the other hand, this table and the cemetery were probably the only places in town they could be alone and not be talked about.

Ice clinked while she stirred the lemon wedge in her sweet tea. He found himself relaxing inside. A quiet meal without the kids was just what they needed.

Charlotte sipped the drink, blotting her lips with the linen napkin after setting the glass on the matching tablecloth. "Did I remember to thank you?"

His eyebrows winged upward. "Thank me... for what?"

"Everything." She leaned forward to be heard above the noise. "When we first met, I had no idea what would become of me and my girls. I guess you could say, we were as lost as the foster kids Mitch and I cared for, but now I've got business partners."

"To add to your other jobs?"

Charlotte's fork stopped in midair. "You're right. I guess it's three jobs now."

"Why don't you give up one of them?"

The silky hair danced around her shoulders. "Just because I've paid off the judge doesn't mean I can give up the jobs. I've checked on health insurance, but it's so expensive. And since we're getting the house ready to open, there's even more work to do."

Having finished his meal, Jake slid his plate aside and reached into his jacket. The little black box had been burning a hole in his pocket since he'd put it there shortly after lunch.

Her eyes flew to the box. "What have you got?"

"Well, it's not a refrigerator."

She slid the glass to the side. "I believe you."

"I was hoping you'd consider giving up Milner's for a package deal. It consists of some guys who love you." Jake couldn't remember the last time he'd been so nervous. He cleared his throat, trying to regain his confidence. "Before you say anything, I'm not much with words, but I care for you, and even if we haven't known each other long, I know we belong together. You're the answer to my prayers."

* * * *

Charlotte's heart soared at his soft-spoken words. She knew the boys loved her. It was the fourth guy she'd never been sure of. Her gaze focused on the blue eyes in his handsome face, trying to ignore the tiny box until light reflected off the solitaire diamond resting in soft, royal blue velvet—the same royal blue as his eyes.

Her brain froze.

"But Jake…"

He shook his head. "Look, I know I'll never have the patience to care for foster kids the way Mitch did—my boys drive me up the wall sometimes, but I love your girls like they're mine."

"Are you sure?" She couldn't take her eyes off the rock, fascinated by its size and clarity. "I know we agree Jesus Christ is our Lord and Savior. We even have similar ideas on raising our kids, but… don't you think there's other things we need to talk about?"

"Like what?" He replaced the ring on its velvet bed, but Charlotte grabbed his hand before he could put the box away.

"Umm, like who wears the pants?"

His eyebrows shot up. "It's a no-brainer. I wear the pants. You look much better in a dress than I do. Not saying I've ever worn a dress but… you know—hairy legs."

"Idiot." She laughed as their fingers intertwined in the same comforting manner their lives had become. "I'm serious. You want me to give up Milner's. What about the shop?"

"Well, you can give it up, too. It's not like you'll have to work."

"So I'm supposed to toss my plans of owning salons out the window? I've wanted to make girls feel beautiful since I was eleven years old. If they strike gas or oil on my land, I'll be able to."

"It's a mighty big *if*," he said, releasing her hand.

Charlotte swallowed tightly, feeling as if she'd been scolded. She'd bet money no one had ever told him to abandon his dreams. "I'm not giving up the shop. And I'm not about to give up my dreams."

"I don't see why you have to be so pig-headed." He crossed his arms, a righteous resolve etched in his expression. "Let's say I understand your point, and I think you should open a business—someday. It's just... a husband, five kids, and a new business is a lot to handle."

She glared at him. "You're being ridiculous. I'm not made of glass."

"I didn't say you were, but I think you should take a break for a while."

Charlotte released a heavy sigh. The feeling of her back against the wall was nothing new. She'd heard basically the same thing eleven years ago, only it was Mitch's reassuring voice back then. *You don't need to finish school. I'll always take care of you.*

Now Jake was offering the same thing, but she wasn't a green-eyed girl anymore. Life being so hard over the last three years had made her cautious. "I have to know I can make it on my own."

He took her hands again, his touch warm and gentle. "Did it ever occur to you God doesn't mean for us to struggle alone. As His children, we're supposed to help one another. I can't promise I won't die, but I can promise you won't be left in a financial mess. If owning a shop means so much to you, there's a building next to our store downtown with its lease coming due next month. News in the grapevine says they aren't planning to renew. We'll check it out, and if it's what you want, then I'll help you get it."

She wasn't sure if he was offering a marriage proposal or another partnership. There was the gorgeous diamond and the belonging together. He even loved her girls, which was nothing new, but as a proposal, it fell short of what she needed. "So what are you saying?"

"What?" His expression was almost comical, as if she'd blindsided him.

"Is this a marriage proposal? Because if it is, you've left something out."

He released her hands and started rotating the diamond in his palm again. "I'm listening."

"For starters, there's 'I love you,' 'I want to spend the rest of my life with you,' and 'will you marry me?'"

Jake slid the ring on her finger. "Yes, I'll marry you. I thought you'd never ask."

Amazed at the perfect fit, Charlotte realized what had just happened. "You tricked me!"

He laughed. "I've been wondering what it would feel like to have the woman I love propose marriage to me."

Charlotte's gaze flew from the ring to his dark blue eyes and knew it was true. "You love me?"

"Of course I love you, but don't ask when it started. It could have been the first time I saw you or heard your voice, or maybe it was the smell of your perfume and pine cleaner. Whatever it was, you won my heart. I can't imagine being without you."

She wiggled her ring finger so the light reflected from the diamond. "You're so romantic."

"I know." He held her hand, a warm sensation filling her heart with love when his expression turned serious. "So—will you marry me?"

She nodded, happier and more content than she'd ever thought possible. "I will, and I've got the perfect sitters for our honeymoon."

Chapter Twenty

They agreed to keep the engagement a secret while tying up the loose ends of the partnership, but it didn't stop Charlotte from thinking of his boys as her own. She'd always wanted a son—now she would have three. The possibility of more children hadn't been discussed, but enough to fill Hidden Hills would be nice. A wisp of a smile drifted across her face... maybe not so many, since they wouldn't have the luxury of living there, but at least one or two more.

No insurance was risky, but she couldn't work both jobs and concentrate on lining up suppliers for the bed and breakfast. She'd handed her notice in at Milner's the following week and booked customers at the Beauty Boutique for mornings only, freeing her afternoons to work from Jake's computer.

Rain moved in on Friday, getting heavier throughout the day. She left home early to get the kids from school, but dark clouds seemed to open up, wrenching the umbrella from her hands when she ran to the car. Winds whipped the trees limbs, rocking the car and setting her nerves on edge. Lightning flashed, momentarily blinding her to the drenching rains hitting the windshield, and the worn wiper blades cut deeper into the glass with each swipe. The storm wasn't letting up, and the visibility dropped to less than a car length when she pulled into the parking lot along with other worried parents. She sat in line, waiting with her foot on the brake until a car parked directly behind her, removing her fear of being rear-ended. When the rain continued to fall in heavy sheets on the flooded parking lot, she knew school would be held until the storm passed.

Cold water dripped under the dash, pooling around her shoes. She moved her feet to the console and noticed more rain trickling down the window inside the passenger door. Reaching under the seat, she found the paper towels kept there for emergencies. Part of the roll went to the floorboard, and the rest were scrunched into a wad to use for wiping until they were saturated. Her faithful old hatchback was falling apart, but she didn't care anymore— being alone sucked. Soon, she would be married to Jake, and even though his warm, strong arms couldn't make her problems ago away, they made her feel a lot better.

She was lost in thought, trying to come up with tonight's sitter when her cell phone rang. The name, William Grant, popped up on the screen. For a moment, everything went blank. Why would Grandpa's attorney be calling, unless he'd found another mortgage? What else could it be? Mr. Grant's voice came through loud and clear, above the pounding rain. His tone brooked no argument— he wanted to see her *today*.

School let out shortly after the storm passed, but the heavy rain started again when she pulled up to Jake's house to let the kids out. She left Jeremy in charge. He opened their back door, and Bruce and her girls followed, getting soaked to the skin. Charlotte had to get to the lawyer's office before four, but she waited until the kids were safely inside, then took a deep breath, said a quick prayer, and put the car in reverse. It was time to face the music.

William Grant had been a close friend of Charles Wills and topped her short list of lawyers to read the contracts Ralph was working on. In his late seventies, he had a lifetime of legal experience and could be trusted. The rain stopped again when she pulled into the small parking lot on Oak Street. She stood by her car a moment watching squirrels chase each other around one of the giant oaks the street had been named for. It was no use. Nothing could erase the feeling of dread churning in the pit of her stomach.

Leaded glass doors loomed in front of her, and she shrank from thinking of their cost. The wealth spent on the building was nothing compared to the worth of the man inside. Pausing long enough to wipe her feet, she entered the office where, to her left, a tall mahogany bookcase lined the wall. Each shelf held an assortment of law books enclosed behind glass doors. An aroma of rich leather filled the air, and she took a deep breath to calm her nerves. The room hadn't changed since the reading of Grandpa's will, but the same couldn't be said for her life.

She remembered sitting next to Mitch, with his parents and Mark occupying the other chairs. All had been calm until the reading of the will. The moment Mr. Grant had read the part saying Mitch inherited everything, Tom McGregor had shot to his feet, shouting at the lawyer until he was red in the face. "Charles was crazy. I could stop him from wasting the money on his useless renovations, but that house belongs to Ellen! And if I have to move heaven and earth I'll see she gets it!" Having seen the judge lose his temper before, she'd cringed in her chair while he stomped around the room, building a hot head of steam. Mitch had

257

been quiet through it all, never once revealing the hurt he must have felt toward his father.

"You wanted to see me, Mr. Grant?"

"Charlotte," he said, his bald head glowing in the watery sunlight coming through the window behind his large desk. "It's good to see you."

He stood, indicated the chair he wanted her in, and sat back down. "Sorry to have to bother you, but this has to do with the final bequeath of Charles Wills. As Mitch's widow, you're the sole surviving heir. I think we can clear this up without any problems."

She eased into the leather wingchair across from the mahogany desk, dread consuming every fiber of her body. William Grant did everything by the book, and she'd forgotten how formidable he could be. He pulled a manila folder with Grandpa's name on it from a drawer to his right, and a cold sweat trickled down the center of her back. There was no way she could ask anyone to invest in Hidden Hills if there was a second mortgage. She'd used the money from leasing her mineral rights and borrowed the rest from Jake to pay the judge. Now she'd have to pay his money back, or else he might feel he'd bought himself a wife.

"Charlotte," William Grant began, and her breath caught in her throat. "I would like you to meet my brother-in-law, Oscar Reynolds. He's a financial advisor from Birmingham. Between the two of us, we've handled Charles' legal and financial matters for the past forty years."

"Ms. McGregor," he said, nodding. "It's nice to finally meet you. Call me Oscar."

"Oscar," Charlotte repeated, shaking his outstretched hand. He must have been in the room, but she'd failed to notice him. Was it taking both men to drop the death blow?

"We've called you here at the final request of Charles Wills. It was his stipulation we wait three years to the day, and... if, you're still the owner of Hidden Hills... you are still the owner, are you not?"

She nodded. At least she was until they told her how many more mortgages she was responsible for. Jake might be willing to stick with her, but Ralph and Shelby would bail, and she couldn't blame them.

Mr. Grant's bald head gleamed in stark contrast to the bushy-haired gentleman she'd just met. Looking at the elderly men, she could only imagine the kind of knowledge they shared. Oscar Reynolds stood behind the desk, removing a piece of paper from the open folder. "Do you want to tell her, or should I?"

Charlotte's nails clamped the arms of the wingchair. Her mind raced. Forget the politeness. *Why don't you just say it? This is it. The house is gone. It's finally over.*

Her prayers had been answered, but it wasn't the answer she'd asked for. God, in His infinite wisdom, had given her what she needed instead. In place of Hidden Hills, He'd brought Jake and his boys into her life, taken away the worry and dread, and given her love. She breathed again, feeling at peace for the first time in almost three years.

"Go ahead, Oscar. You can explain it better."

He removed his glasses, wiped the lenses on both sides, and adjusted the frames on his nose. After scanning the paper one more time, he took a deep breath. "Ms. McGregor, as of this morning your net worth, including but not limited to certificates, stocks, bonds, gold, silver, and oil holdings, is totaled at four-point-five million dollars. This excludes your home and any real estate you may own. I have a few documents you'll need to sign and then... Ms. McGregor... Ms. McGregor?"

"I'ba, I'ba, I'ba." She stammered at the swaying man in the darkening room. A hand pushing her head between her limp knees was the last thing she remembered, until she awoke to the sight of the polished, hardwood floor inches from her nose. She sat up, and the room swirled before her eyes, a cold cloth pressed against her forehead. Someone kept calling her name.

"I—I—I," she tried again before a brown paper bag clamped onto her mouth.

"Breathe, Charlotte! Breathe. Take deep breaths."

The room stilled, lights brightened, and her breathing slowed to the point where they removed the paper bag. Only the trembling remained. "Is this a cruel joke?"

Both men smiled, sitting down on either side of her in matching chairs. "This isn't a joke, Charlotte. It's Charles' way of ensuring his legacy will live on. He knew surviving the first three years would be the hardest for you and Mitch, but he was betting you could do it. After Mitch died, I wanted to pass the second part of your inheritance on to you, but my hands were tied. We had to wait three years, to the day, from when the will was read."

"I can't believe it. This isn't happening."

"Pinch yourself."

She did, her eyes growing round at the sharp prick.

Oscar Reynolds chuckled. "Now do you believe me?"

"What's to stop Tom McGregor? He'll file every lawsuit known to man to get Grandpa's will overturned, even claim he was crazy," she said, still unable to comprehend everything.

William Grant tossed the wet cloth into the trash. "Tom's already tried, but I knew Charles Wills for over fifty years, and I can assure you, he was of sound mind when he wrote the will."

"You mean the judge can't get his hands on Grandpa's estate or his money?"

Oscar Reynolds patted her shoulder. "No one, other than the IRS, can touch your money."

She swayed, the enormity of the amount becoming clear. "How do I... I mean... there's a payment due on Hidden Hills. Can I have enough money to cover it?"

He laughed. "I'll call the bank and get the pay-off. By this time tomorrow, the debt will be history."

The smile on Mr. Grant's face offered a calm assurance. "It's okay, Charlotte. We'll explain everything. Oscar and I will continue to handle your legal and financial matters, if you want us to. Each month, an amount designated by you will be deposited into your bank account. Any time you need extra, you're to let Oscar know. He'll also file your tax returns and answer any investment questions you may have."

"And all I'll have to do is spend money?"

"Sounds like fun, doesn't it?" he said. "There is a bit of advice I'd like to offer, if you don't mind. The fewer people who know about the money, the easier your life will be. I would definitely keep the information from the McGregors, including Mark. Charles gave Ellen a large sum of money before he passed away."

"So the judge finally gets his hands on some of Grandpa's money?"

"I'm afraid I can't say." Charlotte caught the mischievous gleam in his eyes. She'd been privy to several conversations with Mr. Grant and Grandpa. The money most likely had gone into an account for Mark's future.

It made sense. Ellen would leave everything to her

only remaining son after she was gone, and in the meantime, Mark needed to know he could make it on his own.

There was something bothering her. "Mr. Grant, can you tell me why Grandpa left all the debt? Was it to test us?"

His relaxed smile reminded her of the close friendship he'd shared with Charles Wills for longer than she'd been alive. It was easy to picture them with their coffee cups, sitting in front of the rock fireplace, passing the time of day.

"Nothing so simple. You see, Charles borrowed the money to make Tom think he was in financial trouble. He got a kick out of watching Tom plot to get his hands on the estate. Him dying, before he paid it off, was just bad luck for you and Mitch. The wording of the will wouldn't allow Oscar to take care of it."

Another thought hit her. "What about the plans Grandpa and I worked on, the ones for turning the house into a bed and breakfast? He claimed he didn't have money to do it."

"You were such a pretty young thing. Charles said you were the sweetest girl he'd ever met, smart, too. He'd never had anyone hang on his words like you, not even Ellen. Those plans were just a way to keep you coming back with the baby."

"I would've gone anyway," she said. "I loved him."

"You've lived alone out there, Charlotte. It's a lonely life when you don't have anyone to care about you. Oh, he had Eli, but they were like two peas in a pod. You brought a clean freshness into his world. He was an old man, and he felt like one, but you and the baby girl gave him a reason to enjoy life again, made him want to live."

"So, I'm not blocking Ellen or Mark from getting it?"

"Not a dime," he said. "Charles had a few projects he funded, and they'll continue at their present rate for the next five years. When the time comes, you'll have the option of continuing or canceling on an individual basis." He stood, offering her a pen to sign the papers lined up in a neat row on his desk.

She put pen to paper with a shaky hand. This was actually happening.

"Rest assured, Charlotte," Mr. Grant said, after the papers were signed, notarized, and filed away. "Charles' money is right where he wanted it to be."

****

Whoever said bad news comes in threes, hadn't met Charlotte. In her case, the numbers kept mounting. Jake pulled into his drive, worried she would take Ralph's decision personally, and it wasn't. They could always resell the antiques she and Shelby had bought, and he wasn't worried about the money she'd used to pay the judge. What bothered him was he'd gotten her hopes up for nothing.

The rain-soaked yard, covered in red dirt from the old hedgerow, was a reminder of Becky and Maggie's handiwork. He unbuckled Andy's harness, removed him from his car seat, and lifted him onto his neck for a piggyback ride inside. His worrisome day became even more so when he opened the kitchen door to Jeremy tormenting the girls over the cookies and ice cream. The last thing he needed was to referee a bunch of sugar-hyped kids.

"Look Dad, I lost another tooth." Bruce stretched his lip back to show the empty socket. "Why don't we skip the tooth fairy and go to the Pizza Plate instead?"

"Mama's gone, so me and Becky can eat with you."

"Where's Charlotte?"

Bruce crammed a chocolate cookie into his mouth, biting carefully so as not to hurt his sore gum. "Gone to see a man."

"Are you sure?"

"Yep, she went to see him, all right." He wiped the back of his hand across his mouth. "We tried to warn you, Dad, but you wouldn't listen. Now she's got a boyfriend."

"Let it go, son." Jake checked his phone messages. It wasn't like Charlotte to leave the girls during a storm. "Jeremy?"

"I don't think she wanted to go, Dad."

"What makes you say that?" Something must have happened after he'd talked with her at lunch. Maybe the judge... "Did she call his name?"

"Yes, sir, it was Mr. Grant."

William Grant, one of the sharpest attorneys in town, according to Ralph. Why would she need an attorney now? The contracts weren't ready, and unless he missed his guess, they never would be.

It had made more sense for Charlotte to use her talents on their business venture, so he'd talked her into giving up Milner's. Without Ralph and Shelby's money, there would be no Hidden Hills, and as much as he wanted to bail her out, there was no way he could raise the money on his own. He'd failed her, and even though he knew she'd understand, she might not trust him enough to risk marriage.

"Charlotte wouldn't go see a man if she didn't want to," Bruce said. "I don't want to see Ms. Ruff, so I stay away from her."

Jake nodded. "In your case, son, it's a good idea."

* * * *

Charlotte stepped out of her car, stopping long enough to praise the Lord one more time before crossing the red mud to get to Jake's house. When it seemed God's answer would be no, He'd given her more blessings than she'd ever dreamed possible.

Jake met her at the door. Still giddy with excitement, she threw her arms around him, burying herself in his chest. His arms tightened, but she felt something was troubling him. "What's wrong?"

"We have a lot to talk about."

The kids surrounded her, everyone talking at once until he spoke up. "Give her room. She's not going anywhere."

"Guess what, Mama? We're going to the Pizza Plate."

She frowned at Jake. "I've got supper in the crockpot."

"Good, I'm worn out."

"Why don't you kids go play while we clean up this mess?" Not needing a second offer, they disappeared into the other room. She locked her arms around his neck, hugging him tight. "I love you." The safety of his arms had never felt so good, or his kisses tasted any sweeter.

"I was worried about you," he said, coming up for air. "Jeremy didn't think you wanted to go, but according to Bruce, you went to see your boyfriend."

"Not hardly." She snuggled closer. "Grandpa's attorney called. I was afraid he'd found another mortgage, and I thought Ralph and Shelby might bail if he had."

He rocked her back and forth, a comfort gesture when

265

she wanted more. "I hate to tell you, but it's happening anyway."

"What?" A seed of hope sprang to life. "Shelby didn't say anything yesterday."

"It's because she didn't know. Ralph's boss offered him a partnership this afternoon if he'll stay with the firm. It's something he's wanted for a long time. He's probably going to take it."

"Don't worry about it."

"No, Charlotte," he said, deep lines marking his forehead. "You don't understand. Without their cash investment, we'll lose Hidden Hills. I can't raise the money on my own, but even if I could, we'd still have to hire a couple to live there full-time. Unless someone has a vested interest in making it a success, they won't push the business like it'll have to be pushed."

"It doesn't matter…"

"Yes it does. I've failed you, and I'm so sorry."

"You haven't failed me," she said, touched he'd tried so hard. "The day Mitch died, I had twenty dollars to my name, and a funeral to pay for. Our bank account was overdrawn, the credit cards were maxed out, and Mitch had borrowed on his life insurance without letting me know. When the shock began to wear off, it hit me. I also had a mortgage hanging over my head."

"I had no idea it was so bad."

"No one did," she replied, taking a deep breath. "I was so depressed Mama spent the first six months with us, and Dad came up on weekends to help Uncle Eli with the repairs. When Mama realized I'd been selling the furniture to buy groceries, she and Uncle Eli sat me down, and gave me a good dose of common sense. I could pull myself together and live the rest of my life with the good sense

God gave me, or I could wallow in self-pity and never receive the blessings He had in store."

"I take it you pulled yourself up by your bootstraps."

"Not exactly," she said. "Mama went home, Uncle Eli became my babysitter, and I got a job at Milner's and finished the schooling my dad agreed to pay for."

His hands cupped her face, lifting her gaze to meet his probing blue eyes. "And a couple of years later you found me."

"Yeah, I did. You're one of those blessings Mama told me about."

His forehead dropped to hers. "I don't deserve you."

"Well, you'd better, because you've got me." Laughing, she enjoyed the safety of his strong arms. Jake had become her best friend, her confidant, and soon to be, her husband and lover. His warm lips gave the promise of a loving devotion, destined to last a lifetime.

"You never said why Mr. Grant wanted to see you."

"I didn't?" she said, floating back to earth. "Oh, yeah, I meant to tell you… I'm rich."

"Well, of course you are, you've got me."

She laughed. "I'm glad, but I'm also 'blow me down' rich."

"Sure you are." He nuzzled the back of her ear. "Humor me. Just how rich are you?"

"Four-point-five million dollars."

Jake kissed her lobe. "Of course, you are."

"I'm telling the truth." She twisted her ear out of his reach. "At least you're not blubbering like an idiot, the way I did." She felt him go limp the moment he realized she was serious.

"Jake?" She tightened her arms to keep him from falling. "Do you need to sit down?"

"Maybe I should." He grabbed the closest chair he could find and pulled her onto his knees. Big gulps of air seemed to clear his head. "I felt a little woozy there for a second."

"Are you okay?"

He nodded, raising his hands like she was supposed to lay an explanation on his open palms. "What *exactly* did he tell you?"

"Well, it was Mr. Grant and Mr. Reynolds, and they said..."

"Who's Mr. Reynolds?"

"A financial advisor out of Birmingham is all I know. Anyway, it seems Grandpa made a stipulation to his will. It couldn't be read until Mitch and I had owned the estate for three years—that's today."

"So, how much does the house and land account for?"

She shook her head, watching his mouth fall open. "This is the certificates, stocks, bonds, gold, and silver. Oh, and oil... I've got oil holdings, too. Oscar Reynolds said the house and land wasn't included."

"So you mean..."

Charlotte watched the expression in his eyes change with the calculations. Her excitement of being rich did a quick nose-dive at the look in his eyes. Was he going to bail on her?

"Good heavens, woman. You're worth over eight million dollars."

"No." She caught his face, with its day-old stubble, in both hands. "*We're* worth over eight million."

His head started shaking. "Charlotte, I..."

"Now, you listen to me, Jake Weatherman. I love you and you love me—you said so."

"But that was before..."

"I proposed marriage, sort of, and you accepted. There's no backing out."

"Yes, but…"

Sitting on his lap, Charlotte had the upper hand and she intended to use it. Her lips captured his, preventing him from saying anything else. The hot kiss got even hotter when she pressed up against him, one hand cupping the back of his head, the other unbuttoning his shirt to stroke his hairy chest. Seconds later his hands electrified her body, moving down to her waist, then on to her backside where streaks of desire shot through her veins.

"You think they know each other now, Jeremy?"

"It sure looks like it."

Charlotte shot bolt upright, trying to pry Jake's hands from her bottom when she saw his boys standing in the doorway, their innocent eyes wide with wonder. She blushed, smoothing down her shirt. "Um, uh… your dad and I found the money to pay for Hidden Hills."

Becky came around the older boys. "Can we go home?"

"You want to go home, now?" Charlotte glanced toward the house next door. Her weak legs wouldn't hold her up, much less walk across the yard.

"No, Mama, I mean to our old home."

One by one they entered the room, sliding into the empty chairs around the kitchen table in what appeared to be one of the family meetings she'd heard so much about. Jeremy lifted Andy to sit in the chair beside Jake before taking his own seat. "Yeah," he said. "The one with a cool tree house and creek."

"And the pool," Bruce added. "Don't forget the pool. Oh, and everybody gets a horse. We can have saddles and cowboy hats, and maybe a buggy or even a wagon to go on hayrides."

"Mama." Maggie leaned against her leg. "If we move to our other house, can Uncle Eli come home?"

Charlotte ran her fingers through the soft, red curls. She'd forgotten how much her girls loved their Uncle Eli. He'd attended tea parties, read bedtime stories, and chased the monsters from under the beds after Mitch died. Their entire lives revolved around the old man before his surgery, but he'd left the hospital without a goodbye, when his daughter took him to live with her.

Becky leaned against her side. "Yeah, Mama. We miss Uncle Eli."

She turned to Jake. "What do you think?"

He shrugged. "It's up to you, but didn't you say you'd never live there again?"

"It's only lonely when I'm by myself. Maybe we should see if Uncle Eli wants some new nephews." Charlotte relaxed into the strong arms circling her waist. "It'll be nice having a built-in sitter for these little monsters."

A worried frown passed between the older boys, making her wonder what they were up to. She had to learn to recognize their plots and nip them in the bud before they could escalate into disasters. "Something bothering you, boys?"

"Spit it out, son," Jake said.

Bruce eyed her, his angelic expression making her leery. "Well, you see... we know Dad's almost bald, and he's getting kind of old, but we were wondering if you'd marry him anyhow?"

Laughing, she kissed the thickening stubble on Jake's head. "Should we tell them?"

He glanced up, taking the initiative. "At the risk of being further humiliated, it might be a good idea. Kids,

270

you'll be glad to know, I've asked Charlotte to marry me and she said yes. We're going to be a family."

Andy grinned. "I love Mama Char-it."

"Yes, son. I love her too."

Author's Note

If you enjoyed reading Hidden Hills, I would be grateful if you would help others enjoy this book, too.

Recommend it.
Please help other readers discover this book by recommending it to friends, reader groups, book clubs, and discussion boards.

Review it.
Please tell other readers why you liked this book by reviewing it on Amazon or Goodreads. And if you do review it, please contact me so I can thank you with a personal note or visit me at.
http://www.jannettespann.com/

About the Author

Born and raised in northwest Alabama, Jannette Spann still lives there with her husband. The dog died and the cat ran away, so it's just the two of them on his old home place. Travel is in her blood and besides spoiling grandkids, vacationing at the beach is her favorite hobby. Her husband says, "If a car cranks, Jannette's probably in it."

Facebook:
https://www.facebook.com/jannettespannauthor
Goodreads:
https://www.goodreads.com/author/show/7300239.Jannette_Spann
Twitter: https://twitter.com/jannettespann
Website: http://www.jannettespann.com/

Sign up for my Newsletter

To sign up for my Newsletter, visit my website at http://www.jannettespann.com/
I promise not to overload your email but will let you know when I plan to release new books.

Made in the USA
Columbia, SC
13 August 2023

21526730R00167